MW00479028

DISCLAIMER

ISBN (ePub): 978-1-957207-03-2

ISBN (Paperback) : 978-1-957207-04-9

ISBN (Hardback): 978-1-957207-05-6

This is a work of fiction. Names, characters, businesses, places, events, and incidents are either the products of the author's imagination or used in a fictitious manner. Any resemblance to actual persons, living or dead, or actual events is purely coincidental.

THE CHILDREN'S DREAM

ROBERTA KAGAN

PROLOGUE

A SMALL JEWISH NEIGHBORHOOD, A SHTETEL, IN THE OUTSKIRTS OF
Warsaw Poland, 1935
There was a loud shriek, followed by an even louder bang, and
then an eerie, terrifying silence. Naomi Aizenberg jumped up and
ran to her window. Smoke filled the air. And the smell of dynamite
filled her senses.

Mrs. Araonbaum, the woman who lived next door, came running
out of her house. She was clearly frightened, pulling her hair, and
screaming. But Naomi could not make out what she was saying. She
had been so lost in thought that in her mind's eye she could still see
the face of the man she loved, from the last time they were together.
However, this sudden eruption from the neighbor, right outside her
window, had abruptly brought her out of her thoughts and back to
reality. She was not with her lover, but on her knees in the kitchen of
the house she shared with her husband, Herschel, and their three
daughters.

Naomi backed away from the window in horror. *What is
happening out there? Why is Mrs. Araonbaum screaming*, she thought.
Her legs were unsteady. She stood up quickly to and ran to look out
the other window, and as she did, she knocked over the bucket of

water she had been using to wash the wooden floor. She frowned as the dirty water spilled across the kitchen. The old woman from next door let out another scream, and Naomi was again drawn back into the events taking place outside. A crowd of her neighbors were running in different directions. They were panicked. Still inside her house, and too frightened to leave, she tried to listen to make sense of it, but there was so much chaos that she couldn't understand what people were saying. Then she saw them . . .

Soldiers—or were they soldiers? Men with uniforms, and black boots. They were everywhere. Swarms of them, like locusts. Her heart began to race. She saw three of the soldiers pulling the neighbor out into the middle of the street. Not only that, two more of them had grabbed hold of the Araonbaums' two young sons. The soldiers were loading the whole family into a truck. Then another group of soldiers, wearing the same uniforms, came into view. They were holding guns to the heads of three more of Naomi's neighbors. "Get in the truck," one of the soldiers said. "Mach schnell."

Naomi recognized the language. They were speaking in German.

She was paralyzed with fear. She couldn't move to hide or run away. She stood at the window watching in horror. *I almost never see trucks in this neighborhood. And soldiers? Is this a pogrom? But who are these soldiers? They speak German, but they are not civilized like the Germans. They act like Cossacks. But they don't look like the Cossacks that I remember, who attacked our neighborhood in Russia when I was very young. And I know that I will never forget them, because that pogrom forced my family to leave Russia. That was when we came here to Poland. So then, who are these men, and why are they taking my neighbors away at gunpoint?* Naomi trembled as she remembered that her three daughters were outside in the backyard in the chicken coop, gathering eggs. She jumped to her feet and ran outside to find them. But she didn't get very far before one of the soldiers grabbed her by the arm. She let out a scream and immediately wished she hadn't. The sound of her scream brought all three of her daughters running toward her.

"You let go of my mama!" Little Bluma, who was only five years old, cried out fearlessly to the soldier. "What are you doing?"

The soldier didn't answer the child. He just laughed at her, then he kicked Bluma, who fell to the ground. "Shut up, little girl, or I'll shoot you."

Perle, Bluma's twin sister, ran to help her sister back up on her feet. "Are you all right?" she whispered in Bluma's ear.

Bluma was trying not to cry. But she was hurt and humiliated, and most of all, terrified. A tear spilled down her cheek, and she wiped it away with her dirty fist.

Then the soldier called out to one of the other soldiers, who was a few feet away from them. "Fritz, you check the house. Find the man. Make sure you get him. There is no man here. I looked. But we want to make sure we don't leave any men behind. Do you understand me?"

Fritz nodded.

Naomi knew that Herschel was not at home. He was at work in town, in downtown Warsaw. For his sake, Naomi was glad they wouldn't find him in the house, but at the same time she wished he was there beside her to help her. They were four females all alone. And two of them were just little children.

"Please," Naomi said. She was trying to sound as calm as possible. "We have done nothing wrong. Please let us go back into our house. I beg you."

"You are Jews. That's what is wrong. You were born filthy Jews. and now you live in this filthy Jew village. We have to destroy this village. It's infested with Jew rats and it's ruining the country. Not only the country, but the world. Germany has been selected to rid the world of your kind. We have a job to do, and for the sake of our children, we must do it."

"This is madness," Naomi said.

"Shut your mouth. I don't want to hear another word out of you," the soldier said, and he hit her on the hip with the butt of his rifle. Pain shot through her entire side. She fell to the ground. Her face landed in the dirt, which dusted her eyes, her nose, and her mouth.

Coughing, she turned to look up at him. His eyes were cold and emotionless, and as she looked into them, her terror grew even stronger. *My children. Hashem, please protect my children.* Her body was trembling, but she no longer felt the pain in her hip. She was numb. She felt nothing but fear.

"Get in the truck. All of you," the soldier commanded.

The other soldier walked over and spoke to his comrade, who was standing in front of Naomi. "I looked everywhere, outside, inside, everywhere; there's no man in this house. The man must be out working somewhere. But I cleaned out the place. Look here, I took everything of value," he said as he threw a few things on the ground.

"Heavy silver," the first soldier said as he picked up a candelabra from the pile. "Put this stuff in the truck."

The other soldier nodded and began to load all the Aizenberg's valuables onto the back of the truck.

Naomi watched in horror as the soldier tossed the menorah, which had been in her family for generations, along with the candle-holders she had received as a wedding gift, onto the truck. For a moment, her mind flashed to Friday nights when she used this candelabra to hold the candles she lit for her Sabbath service. *They are only material things,* she reminded herself. *Material things can be replaced. It is my children I am worried about. Hashem, let him take the silver. But please make him spare my girls.*

Mrs. Sorrsesky, the old widow who lived around the corner, was lying on the ground. She was crying as one of the soldiers was beating her with his fists and kicking her. Blood from the old woman's face ran into the dirt. Naomi looked away. It sickened her to see this helpless old woman being tortured. But there was nothing she could do to help her.

Bluma looked at her mother, then she pointed to Mrs. Sorrsesky. Naomi nodded. "There is the blood coming out from the old woman's lips and nose," Bluma said. "She's old and sick. If that man keeps hitting her, she will die."

Naomi put her arms around Bluma and pulled her into an

8

embrace, holding Bluma's head against her breast so she couldn't see the bleeding woman. "Don't look," Naomi said. "Don't look."

Then the soldier who had hit Naomi a few minutes ago pushed Bluma's sister Perle with the same rifle butt.

"Leave my sister alone." Bluma stood up and put her hands on her hips. Naomi tried to grab her daughter and make her sit down, but Bluma pushed away.

She has always been my brave one. Oh, Bluma, why did you say anything. Naomi thought as she tried desperately to pull Bluma back into her embrace. But the soldier was angry. He punched Bluma in the face. Her head sprung back like a rag doll. He was a big, strong man, and she was just a bold little girl. No match for him at all. He hit her again. This time the impact of his fist sent her sprawling on the ground. Her dress flew up and blood spurted out of her nose and mouth. Shoshana, the oldest of Naomi's three daughters, reached down and grabbed Bluma, picking her up from the ground with one hand. Then she pulled Bluma to her and held her sister close. "Be quiet," Shoshana warned. "Don't say another word." Bluma's blood covered the front of Shoshana's dress.

"Get in the truck, or I'll shoot every one of you. You swine. You all try my patience too much."

"Please, I am begging you, please, just take me. But not my children. Please not my children. They are only children. They can be of no use to you or anyone else," Tears flowed down Naomi's face as she begged.

"Shut up, you filthy Jew. Get in the truck, all of you," the soldier said to the rest of the people from the village who had been lined up at gunpoint.

"You are moving too slow," the soldier said as he shoved them along with his gun. As her neighbors boarded the truck, Naomi continued to beg. "Not my girls. Please, leave my girls." She was crying, screaming. But the soldiers ignored her. They were too busy trying to keep everyone in line. Blood streamed down Bluma's face onto her dress. Perle held Bluma close to her on one side; Shoshana held on to Bluma on the other.

Then the soldier did something strange and unexpected. He jumped onto the bed of the truck and grabbed Naomi. He laughed as he threw her off the truck and onto the ground. She hit the ground hard. It knocked the wind out of her, and for a moment she could not catch her breath. She tried to speak, tried to beg, but she could not get the words out. Dirt stained her face, mingled with her tears. Then the soldier looked directly into her eyes. She saw that he was heartless and had no feelings at all. Then he smiled at her; the smile chilled her, and she shivered. And then the soldier signaled to his driver to start the vehicle.

Naomi was able to speak again, and she began to scream as the vehicle sprung to life. "No, please, have pity. Do what you want with me, but you can't take my girls. Not without me. Please don't take my children away from me. I am begging you. Please take anything, anything at all, even my life, but not my children." The words were being torn from her throat. "Take me. Take me . . ."

No one paid any attention as Naomi sat in the dirt begging. The truck began to speed away. Naomi saw Perle's face. She was looking directly at her mother. Naomi jumped to her feet and began to run as fast as she could after the truck. But she could not even come close to catching up with it. Then she tripped over a rock, and it sent her sprawling to the ground. She felt something cut into her face, but she could not feel any pain. Her heart was beating hard as the truck grew small in the distance, leaving her behind. Leaving her to lie in the dust alone and weeping. Her dress, and the ground surrounding her, was soaked red with blood.

CHAPTER ONE

"Naomi! Open your eyes!" Her husband, Herschel, was sitting on the edge of her bed shaking her. He shook her hard until she was completely awake. "You were having a nightmare," he said. "You were screaming."

Naomi's three daughters had heard the screaming, and in seconds they came running into their parents' room.

"Mama, are you all right?" Shoshana said as she sat on the side of her parents' bed and put her arms around Naomi. Naomi didn't answer. Her eyes were still wide from the horror of the dream. She was looking at her children and grabbing their hands. Tears streamed down her face as she began to say a prayer of gratitude. She was so grateful that it had only been a nightmare. *My girls are safe. They are right here beside me.* A beam of moonlight filtered through the room allowing Shoshana to see the sweat on her mother's brow. Gently she wiped it away with the edge of her nightdress. "Mama, Mama . . ." Shoshana sighed, shivering, as she took her mother's hand.

"Yes, I am fine. I'm fine," Naomi managed to say. Then she began embracing each of her girls tightly. She was trying hard to stop her own body from shaking because she didn't want to frighten her daughters. "I'm sorry I woke you up."

"Go back to sleep, children. It was only a dream. Your mother is fine." their father said in his practical way. "You girls need your rest."

"Are you sure you're all right, Mama?" Perle asked.

"Your mama is all right," Herschel insisted. "Now go back to bed, all three of you."

Bluma took her mother's hand.

Shoshana studied her mother. "Mama, are you sure you are all right?" she asked.

"Yes, of course, I am fine. Listen to your father and go on back to bed."

Shoshana took her sisters' hands and led them back to their room.

After the girls left Naomi and Herschel's bedroom, Naomi turned to her husband and said, "It was a terrible dream that I had. I wonder what it meant."

"It meant nothing. I know you have this idea that your dreams are visions, but I promise you it was only a bad dream. I've had more than my share of nightmares, and they just fade away when the sun comes up," he said, patting her shoulder clumsily. It had always been difficult for him to express any feelings. Herschel was a practical man. Although he'd studied the Torah when he was young as was required, he'd only done so in order to be qualified to have his bar mitzvah when he became a man at thirteen. Herschel didn't put much stock in anything beyond the material world. Although he never openly said it, he secretly questioned the existence of God. But he tried to follow the rules and do what was expected of him in this neighborhood, where he'd grown up among ultra-orthodox Jews. That was because outward appearances were very important to him. He sent his children to school where they were taught the Word of God. He kept kosher; he celebrated the holidays, and he always observed the Sabbath. But deep in his heart, he thought it was all ridiculous. However, because he followed the rules, he was accepted and respected by his neighbors and friends. In truth, Herschel only cared about two things: one was earning enough money to appear successful and prosperous to everyone he knew, and the other was total obedience from his wife and children.

"But in my dream, soldiers came again. They were terrible, cruel, horrible men. They took our girls away. You were at work, and I was home alone with the children. I couldn't fight the soldiers. They had guns. Bluma was bleeding . . ."

"Naomi, stop thinking about it. It means nothing. Look around you; you are awake now. You just saw your daughters; they are all fine. You are at home, in your own bed. All is well. It was just a dream."

"Herschel, I don't think I can sleep."

"Forget about that dream."

"But, Herschel, I am still frightened. What if it was more than a dream? What if it was a premonition?"

"It wasn't. It was merely a nightmare. That's all. Nothing more. Now, enough about it. As you know, it's only a couple of days until Hanukkah. And there is a lot for you to do to get ready. So, you should get some sleep. After all, you are going to need your rest. Aren't you making latkes and chicken soup and a brisket?"

"Yes, and tonight my sister is coming. So I am making soup tonight too. And fresh challah."

"I didn't know Miriam was coming tonight. I would have thought she would come tomorrow," he said, tapping Naomi on the shoulder. After all, it's the first night tomorrow, and she usually spends the first night with our children.

"I know, but she couldn't make it tomorrow, so I invited her to come a day early. The children would be so disappointed if they didn't see her at all."

"Of course. I agree," Herschel said. "So, I was right; you are busy. Too busy to be exhausted. Get some rest." He smiled and patted her shoulder.

A few minutes passed. "You're not sleeping. I can hear you breathing heavily. Forget about the dream and get some rest."

"I'm trying."

Even though Hanukkah was a minor holiday, the children loved it, so Naomi always made a special effort to make it as perfect as possible.

"Good night. It's time to go to sleep. Tomorrow is a busy day," he said. On the surface, Herschel Aizenberg seemed to be pleased with his life. He had a lovely wife and three obedient daughters. He never complained, not even to Naomi, about how he'd always wanted a son. But Naomi knew the truth. She knew he was secretly disappointed that she hadn't given him a boy. He loved the girls in his way, but having a son was a sign of success, and it was important to Herschel that everyone in his world saw him as a success. Besides that, girls got married, and when they did, they took on the family name of their husbands. But boys carried on the name of their fathers, and therefore the family name continued for the next generation. Since Herschel was his parents' only son, and he had no son of his own to carry on the Aizenberg name, the name would die with this generation. Naomi knew that this mattered deeply to her husband, and she couldn't blame him. All men wanted an heir. Especially successful men with money to pass down to their sons. Herschel Aizenberg was such a man.

Sometimes he treats me like a child, she thought.

"Yes, you're right," Naomi answered him, clearing her throat. She was trying to see his logic. *He's right about the fact that everything is all right. I am awake now; I look around me, and everything is fine. There is nothing to fear. The children are in their beds. And tomorrow I have a lot to do to get ready for the holiday. But I just can't help it, I am so scared that this dream has deeper meaning*, she thought as she wiped the sweat from her face with her nightgown.

Herschel had given her all the comfort he was capable of giving, and she knew it. So there was nothing more to say to him. As she lay there in her bed, her heart felt empty, and although he was in the same room as her, it was as if she were alone. Naomi let out a soft sigh. Sometimes she felt sorry for herself because there was no real communication between her and Herschel. But her mother had told her when she became of marriageable age, that if she wanted to be happy, it was best not to expect too much affection from her husband.

This is my husband; this is who he is. And this is my life. I cannot expect any more from him, because he has no more to give. Then she turned over in her bed so that she was facing away from his bed, and tried to rest. A tear rolled down her cheek and she brushed it away. Naomi couldn't sleep. Every time she closed her eyes, she saw the soldiers. So instead she lay there listening to Herschel's soft snoring until the first light of day when she got out of bed to begin her chores.

As the sun rose, Naomi quietly left the bedroom she shared with her husband and went to wash herself before she started her day. She did this each morning. But today when she removed her nightdress to change into day clothes, she felt a sharp pain in her hip. Looking down she expected to see a bruise. But nothing was there. Gently, she touched the area with her fingers. It was painful. She winced. But what truly frightened her was that the discomfort was in the exact same place where that terrible soldier had hit her with the butt of his rifle in her dream. *But if it was only a dream, why do I still feel it?*

CHAPTER TWO

IT FELT LIKE THE HOTTEST DAY OF THE YEAR AS NAOMI AIZENBERG GOT down on her knees to scrub her kitchen floor. Tiny strands of hair had snuck out of the scarf she wore to cover her head, and now they stuck to her skin with sweat. For as long as she could remember, her mother had stressed the importance of a clean home, and once she and her twin sister had married, they had both kept their small homes immaculate. Humming softly to herself, she felt beads of sweat trickle down the sides of her body, under the long, modest dress she wore. She thought she should have asked her teenage daughter, Shoshana, to wash down the walls. Shoshana would have obliged because she loved her mother. And Naomi reasoned that it was probably good for her daughter to learn to keep house. But Naomi loved to spoil her three daughters. Her precious children.

God had been kind to her, although, because of the things she'd done, she sometimes felt she didn't deserve his blessings. Still, even though she'd broken his laws, God had given her Shoshana, a beautiful and good-hearted child. Then seven years later, she'd given birth to twins, Perle and Bluma. But this prosperous match, this marriage agreement, which her father had made between her and Herschel, had come at a great price to Naomi. She had suffered great pain and terrible loss. And worst of all, she'd endured it all without the support of her husband. She had committed sins, and she carried the shame of them in her heart, but if she had been faced with the same situation again, she knew she would not have acted any differently.

She acted in such a heinous and irresponsible manner that she felt God turn his face away from her. His wrath became more than she could bear. She knew she had to change if she was ever going to live a good life again. So Naomi made a vow to God to stop her behavior, which she knew was against His commandments. And when she did, God smiled upon her. But there was a price to pay. A steep price. Naomi was forced to give up the love of her life. She sighed. It was long ago, too long ago to still hurt as badly as it did.

Twins ran in Naomi's family. Her grandmother had been a twin, and so had her great-grandmother. Having been a twin herself, Naomi knew the joys of sharing a close bond with her sister, so she understood the depth of the relationship between her twin girls, Perle and Bluma. Naomi and her sister Miriam were as close as two people could be when they were growing up. And even now, they had a special bond. But there was something different about the twins in Naomi's family. And it was not until she started having dreams, dreams that predicted the future, that her mother told her about the strange gift that one of the twins in each set in her family's history was blessed with.

"The gift is only bestowed upon one of the twins. And it only occurs with the females. Males don't have it," her mother had said.

"What is it?" Naomi and Miriam asked.

"One of the twins is always a seer. She will have the gift of being able to predict future events through her dreams," Naomi's mother said. "I believe that you are the one, Naomi."

Naomi held Miriam's hand. "I am frightened by this, Mama," she said.

"The dreams are not always correct. Sometimes they are just childish nightmares; other times, they are just dreams. But it is very important that you don't take them lightly. You must pay attention to them because there will be times when they are premonitions. My mother told me about how her mother had a dream that Cossacks would come, and there would be a pogrom. In the dream, the Cossacks came during the springtime, and sure enough, that spring, there was a pogrom. If the family had paid attention to my grandmother's dream, more of them would have been able to get out of Russia in time. But as it was, no one believed, and so just my grandmother and her husband got out. This is why you must not take your dreams lightly," Naomi's mother had told them.

The first time a dream had come to her with a message, Naomi was just six years old. It had happened one night after her mother had misplaced a red scarf and couldn't find it anywhere. In her dream, Naomi had seen the red scarf billowing gently in the breeze as it lay on the ground outside the front door of their home. When she awoke, Naomi told her mother about the dream, and the two of them went outside to look. There, they found the scarf, just as Naomi had seen it in her dream. After that, there were several more incidents where Naomi experienced the power of her gift.

Some of the dreams were frightening, like when she dreamed that the little boy who lived a few houses away would get worms from some milk that he drank. In her dream she saw hundreds of worms crawling out of his mouth. When she woke trembling, she told her mother. Her mother knew better than to go to the boy's mother and say anything.

This gift of inner sight was not something that was to be spoken of to others. It was best kept secret and shared only with the family. If Naomi was branded a seer among the other people who lived in her neighborhood, it could ruin her chances of making a good marriage match. It would also hurt Miriam's chances, because if one child had a trait that the village did not approve of, all of the children in the family would be branded. Miriam and Naomi would be shunned, and any good man would turn away from them as prospective wives. So instead of telling anyone, Naomi's mother waited to see if she ever heard anybody mention anything about the boy having worms. The town was full of gossips even though gossip was strictly forbidden in the Jewish religion. But even so, no one ever mentioned anything about the boy next door coming down with worms. Still, Naomi's mother could not be sure if it was a nightmare or a premonition. That was because illness was another factor that people considered when making a marriage match, known as a shidduch. Illness could ruin the boys' chances, just like being a seer could ruin Naomi's and her sister's. But Naomi's mother was shrewd. She watched the family next door carefully. And when she noticed that they slaughtered one of their cows and took it to market, she was certain it was because the milk had caused the child to have worms. Therefore, she believed Naomi's dream was a premonition, and the boy's mother had kept it a secret.

Since Naomi's mother had taken her dreams so seriously, now that Naomi was married and had twins of her own, she watched and waited to see if either of them had the gift. It had not taken very long for Naomi to find out that Perle was the one. She had not been surprised at all when Perle began to show signs. Of Naomi's twins, Perle was physically weaker. Bluma was strong and athletic. Even as a young child, Bluma was brave and capable of physical activities. Bluma crawled before Perle; she stood up before Perle, and she walked before Perle.

But then, as Naomi suspected it would happen, Perle had her first dream when she was only four, and that was the beginning. Naomi listened to Perle describe her dreams in detail, and she tried to figure out what they meant. This caused arguments between Naomi and Herschel, who demanded that Naomi make light of the dreams so as not to, as he called it, fill Perle's head with nonsense. However, she couldn't. She had experienced this herself, and she knew Perle was frightened by it, because she herself had been frightened by it as a child and sometimes she still was. Therefore, Naomi didn't ignore Perle's fears. Instead, she offered Perle comfort and understanding, which infuriated her husband.

One evening after dinner, Herschel called Naomi into their bedroom. He asked Naomi to please sit down. Although he seemed calm, there was an underlying threat in his voice as he explained to his wife that the more she nurtured Perle, the stronger the dreams would become. Naomi looked into Herschel's eyes. *He thinks he knows everything*, she thought. *But the truth of it is, he knows very little.* She was annoyed, but she had been married to Herschel long enough to know that he would not listen to her if she tried to explain why she felt she must be available for Perle when Perle needed someone to talk to about this matter.

Herschel was a stubborn man, and he had already made up his mind about this. The look in his eyes told Naomi that she had better not argue, or he would get really angry. He was insistent that she follow his rules. Besides, she was tired of arguing. It would get her nowhere with him. It never had. So when he said, "You understand me? You will do what I say?" she just nodded. He was satisfied. He believed that meant she would obey. It didn't. All it meant was that she would not discuss the situation with him anymore, ever, and she would discourage Perle from doing so too. But Perle was just a child, and Naomi worried about this because she believed Perle trusted her father. Herschel was the biggest and strongest person in the house; it would be only natural that Perle would go to him to offer her protection if she had a nightmare. To Naomi's surprise, Perle was wise beyond her years. She seemed to understand that her father was not advanced enough to help her navigate this strange gift. So when she had a dream, which seemed like it might be a premonition, she went to her mother or her sisters for comfort. Together they did what they could to make sense of the dreams.

Miriam and her husband, Aram, were coming over to have dinner with Naomi and her family tonight. They came once a week to see the children because, try as they might, Miriam and Aram were unable to conceive, and it was Miriam's greatest wish to have a child. But since they could not, they had become like second parents to Naomi's girls. Naomi was glad that Herschel had not seemed to be opposed to their constant visits. If he had been, she knew he would have found a way to put a stop to them. But as it was, her sister and her brother-in-law indulged the children by bringing them small gifts. And although they adored Perle and Bluma, Miriam had a special soft spot for Shoshana. Naomi knew why. It was because when Shoshana was younger, Miriam spent a lot of time watching her for Naomi, and the two had developed a bond.

Naomi sat back on her haunches. The scarf she wore as a head covering had fallen down upon her forehead. She pushed it back away from her face and wiped the sweat from her brow. Then she stopped cleaning for a moment. The little house where they lived always seemed so large when she was faced with scrubbing down the walls and washing the floors. But she liked to make sure that the house was spotless on the nights when her sister and brother-in-law came to dinner.

Leaning back, squatting, Naomi sucked in a deep breath and sighed. Her heart was filled with gratitude because, even though she'd faced some daunting challenges which had threatened to ruin her marriage and the lives of her children, she was grateful to have three healthy daughters and a husband who was a good provider. These were the important things. At least that was what her mother had always told her. And having been an obedient child, in the end, Naomi had sacrificed her own happiness in order to do right by her family.

She gazed out the window for a moment, and her mind drifted back to the young man who, long ago, had turned her head and made her feel alive. It had been years since she thought of Eli, the handsome yeshiva boy she'd fallen in love with. At first, it was only from afar. But there was something about him, something different. Something that touched her in a way no other boy ever had. They had never even spoken to each other. When they saw one another at the marketplace or passed each other on their way to their respective areas of the synagogue—Eli to the men's section and Naomi to the women's section—they would avert their eyes from each other shyly. But Naomi's mother knew her daughter, and she could see that Naomi was attracted to Eli. She also knew that Eli was a scholar, and he would need a wife whose family had the money to support them while he continued his studies.

Naomi's family was poor. Her father was looking to make a match for her with a successful businessman, someone who could help him financially. Naomi was pretty enough to attract a man like this, and because of that, her parents had high hopes for a wealthy son-in-law. Her mother, seeing Naomi and Eli exchanging glances, took her daughter aside and discouraged it. "Your father has someone else in mind for you," Naomi's mother said. "He has been talking to the Aizenberg boy's father. I think he is arranging a match between you and his son, Herschel Aizenberg."

Naomi's heart sank. She'd never liked Herschel Aizenberg. He was too flashy, and too conceited. But he certainly was successful, and that was what her father was looking for. Even though she and Miriam were identical twins, Naomi was the prettier one; she was more vivacious, slightly more delicate; her hair was thicker and shinier, and every boy seemed to glance her way when she walked down the street. Therefore, Naomi was her father's great hope for a wealthy match. Although, according to Jewish law, the potential bride was to make the final decision as to whom she would marry.

Naomi knew that once her father made a match for her, she would not argue. She'd grown up to be an obedient daughter, so she would do as he commanded. Miriam and Naomi were raised to respect their father and obey him, no matter what he said. He was a cold man who always kept himself apart from the rest of his family, and because of this, his daughters were always afraid to speak to him. They didn't dare tell him what they felt or what they wanted. Most of the conversations he had with his offspring consisted of him telling them what they were to do, with both of the girls dutifully answering, "Yes, Papa."

Naomi and Miriam loved their father, not the way they loved their mother, because she was much easier to feel close to, but they loved him all the same. After all, a child must love their parents no matter what they said or did. This was what Naomi and Miriam had grown up to believe. They also chose to believe that, in his way, their father loved them too. He was just not a man to show his feelings, and it was clear to his family that he was more concerned with outward appearances than he was with his daughters' needs.

Later Naomi would learn that this trait of worrying more about what people thought of him, than about the happiness of his children, would also be a strong characteristic found in her husband. But for now, she didn't know anything about Herschel Aizenberg except that her father wanted her to marry him. Naomi knew that once she was married to Herschel, there would be no turning back. So although it was very difficult and frightening for Naomi, she had to speak to her father and tell him how she felt about Eli. She discussed this with her sister, and they decided that Naomi's only hope was to beg their father to allow her to marry Eli instead of Herschel.

"I have to at least try. I can't marry Herschel without first at least trying to convince Papa," Naomi said.

"I understand how you feel, but you know Papa. If he's made up his mind, there will be no convincing him otherwise."

"I hope you are wrong."

"I hope so too," Miriam said. "If you are going to do this, wait until after he eats. Don't try to talk to him as soon as he walks in from work. He's easier to talk to when his stomach is full."

"I don't think he's ever easy to talk to," Naomi said.

"I didn't say he was easy to talk to; I said he was easier to talk to," Miriam said, and then they both laughed.

That night, Naomi set the table. Her father walked in, hung up his coat, then he went to wash his hands and face. He sat down at the table, and his daughters and wife began to serve their evening meal. After the food was placed on the table, Naomi and Miriam took their seats. Naomi's heart pounded. She couldn't eat as she watched and waited for her father to finish his dinner. Once he was done, he stood up and yawned. Then he went to sit in his chair by the window while Naomi's mother and the two girls cleaned up the kitchen. Once they were done, Naomi and her sister had both decided that this was the best time to approach their papa. Gingerly, Naomi walked over to her father, and in a very soft voice, she said, "Papa, can I speak with you?"

"What is it?" he said, and she knew by his tone of voice that he was annoyed at being disturbed. He worked long hours, and when he was at home in the evening, he liked to relax and sit silently. If he was able to afford it, he would purchase a bottle of Russian vodka and sit sipping it from a small glass and savoring the flavor.

"I . . . I know you are planning to speak to Mr. Aizenberg about arranging a match between me and his son, Herschel."

"Nu? So, yes, you're right; it's true. I should think you are quite happy about it. I am hopeful that the Aizenbergs will have you. After all, they have a lot more than we do. Herschel was educated at the University of Warsaw. He has a law degree. You are just a girl from a poor family." He sighed. "But at least you're pretty and you're frum, a good religious girl. You have an impeccable reputation. No one in this town could have anything bad to say about you. His father should like that."

"Yes, Papa." She could hardly breathe. Her father thought she was excited about the match, and now she was going to have to tell him how she really felt. For a moment, she considered walking away. *But I can't walk away. My whole life depends upon this. I have to at least try to convince him. I am terrified of what he'll say, but I have to try.*

"Papa." Naomi cleared her throat. "I know it is highly unusual for a girl to ask this of her father. And you are usually right about everything. I just have to ask you this one favor. Just this one time. I wouldn't ask if it wasn't important. Very important. You see, I have a request, an important request."

"You're rambling on, Naomi. What is it? What is it that you want? Speak, child. You are starting to bother me. I like to relax after a long, hard day at work. So, what is it you have to say already?" he said, and she felt his impatience. She wanted to run away, but she had to say what she had come to say.

"Papa, you know the boy, Eli Silberberg? The young yeshiva student with the dark hair and long payot?"

"Yes, I know who he is. Everyone knows who he is. I hear he's one of the rabbi's favorites. They say he's a good student. So, what about him."

"I was thinking. I mean I was hoping. I mean, Papa, I was praying, that maybe you would consider him as a possible match for me."

"Are you crazy? Eli Silberberg is a scholar. He's not for you. He needs a rich father-in-law so he can continue his studies. He wouldn't want you. And I don't want him. You should be hoping and praying that the Aizenbergs agree to this match. It would be the best thing for you and for your family." His voice was loud, and there was a degree of anger in it. "Don't tell me that you and this boy Silberberg have had any contact with each other. Don't you dare tell me that you have brought shame on your family. Go on, tell me. Have you?"

"No, we have never even spoken. I just saw him at the synagogue on Friday night, and sometimes I pass him at the market. But I have not brought any shame upon you, Papa. I promise. I was just hoping that my happiness would matter to you. I . . ."

"It's out of the question. I have already decided. I have made the match with Herschel Aizenberg's father, if he will have you, and that's the end of it. You will marry Herschel."

She gasped. "Papa."

"Enough. Go to your room now. I am tired, and there is no more to discuss."

Tears ran down her cheeks as she fled to the room she shared with Miriam. Miriam had been waiting. She knew this would be the outcome. She held her twin sister while Naomi wept. The following day, Naomi's father went to see Herschel's father. They made the match, and she and Herschel had been wed.

CHAPTER THREE

NAOMI'S PARENTS DIDN'T HAVE A LOT OF MONEY FOR A WEDDING. BUT that didn't bother Herschel or his family. He was ten years older than Naomi, and he was excited to be marrying one of the prettiest girls in town. Everyone knew he was an ambitious young man who owned shops in town, which he rented out to store owners. Besides that, he'd left the town for a while when he was younger and studied at the University of Warsaw, where he'd earned a degree in law. His father was a lawyer who worked with a large non-Jewish clientele outside the neighborhood. And as soon as Herschel joined his father's practice, his father planned to retire and pass his clientele on to his son.

Money was not a problem for Herschel Aizenberg, so he didn't mind paying for the entire wedding. It was a lovely affair. Far more than Naomi would have ever thought possible for herself, being a girl from a poor family. Her mother had insisted that she wear the wedding dress that had been in their family for years, but if Naomi had wanted a new dress, Herschel would have had one made for her. He bought her a real gold ring with a two-carat diamond. She should have been impressed. She should have been overjoyed. But something felt wrong. There was something missing between them.

Every girl in town, especially Frieda Bergstein, was a little envious of Naomi that she was marrying such a successful man. After all, a man like Herschel was quite a catch. But most of the girls at least tried to pretend to be happy for the newlyweds. At the wedding, they handed Naomi their gifts and wished her and Herschel well. All of the girls except Frieda. She and Naomi had once been friends when they were very young children. Even as a child, Frieda had loved Herschel Aizenberg. She was certain that she would marry him someday. But then Naomi had come between them, and Frieda had come to hate Naomi. The three of them had all grown up in homes located within a mile of each other. Herschel being the oldest, then came Frieda, who was only a few years younger. But Naomi was almost ten years Herschel's junior, and even as a child, everyone said she was the prettiest girl in the village.

At first when they were just children, Frieda began to do cruel things to Naomi. She would knock her down when she thought no one was watching or pinch her arm when the adults were too busy to notice. Things progressed as the three of them grew older. It seemed that no matter what Herschel decided to do, Frieda was there at his side to make his life easier.

After he returned to the small village from attending law school, he went to work at his father's practice. Frieda had been waiting for him to graduate. While he was in Warsaw, she had spent her time learning to read and write as well as to take dictation and use a typewriter. She planned to work as his secretary. He knew her, and he knew how efficient she was. So when she came to him with her credentials, he hired her immediately. It turned out that she was good for his business. But not only for his business, she was good to him personally. Each day when she came to work, she made sure that she brought a kosher lunch for him. She often insisted on taking home his dirty clothes so she could do his wash and press his shirts.

Most days she stayed after work to discuss his cases with him, and she always made sure to give him relevant suggestions on how to handle things. He liked her. But he liked her only the way a man likes his sister. Herschel was not attracted to her as a woman. He found her unappealing. Herschel Aizenberg was ready to get married, and he had his sights set on Naomi. He didn't know that her father was hoping he would accept Naomi even though she was from a poor family. All Herschel knew was that he had the means to convince her father of his worthiness, and he planned to do just that. He didn't care what he had to promise her family; she would be his. And like everything else Herschel Aizenberg set his sights on, he achieved his goal.

One night soon after the wedding, Herschel was working late, so Miriam came over to spend some time with Naomi. She was soon to be married, and the two of them spent endless hours talking about their plans for the future. But on this particular night, Naomi had something on her mind, and she wanted to discuss it with her sister.

"Frieda Bergstein is here at our house all the time. She brings special fruits and vegetables for Herschel. Whenever she goes to the market, would you believe she stops here on her way home? On the Sabbath, she bakes for him and comes rushing over here before sundown. As if I can't bake or go to the market for my husband. Frieda makes me feel very uncomfortable when I am around her. She has always disliked me. You know she never even congratulated me or Herschel on our wedding."

"I'm not surprised," Miriam said. "You're beautiful and she is ugly. You have the man she wanted. Poor Frieda is burning up with jealousy."

"She's only ugly because her heart is ugly," Naomi answered.

"Yes, it's true her heart is ugly, and her face is ugly too."

"Don't say that. It's not nice," Naomi said.

"Not nice, yes. But true, no?" Miriam said.

Naomi had to laugh. Then she nudged her sister's arm and play-fully said, "What am I ever going to do with you? You are absolutely incorrigible."

They both laughed. "I meant to tell you that Papa chose a husband for me." Miriam said.

"Oh, who is it?"

"Aram Fishmann."

"He's not bad looking."

"No, he's not," Miriam agreed. "I'm not disappointed. I think I will be happy with him. At least I hope so."

"He's better looking than Herschel," Naomi said.

"But Herschel is rich. Papa likes that. He's always wanted a rich son-in-law to take care of him and Mama."

"Yes, and so he sells me to the highest bidder. And that bidder is Herschel."

"I know he wasn't your choice."

"No, he wasn't, but that didn't matter to Papa at all. All he ever cared about was what was good for him."

"Don't be sad. You will have a good life with Herschel. He can give you things other men wouldn't be able to give you."

"I know. You're right. I should be happy."

"But you're not," Miriam said.

"No, unfortunately, I am not."

"Well, it could be worse. There are worse husbands out there. Some of the girls I know have husbands who are violent. He doesn't hit you, does he?"

"No, he doesn't. He's demanding, and in many ways he's just like our papa. Distant and expects obedience. But that's not all of it. What bothers me the most is that when I am with him, I feel so lonely. It's worse than being alone."

"Come on, Naomi. You know that you are never really alone. You and I will always have each other. I'll be married soon, and then hopefully we will live near each other and spend all our time raising our children together. Nothing will ever come between us," Miriam said, reaching for Naomi's hand and gently squeezing it.

"You're right. No matter what, at least we have each other,"

"I have often wondered how people who don't have a twin sister can survive. You are my best friend," Miriam said.

"And you're mine," Naomi replied.

Naomi smiled at the memories she had of that day long ago when she and her sister were both so young. Naomi had been so hopeful then. Looking back on it, the day she had married Herschel seemed like a thousand years ago. And now that she knew what the future would hold, she realized she had been right all along about Herschel. Something was missing between them, something that would never be right, no matter how many years they spent together. They should never have married. They were not each other's bashert. And as far as she and Miriam were concerned, that had not been perfect either. The promise they made that day, to always be there for each other had not been easy to fulfill.

There was a knock on the door. Naomi ran to answer it, thinking her sister had arrived early for dinner, but when she opened the door, she was disappointed. It was Frieda Bergstein. Naomi found it hard to believe that there had been a time, early on in their relationship, when she and Frieda had actually been friends. But then, Herschel had shown an interest in Naomi, and that had turned Frieda's affections toward Naomi to hatred. Although Frieda pretended to be Naomi's friend, Naomi knew that she was always looking for a way to win Herschel's attention.

"Hello, Frieda," Naomi said.

"Hello. If I don't see you before the end the of the holiday, happy Hanukkah." Frieda paused for a moment. "Aren't you going to invite me in? What kind of manners do you have?" Frieda said with a smile, but deep down Naomi felt the dig.

"Yes, of course," Naomi said, wishing she didn't have to be cordial to this woman.

Frieda walked in and went right into the kitchen and put a plate down on the table. "I brought a little rugalach. I know that apricot is Herschel's favorite, and when I saw it in the window at the bakery, well . . . I thought of Herschel."

"Thank you. That was very nice of you," Naomi managed.

"Yes, it was." She smiled. "I am a nice person. A good friend, no?"

"Of course you are," Naomi lied.

"So, where is Herschel?"

Just then there was another knock on the door.

"Excuse me," Naomi said, opening it. She was relieved to see her sister and her brother-in-law standing there.

"Come in," Naomi said, her eyes telling her sister Miriam everything that she could not say aloud because Frieda was standing there.

"Oh, you are having company for dinner," Frieda said. "I should go, unless you have room for another person."

"I don't think she does," Miriam said coldly. "The table is set. This is something we do every Hanukkah. It's a family event. I am sorry."

"Oh, no, of course. I'll go. I wouldn't want to intrude. But, Naomi, you'll be sure and let Herschel know that I brought the rugalach just for him?"

"Yes, of course, I'll let him know."

"So, I'm going to leave now."

"All right, goodbye, then," Naomi said as she opened the door again. Frieda tried to look past Naomi to see if Herschel was coming out of the bedroom, but Miriam was blocking her view.

Finally, Frieda left.

Miriam and her husband carried a gift for each of the children.

"Come here, all of you. Come on," Miriam said, and the girls gathered around their aunt. She handed each one a gift. "You will open these tomorrow after you light the candles," Miriam said.

"I wish you could come for the first night of Hanukkah. I wish you and Uncle Aram could be here when we open our presents," Shoshana said.

"I wish so, too, but we are planning to go and eat with Aram's parents tomorrow. They are expecting us."

"We'll miss you both," Shoshana said.

"And I'll miss you too."

"So you'll come again next week, Auntie Miriam?" Bluma asked.

"Of course. You know I'll come."

Miriam and Aram stayed late into the night. They sat on the floor and played dreidel with the girls, and they laughed and sang Hanukkah songs. It was a day early, but it was to be expected that if

Miriam's husband wanted to go to see his family on Hanukkah, his wishes would come before his wife's.

After they left, the girls went to bed, and Herschel followed. Naomi straightened up the living room, then she, too, went to bed. She was so tired that she fell asleep and did not think about the dream at all.

CHAPTER FOUR

THE FOLLOWING DAY, HERSCHEL GOT UP IN THE MORNING, ATE THE breakfast Naomi prepared for him, in silence, then left for work with just a quick goodbye. After he was gone, Naomi spent the entire day cooking. She peeled and shredded potatoes to prepare her special latkes, potato pancakes, for their dinner; she mixed the dough and then kneaded it for challah. Then she killed and plucked a chicken, which she put into a pot with sliced carrots, parsnip, onion, and celery, for soup. Once she'd finished, she washed and dressed for dinner.

That night after they finished eating, the Aizenberg family gathered around. They planned to light two menorahs. One, a candle menorah, that had been in Herschel's family for generations, and the other an oil menorah, which had been Naomi's mother's silver treasure. Naomi looked at her mother's menorah and shuddered as she remembered her dream. But she didn't say a word about it to anyone. Instead, she forced herself to smile as she filled only one of the small glass cups with oil, because it was the first day of Hanukkah, but she also filled the shamash. This was the flame that was used to light all the others.

The three girls gathered around their father as he closed his eyes and prepared to sing the special Hanukkah prayer. Although prayers would be sung each night of the eight nights of Hanukkah, the first night of the holiday was special. On this night the prayer was longer. On the first night the Shehecheyanu was sung.

Naomi watched her girls and thought of how beautiful they were as they waited for their father to begin: their faces illuminated by the soft flame and their heads turned upward to watch their father. The wonder in her daughter's eyes filled Naomi with so much love that she thought her heart might burst. The room was silent. Then Herschel, in his deep baritone voice, began to chant the ancient Hebrew prayer.

> *Barukh atah Adonai, Eloheinu, melekh ha'olam*
> *Blessed are you, Lord, our God, sovereign of the*
>   *universe*
> *asher kidishanu b'mitz'votav v'tzivanu*
> *Who has sanctified us with His commandments*
>   *and commanded us*
> *l'had'lik neir Shel Hanukkah. (Amein)*
> *To light the lights of Hanukkah. (Amen)*
> *Barukh atah Adonai, Eloheinu, melekh ha'olam*
> *Blessed are you, Lord, our God, sovereign of the*
>   *universe*
> *she'asah nisim la'avoteinu bayamim haheim*
>   *baziman hazeh. (Amein)*
> *Who performed miracles for our ancestors in those*
>   *days at this time*
> **Shehecheyanu**
> *Barukh atah Adonai, Eloheinu, melekh ha'olam*
> *Blessed are you, Lord, our God, sovereign of the*
>   *universe*
> *shehecheyanu v'kiyimanu v'higi'anu laz'man hazeh.*
>   *(Amein)*
> *Who has kept us alive, sustained us, and enabled us*
>   *to reach this season (Amen)*

"Amen," the family said.

Herschel Aizenberg smiled at the girls. Then he asked, "Nu? Which one of you can tell me the story of Hanukkah? Who knows this story?"

"I do," Bluma said loudly.

"All right, Bluma, you can tell me. So, why do we light the oil?"

"Because long ago, in biblical times, the Jewish people were being treated very badly by the Syrian government. So, the Maccabees went to war. They beat the Syrians who were idol worshipers. Then they cleared the temple of all of the idols that the Syrians had put there."

"Do you know what an idol is?" Herschel asked gently.

"It's a statue," Perle said.

"That's right. So, the Syrians were worshiping statues, and according to the first commandment, the Jewish people are never to take any God above Hashem. Isn't that right?"

"Yes, Papa," Bluma said.

"You know your commandments. That's very good. All right, Bluma, finish telling us the story."

Naomi watched her husband and the children. *He is a good father, in his way, even though I know he doesn't believe in anything really. He is kind as long as they obey him. And he tries hard to be patient. He also does what he can to teach the girls what they will need to know when they marry and have families of their own.*

Bluma was sitting up proudly as she finished telling the story of the Maccabees. "So, the Maccabees found that their menorah had been stolen. They were very upset. But they made a new one. After they finished making it, they needed to light it, but they had no oil. Then Judah, who was the leader of the Maccabees, searched everywhere for oil because they needed it for light, otherwise they would be in the dark, right Papa?"

"Yes, Bluma, that's right. I can see you have been paying attention in Sunday school. What a smart girl you are. You remind me of myself. And, nu, for your age, you're a genius." He smiled and winked. "You give your papa such nachas, such joy. I kvell, with pride, when the teachers tell me how smart my daughter's are. Now go on and finish the story." Herschel smiled at Bluma as he leaned back to listen.

Bluma continued, "Even though Judah Maccabee searched very hard, all he could find was just a small jug of olive oil. And that would only be enough to light the menorah for one day. He lit it because he had to. And the people were very worried. But then do you know what happened?"

"Why don't you tell us?" Herschel said, and he smiled at Naomi who returned his smile.

"I will! Hashem made a miracle. He made that small amount of oil burn for eight long nights. And by then the Maccabees were able to get more oil," Bluma said, sitting up straight and smiling.

Perle hugged her twin sister.

"That's absolutely right. What a smart girl you are." Herschel beamed at his daughter. He favored Bluma because she made the best impression on people, out of all of his daughters. She was not shy like Perle or introspective like Shoshana. She spoke up when she was asked a question; she was quick to learn, and whenever she was given a chore, she would work very hard to prove herself capable. He imagined that she would be quite an asset when she grew up. She would marry well and make him proud.

Naomi wrapped her arms around herself. *I have such a beautiful family. I should be the happiest of women*, she thought as she watched her husband and children as they laughed and talked about the meaning of the holiday. *I have been so blessed. My husband, although he is strict and sometimes cold, tries his best to be a good father. I know he loves our children with all his heart. And there is no doubt that he's a good provider. He works hard. And we never go to bed hungry. The girls have everything they need. I just wish he were not so cold and emotionless. But I can still remember that my mother always said that men were like that. And that a wife must accept her husband as he is. I try. I really try. But Herschel can also be very unreasonable at times, like when he doesn't get his way. I suppose the only thing I can do is keep my focus on his endearing qualities, like now when he has his daughters gathered around him. All I want out of life is to just be happy.*

Why can't I be satisfied with what I have? What is it inside of me that makes me want more? Why do I need love so desperately when I know that love is not something we Jews strive for or even believe in. Yet, I believe in it wholeheartedly, and I need it desperately. Then she put her hand on her hip where she had felt the fantom bruising that morning. White hot pain shot through her, reminding her of the dream she had the previous night. No one noticed, but Naomi shivered at the memory.

My babies, she thought. *My precious children. What a horrible dream that was. And I don't understand how it is possible that I could feel such discomfort in my body, if it was only a nightmare? I am so afraid it was something more, something sinister. A warning perhaps. What can I do even if it was a premonition of what is to come? I have no idea of how to interpret this. Herschel is so certain it was just a nightmare. I wish I could accept that,* she thought as she rubbed her hip. *I've had dreams like this before and nothing has happened. But I never woke up with any physical evidence from the dream. Nothing like this shooting pain has ever happened before.*

She went into the kitchen to clean up the rest of the dishes from dinner. But she couldn't take her mind off her dreams. *This is not the first time I have seen the same soldiers in the same uniforms in my dreams. I remember when I had a strange nightmare last year in which I saw the same uniformed soldiers carrying the same flags as the ones in my dream last night. I could never forget those flags; they struck terror in my heart from the first time I saw them. Although I have never seen them anywhere, except in dreams. So I don't even know if they are real. But when I close my eyes, I can still see the red flag flying in the wind with that same black spider in the center. It makes me shiver. But I have to remember that just as Herschel promised, nothing has ever happened. Nothing came of the dream last year. So maybe nothing will come of this one either. Still, I can't help but wonder why I would dream of those same soldiers. Does any of this have meaning, or is it just a nightmare, like Herschel says?*

Once again, she touched her hip, where the soldier had wounded her in her dream. The area felt very tender.

CHAPTER FIVE

AFTER THE MENORAH FINISHED BURNING, THE GIRLS EXCHANGED THE small gifts they gave each other on the first night of the holiday, and then they opened the gifts their aunt and uncle had given them. Once they had finished, the family put on their coats, and as was their tradition, they walked to the orphanage where each member of the Aizenberg family brought one of their possessions to give as a gift to the poor children in need. This was Herschel's way of showing the others in the neighborhood that he was a good man who was teaching his children about Tzedakah, the joy of helping others.

Every year, the children were told that they were to take special care in selecting the perfect gift to give away, from among their own possessions. They were told they were to find joy in giving things to those who were born to mothers who had died, or families too poor to care for them, and therefore they were less fortunate than the Aizenbergs. Shoshana loved this part of the holiday. She loved to see the joy on the faces of those who would receive her gift.

The Aizenbergs were not extremely wealthy, but they were very comfortable. In fact, they were more comfortable than most of the families in the village. Herschel made it clear to his wife and children that he was very proud of this fact. He let them know that they were very lucky to have a father who was such a good provider. Although it was kind to give things to those in need, Herschel had an ulterior motive. He liked the feeling of being seen as a prosperous man. And giving gifts to the poor was his way of letting his neighbors know that Herschel Aizenberg could afford to give things away, and that meant that he was a successful man.

Each year he made a sizable donation to the shul and to the orphanage, but he never gave anything anonymously. It was important to him that everyone knew where the gifts came from.

This year, Shoshana had knitted a scarf to give away. She'd purchased some pretty white yarn to make the scarf. It had taken her weeks of working on it because she'd had to do her knitting between her other chores. But now as she looked at the scarf, she was proud of the final result. The twins each chose one of their toys to give away. Bluma never gave away anything that was important to her. She always gave something she cared very little for. She found it hard to part with things she loved. Today she gave away an old fabric doll that she had never played with.

However, Perle was not like her sister. She had a big heart, and each year she chose to give one of her most precious possessions away. Today she gave away a special sweater that had been given to her by her Aunt Miriam. It was a store-bought sweater that Miriam had purchased when a salesman had come through town. The sweater was made of soft wool. She'd given one to Perle and one to Bluma. The girls both loved the sweaters because they had never owned a such beautiful garments before. And they had only worn these sweaters for special occasions so as not to wear them out or get them dirty. Shoshana knew that aside from Perle's teddy bear, which she would never give away, this was Perle's favorite thing. Perle loved her teddy bear. It, too, had been a gift from Auntie Miriam. She'd given one to each of the twins. Bluma had no use for hers. It sat on a shelf in her room. But Perle immediately named hers Alana. And she took Alana with her wherever she went. No one ever saw Perle without her bear.

As they entered the poorhouse, Shoshana looked at the sweater in one of Perle's small hands. In the other, she carried Alana.

"Perle, are you giving away your bear or your sweater?"

"The sweater. I love it, but I love Alana even more," Perle said.

"Perle, I know you love that sweater, and it is your prettiest one. Why would you give that away? You have other sweaters that you could choose from to give to a poor child."

Perle smiled at Shoshana, and for a moment she looked far too wise to be so young. Then she said, "I love this part of the holiday. Giving feels good. It makes me happy to know that a very poor little girl will be warm and happy this Hanukkah, and it will be because of me."

Shoshana was so filled with love for her sister that she couldn't speak. She just pulled Perle into her arms and hugged her tightly.

CHAPTER SIX

Naomi brought a pot of hot soup to the poorhouse. It was heavy and difficult to carry because of the temperature. She wished that Herschel would offer to help her. But he pretended not to notice that she was struggling. And she didn't feel comfortable asking him to carry it for her. She had spent the day preparing this pot of soup, along with the meal she'd prepared for her family. But then as they were walking by the house Frieda lived in with her parents, Frieda came outside. *She must have seen us through her window,* Naomi thought. *She's so nosy, always watching out the window.*

"You are going to the orphanage?" Frieda asked. Naomi wondered how she knew. *Perhaps, Herschel told her?*

"Yes, we do it every year," Naomi said, still struggling with the pot of hot soup.

"I know. I have seen you go there before," Frieda said. "Herschel is such a generous man. You are very lucky to have him."

"Yes, thank you. He is," Naomi said. *She is giving me a kenahora. The evil eye. I can feel it.* It was a relief when they finally arrived at their destination.

"Let me hold the cauldron for you, so you can take off your coat and get your girls situated," Frieda said.

Glad to be relieved of the heavy, hot soup, Naomi handed it to Frieda. They walked inside, and Frieda set the ponderous cauldron down on the table. The orphaned children lined up, and Frieda began ladling Naomi's soup into small bowls.

Once they'd all been served, Naomi overhead Frieda talking to one of the teachers. She was implying that she had brought the soup and acting as if she was Herschel's wife.

"It warms my heart to bring food for the orphans," Frieda said. "Herschel and I are so alike. We both have very generous hearts."

Naomi rolled her eyes. But since this was a mitzva, a blessing to do good for others, she didn't want to start an argument. *Let her have the credit. I don't care. It's not about who gets the credit anyway. It's about true generosity and having an open heart to help those in need.*

And as Naomi watched the orphaned children eat, she was glad to see how much everyone was enjoying having a hot meal. Naomi was generous; she believed fully in giving; it was in her nature. But she felt that sometimes Herschel went too far in asking the girls to give away something of their own. They weren't starving, and they weren't as poor as so many others. Wouldn't it have been easier to just buy gifts for the needy children? *I suppose maybe he's right. Maybe he's teaching them properly, and it's good for them to do it this way,* she thought as she watched Herschel. He was standing across the room and making a speech to all of the orphaned children, who were listening intently. Naomi knew that they all looked up to him. And why wouldn't they? He was everything they were not. He was everything they wished they could grow up to be.

Herschel Aizenberg was rich, and to those who suffered, he was like a god. He was always dressed in his finest clothes on the days he and his family went to present their gifts to the poor on Hanukkah. This had always made Naomi feel uncomfortable. She didn't think he needed to wear his nicest suit. It would be less intimidating if he were dressed more casually. But the truth was that she knew why he did. Naomi understood Herschel in a way no one else did, and she knew he loved showing off. This made her feel sick, because this behavior was not in the true spirit of giving. But she said nothing; there was nothing to say. If she criticized her husband, it would not change him; it would only make him angry.

Naomi sat alone in the back of the room. She didn't need to have everyone thank her for her kindness. Just seeing the children enjoy the food she prepared was enough. So she quietly waited for her family to be ready to leave. A little girl with a dirty face and torn dress received the doll that Bluma had donated. The joy on the child's face made Naomi smile. Then she saw the girl who received Perle's sweater. She had put it on. Her hair was matted, and tears were streaming down her face. *My Perle is just a good child. She has such a true and generous heart.* Naomi searched the room for Perle, who was standing with Bluma, waiting for their father to be ready to go. They had given their gifts, and now they wanted to leave. Naomi assumed that seeing the poor children made her girls a little uncomfortable. She assumed that they felt some guilt at having so much, while others had so little.

Naomi agreed with them. She felt a little uncomfortable too. And . . . it was then that Naomi looked up and saw him. Eli, the boy she had known when she was single. She remembered how she had wished, hoped, and prayed that Eli would be her husband. And then when her father had chosen Herschel, she thought it was over with Eli. But it wasn't. In fact, it had not yet begun. Her face was red with shame, but her heart was on fire with love.

Eli had just walked in, his dark hair and beard covered with snow. He shook off the snowflakes. In his hands, with those long, perfect fingers, he carried loaves of bread that he'd brought, which were from the rabbi for the poor. Quietly and without bringing attention to himself, Eli laid the bread down on the table in the back. Again, he shook the snow off his coat, and it was then that he looked up. His dark, soulful eyes caught Naomi's. She felt her face grow even hotter as she turned away. But then she turned back, and there he was still looking at her. Tears threatened to fall from her eyes. The longing in her chest was almost painful.

It had been five years since they had ended their relationship. Saying goodbye was the hardest thing she had ever done. But she was married, and she had made a vow. It had to end. And since that day when she'd embraced him for the last time, they only saw each other on a handful of occasions in passing, but whenever their eyes met, it brought back all the memories as if they had ended it only yesterday.

CHAPTER SEVEN

The following day, the second day of Hanukkah, the sky was a bright shade of sapphire. Herschel was at work, and the children were busy. Naomi sat at her sewing table. She was busy making a special dress for Shoshana because Herschel had been talking about bringing home prospective husbands for her. Last week, he'd given Naomi money, insisting that she buy expensive fabric to make this dress for Shoshana. "It needs to look impressive. We want to make a good match for our daughter," Herschel said.

As Naomi pulled the needle through the fabric, she thought about the fact that soon Shoshana would be married. *She's so young. I hope she's ready,* Naomi thought. *I suppose every mother must feel this way when her daughter approaches marriageable age. And I hope she doesn't suffer. I hope Herschel chooses a man who will make her happy.*

The house was quiet as the soup that Naomi had put on to boil for dinner was simmering. The twins were in the small room they shared, playing quietly while Shoshana and Neta, her best friend, who had come to visit, were in Shoshana's room busy mending socks.

Naomi felt sorry for Neta. She knew that Neta's father was not successful, and to make matters worse, Neta was not very pretty. Therefore, the boys who would be presented to her as potential matches would not be as good a quality as the ones who would be chosen for Shoshana. She hoped Neta would find happiness too. *It's hard to be a woman in our world*, Naomi thought. She knew that her husband had been considering Albert Hendler as a potential match for Shoshana, and she had to admit he was a handsome boy. But more important to Herschel, Albert's father had a thriving business, and Albert would apprentice under him. He would be a good provider. Naomi's eyes began to blur from the tiny stitches she was making in the fabric. She closed them for a moment, and when she did, in her mind's eye, she saw Eli. Her mind drifted back to the first time they made love in a field. The field where the mushrooms grew wild. The mushrooms had a yellowish hue and were as soft as velvet. They were easy to pick, and once you had them in hand, they were slippery in the fingers, like angel's wings. The perfume of wildflowers filled the air.

It was a light fragrance that tickled her nose, a delicate, mild scent that was somehow familiar. How afraid she had been that day, but how she had wanted him. His voice lingered like a melody in her heart. If she allowed herself to close her eyes and remember, she could still smell the fresh fragrance of soap in his newly washed hair. The recollection was so vivid that she felt tears begin to form in her eyes. *How I long to be in his arms again. I miss him every day*, she thought, then she reminded herself: *But I must stop this. It's pure madness. After all, he is getting married now*. Eli had become engaged a few months ago to a young girl with a rich father who had chosen him because he was a Torah scholar. It was an honor to have a Torah scholar for a son-in-law. And this girl came from a wealthy family who relished that honor. So now, Eli's father-in-law would support him for the rest of his life, so he could spend all of his days studying.

I should be happy for him, but I am not. I am miserable. I want him to be happy. But I still wish it could have somehow been with me. But even if my parents would have accepted him, which they didn't, they would have been appalled by the fact that not only is he poor, but he is also a convert. My parents are not wealthy. They depend upon Herschel to help them financially. Eli couldn't have done that. He would have had to work at a job just to earn enough for him and I to get by. He is so smart, and he would have had to sacrifice his studies in order to work, if he married me. I know he still loves me. I know he has always loved me. And, oh, how I loved him. But I pushed him away because I knew there was no future. And even before I married Herschel, my father made it clear that he didn't care about my feelings. He wanted my husband to be a man who could provide for me and help him and my mother out too. So when Herschel came along, he thought that he'd made the perfect match for me. I suppose he did what he believed was best for all of us.

Then she thought about Eli again. She could feel his hands on her, and her face turned red with shame as she remembered those very special months when she and Eli had met with each other under the shade of an old oak tree. The air smelled of damp earth and age. Under the shade of the oak was the sound of leaves rustling, and here and there, the sound of the wind. Their lips met and pressed together in a soft, sweet kiss and she could feel his breath as it brushed across her cheek. She could taste his lips against her as he leaned in, his lips a sweetness and a promise. A promise that he was willing to keep, but she could not. It was years ago. It was when Naomi was very young. Shoshana had not yet been conceived. In fact, Naomi and Herschel had only been married for a short time when things began between Naomi and Eli.

Herschel had gone to work that morning. It was a lovely spring day, and she had to get out of the house. So she grabbed a basket and was on her way out of the crowded city into a more rural area, where she planned to pick wild mushrooms. There was no one around for miles, and she enjoyed the peace of being alone. But then she thought she saw the figure of a man in the distance. At first, she was frightened and thought about turning and running for home. But then as he got closer to her, she realized it was Eli. Gazing at him in the distance, she wondered why he was on this road when he should be at the yeshiva studying. Where was he going? She knew that he saw her.

For a moment, he stopped walking and just stood there staring at her. And to Naomi it seemed as if the world stopped turning. The sun shone behind him like a halo lighting his hair. Her breath caught in her throat. She couldn't believe how handsome he was. But being a newly married woman, she knew these were not thoughts she should be having. And yet she could not stop them. Her heart raced. The basket handle grew wet with sweat in her hand. And for a single moment she wished with all her heart that he was her husband and that they were meeting here alone in this field of sunburned grass.

She closed her eyes and imagined him taking her in his arms. *I am a sinner. I am sinning in my thoughts, and that's bad enough, but I should run home before I do something I will regret.* Then Eli began to walk toward her quickly. A million thoughts ran through her mind. *We are all alone here in this field. There is no one else around. No one to chaperone. No one to protect my honor. A girl and boy should never be alone like this, not even a boy and girl who are single, let alone a woman like me who is married. I should not be here. I owe it to Herschel to go home right away. I should turn and run as fast as I can. But I can't move. My feet feel like they are stuck to the ground. He is approaching. What if he talks to me? What should I say to him? What should I do? Oh my, he's getting closer. I should run home.*

"I've seen you around," Eli said as he approached. "I'm Eli Habersky." He was toying with the button on his jacket.

She thought he looked nervous. For a moment, she watched him. Then she turned away. "I should go," she said.

He nodded. Then he cleared his throat and blurted out, "Your name is Naomi, isn't it?"

She nodded quickly. She was surprised that he knew her name.

"Someone at the shul said you make the best luchen kugel, noodle pudding, of anyone else in town."

She giggled. "I don't know if that's really true," she said. His compliment caught her off guard.

"I'll bet it is. And"—he hesitated, then added clumsily—"you're very pretty too. I shouldn't speak so brazenly. But I am sorry. I can't help myself."

"Oh, I really should get home. I am married, you know. My husband is Herschel Aizenberg." She felt better about speaking to Eli when she mentioned Herschel's name. It didn't seem like such a sin, for some reason.

He nodded. "I know." Then he cleared his throat again and managed to say, "I know I shouldn't say this to you, but I must. You see, I don't know if I will ever have another chance to speak to you alone. So I must tell you what it is that I have to say."

She sucked in a deep breath. "Tell me, then. Whatever it is, just please tell me quickly. I must leave here soon. I must get home before my husband returns from work."

"It's early in the day. You have a few minutes. I promise not to take too long." He sucked in a deep breath. It appeared to her that he was mustering up his courage.

She stood there looking at him, too fascinated to leave. *I can't believe I am speaking to him like this. We are all alone, and this is so forbidden. I dare not think about what my mother would say if she knew. Or even worse, what Herschel would say if he ever found out. But I can't leave here until I hear what Eli has to tell me. If I leave without knowing, it will haunt me for the rest of my days.* "Go on, then. Please, just tell me."

"I wished it were me," he blurted out.

"I'm sorry, but I don't understand."

"I wish I were your husband. I was hoping that your father would speak to my father about a match for us. Instead, he chose Herschel Aizenberg." He was speaking quickly, forcing the words out. "When I found out that you and Herschel were going be married, I was heartbroken. I tried my best to accept it. I really did, because I wanted, more than anything, that you should be happy. I even spoke to the rabbi to get advice. But . . . well . . . in the end, I followed you here, so I could speak to you and tell you everything that is in my heart. And now here I am standing across from you and looking at your beautiful face, and all I can say is that I am still wishing that somehow things could have been different. That you could have been mine."

"You shouldn't say such things," she said.

"I must say them because I can't hold them inside of me any longer. If I do, my heart will shrivel up with sadness. I realize that you are married, and there is nothing that can or should be done to change that. And I would never do anything to hurt or embarrass you. But . . . I had to tell you how I felt." He hung his head. "I know it was selfish."

She thought he looked like a little boy, so vulnerable. "I understand."

Then he turned and began to walk away, and she knew that if she let him go, she would spend the rest of her life wishing she had said something to let him know that he was not alone in his feelings. "Wait." Naomi's voice cracked as she called out to Eli. He turned to look at her. She couldn't look directly at him, but she knew she had to speak. "I felt the same way. I prayed that my father would choose you."

"Then why didn't you tell him?"

"I did. I tried. Believe me, I tried. But my father is stubborn and selfish. He's never been the kind of man who cared what anyone else wanted. So, he wouldn't have listened anyway. My husband is the same way. My mother says that all men are like this."

"Not all men, Naomi. Not all men."

"All the men I have ever known," she said. "My husband, like my father, makes the rules, and it is my place to obey. He makes it clear that I am not to question his decisions on anything."

"You mean you can't talk to him at all?"

She shook her head. "He and my father are the same. They don't listen to what women have to say. They make the decisions, and they believe that it is the woman's place to do as they say."

"And what about you, Naomi? What do you believe?"

"I believe that this is my destiny. I am married to Herschel Aizenberg. I will give him children and keep his house. I will prepare kosher food and observe the Sabbath. And in the end, my life will be just like my mother's and her mother's before her."

He walked toward her and then stopped. He stood close beside her. "I've never stood this close to any woman before. But you are different. I believe in my heart that you're my twin soul," he said softly. "My bashert."

"No, that is not right." She shook her head and looked away from him. "You must never say that again."

"Yes. I must say it. Because I know it's true. Do you know the story of the twin souls? It's a story from the Talmud," he said.

"I don't know it. All I know is that I think I should go home."

"Let me tell you the story, then you can go. Would that be all right? I'll be very quick."

"All right. Tell me the story," she said. Naomi agonized. She wanted to stay and be with him, and yet she knew that she should run away.

"Before a child is born," he said, his voice soft, deep, and mesmerizing, "its soul divides into two parts. These two parts become two people. These two people will then come to earth separately. They might be born in two different countries, or they could be born to families who live right next door to each other. But either way, these two halves of one soul are destined to find each other so that they can become complete again. This is because they are basherts. Naomi, I have to tell you that I knew the first time I saw you that you were my bashert. I looked into your eyes, and my soul stirred, telling me this is your other half. You have found her. She is the only person who can make you compete. So, you must never let her get away. You must spend your life together, and if you do, you will always be happy."

"I can't listen to this anymore. I am leaving. I'm sorry," she said and picked up her basket and ran home. As she ran, tears fell down her cheeks. He'd touched her soul, and the magnitude of her feelings terrified her.

When she arrived back at home, she started frantically cleaning her house. *I have to stay busy*, she thought. But try as she might, she could not forget the words Eli had spoken to her that day as they stood in the field with the golden grass blowing in the wind and the sun shining on their shoulders.

Days passed. She did everything she could to think of ways to force him out of her mind. However, the harder she tried, the more she thought about him. He began to appear in her dreams. And finally, she could not bear it anymore. So she watched him come and go on his way to the yeshiva, and one morning after Herschel left for work, she waited for him outside the yeshiva, hiding on the side of the building where she would not be seen. When he came walking up to the door, she was glad to see that he was alone. "Eli," she said, her voice barely above a whisper.

Even though she spoke very softly, he heard her. He followed the sound of her voice. "Naomi?"

"Yes. I had to see you. I can't stop thinking about what you said."

He reached out and touched her hand. She trembled, but she couldn't pull her hand away from his. No man other than her husband had ever touched her, and Eli's fingers burned like fire, igniting her passion as they connected with her own. "Will you meet me tomorrow, early in the morning?"

She nodded. She couldn't believe that she was agreeing to this. If her parents saw her now, they would be mortified. Her husband would be appalled. She would be shunned by all of her friends and family. Yet, she knew that no matter what the consequences might be, she would meet him. "Where?" she asked in a very small voice.

"Where we saw each other in the field yesterday."

I shouldn't. I know that I shouldn't, and you know it too. What we have done thus far is bad enough. I know you want me. I want you too. And we both know that this is forbidden. What am I doing here? This can only lead to no good. I should return to my home, to my husband, to the safety of my present life. But when his eyes met hers, she melted. "I'll be there. Around eleven?"

"Yes, I'll be there too," he said, and his eyes bore into hers. Then he turned and walked away, leaving her shaking, terrified, yet excited too.

Naomi ran all the way to the edge of town. She had to get home and start dinner. It was getting late. But when she arrived at the village, she stopped running. She knew that if anyone in town saw her running, they would be curious as to why. Straightening her dress again, she began to walk quickly toward home. When she arrived, she noticed that her door was slightly ajar. A pang of fear shot through her heart. *Who is in my house? Is Herschel home early? Is he ill? Or is it something more sinister?*

Naomi entered gingerly and stood in the doorway. "Herschel?" she called out.

"Herschel's not home yet. He sent me home early. So I came over to mend the hem on the pants he wore yesterday. I noticed that the hem was coming down," Frieda said.

Naomi glared at her. "You came into my house when no one was home?"

"I am just here taking care of the wifely duties that you are neglecting. Where were you? Where are you busy running around to so that you can't take care of your husband? You were gone for such a long time with only a basket of mushrooms to show for it? Very strange, Naomi."

"Where I go and what I do is none of your business. You had no right to come into my house and take my husband's things out of his closet. How dare you!"

"If you were a better wife, I wouldn't have to."

"Get out of my house. Get out!" Naomi screamed.

"You're making a mistake pushing away my generosity. You'll be sorry for this. That, I promise you," Frieda said, then she picked up her handbag and walked out the door with her head held high.

Naomi sank down onto the sofa. She felt violated. *I wish Frieda would just leave me alone. I am afraid of her. I am afraid she will follow me and find out about Eli and me. And I have no doubt she would use that information to try to win Herschel. But I know for sure that it wouldn't work. He has no interest in her. However, the consequences for everyone I love would be terrible. Just terrible. She thinks Herschel is such a prize, but she doesn't really know him. She doesn't really know anything at all. But what is so dangerous about her is she thinks she knows everything.*

Herschel never seemed to notice that anything was on Naomi's mind. He never looked deep enough into her eyes to see that she was experiencing extreme inner turmoil. He ate his dinner as he always did, and without a word, he walked into the living room and sat in his chair. Then he began to read quietly.

Before she started to clean the kitchen, Naomi watched him from the little hallway into the living room. He didn't even realize that she was standing there looking at him. His expression was serious, and his face was buried in his law book. *There is something he is researching for work,* Naomi thought. Out of nowhere, Eli's face crossed through her mind's eye. She was ashamed because she imagined having intercourse with him. In her imagination she saw his eyes staring into her own, shooting rays of desire and passion that left her breathless.

Herschel made a small grunting sound at something he read. Realizing where she was, she was suddenly ashamed. Her face grew red and hot, and she turned and walked quickly into the kitchen. Then she began to clean furiously. But as she did, her mind drifted again, and this time she remembered the first time she and Herschel had intercourse. It was a clumsy and awkward event that took place in the little room in the synagogue that had been set aside for newly married couples to have their first sexual encounter. The wedding guests were in the banquet room. They were waiting for Herschel to bring out the bloody sheet so they could bear witness to the fact that Naomi had been a virgin bride. She didn't disappoint them.

When Herschel penetrated her, he was quick and forceful. She knew he didn't mean to hurt her, but he was unsure of himself, so he forced himself inside of her, so that he wouldn't look as if he was inexperienced. She knew he was. It was easy to tell. It was over quickly, and she was left with blood staining her thighs and the sheets beneath her. When Herschel brought out the sheet, the wedding guests all cheered. Naomi wanted to cry, but she didn't want him or the guests to see how disappointed, embarrassed, and humiliated she was. But she was also relieved that it was over. She got dressed. For years she'd wondered what her first time would be like, and now she knew. It was not pleasurable in any way. In fact, she hoped it would be a while before she had to do it again. But at least he was quick, and the entire thing was over in minutes.

Naomi couldn't say that she disliked her husband. He had some good qualities. Since the day she had become engaged to him, she had not gone to bed hungry even once. He brought enough food to her house to feed her entire family. She remembered how many times before Herschel came into her life, she and her sister lay in bed listening to their stomachs rumble but being afraid to complain, knowing all the while that it wouldn't do any good anyway. Their father could hardly make a living. Everyone in the neighborhood knew that Naomi's family was dirt poor. The parents did what they could for their children, but often there just wasn't enough to go around. Naomi and her twin sister had two older brothers and a younger sister. That made for five children in the family, five hungry mouths to feed. Sometimes, if the neighbors could afford to, some of them brought food. Naomi was embarrassed that people knew her family needed the charity. But shame took a back seat to hunger, and the family took whatever was given. And they were very grateful.

Meanwhile, Miriam and her husband, Aram, both worked. She taught Hebrew school, and he worked in town for the blacksmith, shoeing horses. It was a dangerous job, but he was young and strong. One evening after Miriam and Aram had dinner at Naomi and Herschel's home, the women were cleaning the kitchen when Miriam told Naomi that she was often worried about Aram's job. "I have heard so many terrible stories of horses who fell on top of the black-smith while he was shoeing them. The blacksmiths were maimed and sometimes even worse. Those animals are so heavy. If they fall on a man just right, they could easily kill him. I would die if a horse even stepped on Aram. It could break his foot or his leg. And when I think of those hot irons, I shudder. Do you know that my poor husband has got scars all over him from being burned? I wish he could do some-thing else. I wish and pray he could find another job. Something less dangerous," Miriam admitted.

"You love him, don't you?" Naomi asked, surprised, because it was rare for a woman to love her husband in their religious world. Marriage was a duty, an obligation that was expected and that must be fulfilled.

"I do. I never expected to love him. But I really do. I know that word 'love' is not common here in our village. In fact, it's not some-thing we strive for in a marriage. But I am fortunate. I thank Hashem every day, because Aram and I are very happy together. It has been this way since our wedding," Miriam said.

"I envy you," Naomi said, shaking her head. "I don't love my husband."

"But Herschel is a very good provider. You have everything in the world that any woman could need. And at least Herschel isn't in danger every time he goes to work the way my husband is. Herschel works in a clean office. It's a safe place. You know he is not lifting anything heavy or extremely hot, that could drop on him and break his leg or even kill him, God forbid. My husband works with such heavy equipment. At any time he could be injured or worse." She clicked her tongue and then spit on the floor. "God forbid." She said again.

"Yes, but I would trade all of that to be as happy as you are. You see, unlike you, I am a not eagerly awaiting my husband's return each night. The only time I feel at peace is when he is at work. It's the only time I feel that I am not being judged and failing. Herschel never seems happy with anything I do, and he always seems to be demanding more. He's just never satisfied. But I'll bet that you are waiting for Aram each night, aren't you? I can see it. You are looking out the window with eager anticipation each day when it's time for Aram to return home. Am I right?"

"You are. You know me so well," Miriam said.

"I'm not surprised. So, let me ask you something," Naomi said. "Do you enjoy having sex with him?"

"Naomi! How could you ask me that?" Miriam blushed. "That's a very personal question."

"Please don't act like we are strangers. You know that I could ask you anything. And you could ask me anything. We have talked about everything over the years. You are my twin, my best friend, my sister. We know each other better than anyone else could ever know us. So, please, just tell me, do you enjoy it? The sex, I mean?"

"Actually, yes. I do. When we are forced to separate because I am unclean during my menses, I am miserable. I know he is miserable too. The days pass slowly until the blood stops flowing and I test clean. Then I am so excited to go to the mikvah because I know that I will become clean and be ready for him. I can't get home fast enough. When I arrive home, he can hardly contain himself. He pulls me to him, and we are lost in each other's arms. I find him so beautiful inside and out. He is muscular and strong, and when he takes me in his arms, I feel warm and safe."

"I wish I felt that way with Herschel."

"You don't at all?"

"No, not at all. In fact, he doesn't even really take me in his arms. He just puts himself inside of me while I lie there and take it."

"Naomi, you say the crudest things! But that's awful. It really is."

"But it's true. I am glad that at least we sleep in separate beds. I couldn't bear to share a bed with him. He doesn't caress me or kiss me very much. I feel like he is just trying to get the job done. I mean, we all know that we are supposed to have children; it's what's expected of us. So, I guess he is trying to fulfill his obligation."

"I wish Aram and I were able to have children, but it doesn't look like we are going to. I haven't ever been late with my period. I am always right on time. It disappoints me. I am disappointed in myself. But Aram says he's not disappointed in me. He says it's all right with him that I can't conceive. He says he loves me anyway. And I know he does. But I wish I could give him a son."

"He is so generous. And so willing to help our parents out financially."

"Yes he is. He is so generous. And what makes it so touching is that he is not a wealthy man, and yet he is willing to share what he has. I think he would help our papa and deny himself if he had to. He is so kind."

"Papa," Naomi scoffed. "He's got us all working for him now. You and your husband help our parents; Herschel and I give them money too. They are doing better than they ever did. Papa must be quite happy. He doesn't have to work much at all anymore. And he was always quite lazy. If he had his way, he would sleep all day," Naomi said bitterly.

Miriam put her arms around her sister. But she didn't argue the facts.

The rest of Naomi's siblings did not help their parents. Her brothers both worked at trades; they had two children each and hardly earned enough to care for their own families, but at least they'd married poor girls who expected very little of them. Their baby sister had recently married a farmer, and as of yet they didn't have any children. When the crops were good, he would sometimes send food for her parents. But for the most part, they didn't help much.

Naomi's father liked Aram, and he was grateful for everything Aram gave him. But Herschel was, by far, his favorite son-in-law. And Naomi knew her father often bragged to his friends that Herschel gave him more than enough money to keep him comfortable in his old age. Naomi knew that she should be grateful to her husband for all that he did for her parents. But as much as she tried to see Herschel's good qualities, she had to admit to herself that living with him, often felt like living alone.

She longed for human companionship. She was starved for human touch. Not necessarily sexual touch, but a touch of his hand on her shoulder or a gentle caress would have meant so much to her. If he would only have taken the time to sit and talk with her, to laugh with her, to make her feel appreciated, she would have done anything to try to care for him. And she would have tried harder to find a way to get over her feelings for Eli. But Herschel wasn't capable of this. Even though they'd been married for a while now, he still didn't know how to really communicate with her. And he didn't try to learn. Most of the time when they spoke, his answers to her questions were limited to one or two finely chosen words: "Yes" or "No" or "Do as I say."

CHAPTER EIGHT

THE GUILT SHE FELT FOR WHAT SHE WAS ABOUT TO DO WAS CONSUMING her as she walked out into the countryside to meet Eli the following day. *What am I doing? Where am I expecting this to go? No good can come of it*, she thought, but still she walked toward the open field, where she knew Eli would be waiting for her.

And he was waiting. He was sitting on the ground under the shade of a large old oak tree, his long legs crossed under him. When he looked up and saw her, his face lit up. "Naomi," he said. "You came. I was afraid you wouldn't."

She nodded. "I know I shouldn't have. But yes, I came. I am here."

"I'm glad. I was worried all night that you would change your mind."

"I changed my mind a hundred times. But in the end, I had to come. I had to see you."

He admired her with his eyes. And each admiring glance made her feel warm and wanted as she had never felt before.

Then in a soft voice barely above a whisper, he said, "You are my bashert. I know it. I am so certain of it."

She shook her head, and tears began to form in her eyes. "Then why didn't things work out differently with us? Why are we meeting here, sneaking around like criminals? If I am really your bashert, we should be married. Not meeting here doing this against Hashem's commandments. We are sinning, Eli." Naomi looked away from him and down at the ground.

He touched her cheek gently with his fingers. "I don't believe that. I refuse to believe that true love is ever against Hashem."

"I am an adulterer," she said soberly. "I am doing wrong, and I know it. But I can't stop." She looked away. There was silence for a few seconds, then she said, "I've heard you're a convert. Is that true? I heard that you were adopted, and your birth parents are not Jewish."

"Yes, it's true. My birth mother was not Jewish. I don't know who my birth father was. I was adopted as a baby by my current parents, and they are very Jewish. So, from the time I was very small, I began to study the Torah. I would say that this makes me Jewish, no?"

"I have heard even more about you. People say that you are a scholar. So, I am sure you are familiar with the commandment about adultery?"

"Yes, but it's different with us."

"You can't really believe that. You study the Torah. I am sure that you must know the truth about us. You just don't want to believe it as I don't want to believe it."

"Maybe you're right. Maybe I just can't let myself accept it. I have to believe that our love will prevail somehow."

"I've also heard it said that the rabbi favors you, because you have a good mind. Everyone says you are a true scholar."

"I am a seeker. I am trying to understand and to learn. But I suppose I am a bit of a rebel, too, because I don't believe everything I read in the holy books. Sometimes I just follow my heart. I believe that sometimes God wants us to follow our hearts."

"Instead of his commandments? I highly doubt that," Naomi said.

Eli shrugged.

"Then, I guess you just can't understand what I am going through. These feelings I have for you are a sin. I can't just ignore the fact that I am a married woman."

"I know the laws. And believe me, sometimes I feel guilty too. Oh,

Naomi, if you only knew how hard I tried to stay away from you. But I couldn't. That's why I knew for certain that you are my bashert. I have never felt this way before about anyone."

"So what happens now? There is no possible future for us. I'll tell you what happens now. Now I go home to my husband, and forever I have to carry this secret inside of me. This secret of meeting with you, alone. This secret of all these strange, wonderful . . . terrible . . . unexplainable . . . feelings." She was crying softly. "I am sick with guilt."

He reached over and took her hand. She didn't resist even though she knew she should. Then he leaned over and kissed her. She was lost in his kiss. *I am starved for human kindness; I am hungry for human touch*, she thought as a dizzying feeling came over her. *I should push him away.* Her resistance lasted for only a moment because when he kissed her, she felt her body surrender to him completely.

Eli removed her headscarf and touched her hair as it fell about her shoulders. He kissed her neck softly and gently until she was moaning, and then he unbuttoned the top of her dress. She couldn't think straight. Her mind was blank, so all she could do was feel. It was like her entire body was a hypersensitive organism incapable of thought or reason. All she knew was that she wanted him, needed him, could not walk away from him. He made love to her under the tree that day. And for the first time in her life, she knew what it felt like to be loved. He did not rush; he made sure she was ready before he entered her. Then he was so gentle that her body moved in rhythm with his. When they were finished, he climbed off her and lay down beside her, kissing and caressing her shoulder. "I've never made love to a woman before," he said. He spoke so openly that it made her turn away with embarrassment. But he did not stop speaking. Gently he put his hand on her chin and turned her head, so she was facing him again. Then he looked into her eyes and said, "I love you. I loved you before today. I love you even more now."

"I am frightened. I feel like my life is falling apart," she said.

"There's no need for you to be frightened. There is no need for your life to fall apart. If you want to file for a 'get,' a Jewish divorce, I would be honored to marry you."

"I can't do that. I dare not. My parents would be mortified if I divorced Herschel. Besides, you are a scholar; you don't earn any money, and I am a girl from a poor family. How would we afford to live?"

"I would give up my studies and I would find work."

She took his hand in hers. The skin was soft, the hand of a student. Not the hand of a hardworking man. "What would you do?"

"Anything. I would do anything to be with you, to be your husband."

"I can't do that. I can't take you away from your studies. It would be another sin. What we have done here today, is sin enough."

"Please, I am begging you not to say that this is the end of us. Please don't say that we can never meet like this again."

"I should say that. And I should mean it. But I know better. I want you as much as you want me. We will meet again."

"When? When can I see you again? Can I see you tomorrow?"

"Not so soon. If we pace ourselves, and we don't meet every day, we will be less likely to get caught." She sighed and shook her head. "Eli, I just can't get caught. My parents would die."

"Then we won't get caught. How often do you think you can come up here to this valley without anyone taking notice?"

"Once a week should be safe. We must be very careful. So, each time we meet I will have to return with a basket of mushrooms. You know how people in our village are. They will notice if I go and then return empty handed. But if I bring back a basket of mushrooms, they will think that's why I go out to the country, and hopefully they won't look into it any further."

"So, bring your basket, and I will help you gather mushrooms. I will do anything that you need me to do so long as I can see you and be with you."

She smiled at him. "I have to go now. We have been here for at least two hours. I'll see you next week on Wednesday at the same time."

"I'll be here waiting," he said. Then as she started to get up, he gently pulled her arm, so she sat back down. Then he kissed her softly and touched her cheek, slowly running his fingers down to her chin. "My bashert," he said.

That day, as she made her way back home, she realized that she hadn't gathered a single mushroom. When she left her house that morning, she'd been so nervous that she hadn't even thought about gathering them. Therefore, she hadn't brought her basket with her. A pang of guilt and fear ran through her. If anyone asked her where she had been, she would say that she had been taking a walk and praying to conceive a child. Straightening her back, she began to walk quickly toward home. When she got to the outskirts of the village, she looked around to see if anyone was sitting outside watching. After all, it was a beautiful day, and people often sat outside. But she saw no one. Before she knew it, she had arrived at home. To her relief, no one was paying attention as she strode up the walkway and entered the house she shared with Herschel. Immediately, she started to prepare dinner. Herschel would be home soon, and he would expect a hot meal. As she cut the vegetables for the stew she was going to prepare, her thoughts drifted to Eli: *Why was this afternoon so wonderful? Why was it so beautiful? And why can't it be that way with Herschel?*

Naomi was nervous about facing Herschel. She was afraid he would be able to sense that there was something different about her, or perhaps even see it in her eyes. As he walked into the house that evening, she felt her body tremble with fear. But he didn't notice a thing. That night was just the same as every other night since the day she'd married him. He walked into the house and hung his hat and coat on the rack by the door. Then he said, "Good evening."

"Good evening," she answered as she always did.

There was no other exchange of words as he walked into the bathroom to wash up. Then he sat down at the table, and she served him. He ate his dinner in silence. When he was finished, he wiped his lips carefully with his napkin, stood up, and walked into the living room, where he quietly sat down in his overstuffed easy chair and began reading from one of his law books while she cleaned up the kitchen.

Once her kitchen was spotless, she got ready for bed. "I'm going to sleep," she said softly. He never looked up from his book; he just nodded.

She hoped he would think she was asleep when he came to bed an hour later. He never checked to see if she was awake before he climbed into her bed and began to have sex with her. She was worried again that her body would somehow feel different to Herschel now that she had been with Eli. However, if it did, he never said a word about it. He did what he had to do to finish, and then with a grunt he went back to his own bed. "Good night, sleep well," he said.

"Yes, the same to you."

Naomi felt a chill that was more than physical. It ran through her body and then penetrated her very soul. She wept softly into the pillow. There was no point in waking him up. Where in the past she'd always hoped he would want to talk afterward, today she was glad he was snoring. After making love with Eli she knew for certain that Herschel was not in love with her, and he never would be. He thought of her as the perfect wife. She made the right impression on people. And that was what was important to him. When he went to her bed, he did not want to be intimate with her; he was only doing his duty to get her pregnant. This was to be her life.

When she'd signed the ketubah, the marriage contract, that day she married Herschel, she had signed away any chance of happiness. They had both been raised to know and understand what would be expected of them as adults. It was his job as her husband to impregnate her, and as his wife, it was her job to lie there and allow it. But now that she'd tasted the exquisite pleasure of being loved, she yearned to taste it again. *I am a terrible wife. I am a terrible person, because I no longer care about my marriage. I no longer want to try to find ways to make things better between Herschel and I. I am a sinner because all I can think of is Eli and the next time I will feel the heat of his lips on mine.*

CHAPTER NINE

ELI HAD ALWAYS LOVED TO LEARN. THAT WAS WHY HIS TEACHERS AT THE yeshiva had been impressed with him since he was a small child. Even the rabbi had taken a special liking to him. He'd come from a difficult background. Although he didn't know his parents, he knew enough to know that he was born out of wedlock to a non-Jewish woman. He'd always felt blessed to have been adopted by his Jewish parents. However, when he was growing up, his past had felt like a burden he had to overcome. And maybe, he reasoned, that was why he'd worked so hard to be a good student. But after that day in the field with Naomi, he felt a change in himself.

Now, Eli had a hard time focusing on his books, and he didn't enjoy studying or having religious discussions with the other scholars the way he had in the past. His thoughts were of Naomi, and they constantly crept into everything he did. When he wasn't lost in the memories of making love to her, he was on his knees praying for forgiveness. There was no doubt in his mind that what they were doing was wrong. And he felt terrible for having dragged her into this. After all, he knew from the start that she was married to another man. But he justified it by telling himself that she was his bashert. *Naomi is the other half of my soul. Isn't it obvious by the glorious way that we feel when we make love? I have to believe that this is an indication from Hashem that we belong together. But if it is so, then why has Hashem not made her my wife?*

Two days after Eli and Naomi had their first physical encounter, Ari, Eli's best friend and roommate at the yeshiva, confronted Eli. They had been friends for a long time. He was one of the only boys at the yeshiva who wasn't jealous of the favoritism the rabbi paid to Eli. Because of this, they had been like brothers since the day they met, when they were just small children. And even though the rabbi's attention to Eli grew as the boys got older, the friendship between Ari and Eli never changed. Ari knew Eli very well, and because he did, he could tell that something wasn't right with Eli. "I want to talk to you," he said. "So, what's wrong with you lately? You've been so distracted. You can't even have a decent Talmud discussion. Your logic is off. Are you feeling well?"

"I have a problem. I don't know if I should discuss it with you or not. It feels like a betrayal to her if I tell you."

"Her? There's a woman involved?" Ari said, shocked.

Eli nodded. "Yes, a very special woman."

"One you are planning to marry? Have you spoken to her father? Don't tell me you have spoken to her?"

He shook his head. "Yes, I have spoken to her, and not to her father. You see, Ari, this situation is far more complicated than that," Eli said.

"What is it? She's betrothed to someone else?" Ari guessed.

Eli turned away. Then he said, "If I tell you, you must promise me that you will never tell anyone else. Not anyone, not ever."

"I promise you," Ari said. "You've told me plenty of things that you wanted me to keep secret, and I've never told anyone. You can trust me, Eli. Nu? What is it with you?"

Eli felt confident that he could trust Ari with his secret, and he had to tell someone, or he felt sure he was going to explode. "I am in love," he said.

"Love? That's a real goisha word. We don't marry for love here. You know that. Marriages are practical arrangements."

"Ahhh, so they say. But for me, it's different. You see, I've met my bashert."

"Your bashert? Really? Are you sure of this? I have never spoken to anyone who said they met their true bashert before."

"I am sure. One hundred percent, I am sure."

"I don't know what to say," Ari said, rubbing his thin dark beard. "Nu, if you're so sure, then you should go and speak to her father. Tell him you would like to make a shidduch. Tell him that you are a scholar, that you are a favorite of the rabbi. These things will impress him. I am certain of it."

"I can't."

"Nu, so then go to a matchmaker, and have her talk to the girl's father for you. You need money for the matchmaker? I have a little bit that I can give you. Pay the matchmaker, and have her arrange things for you."

"I wish it were that easy." Eli sat down on the bed and put his head in his hands. "I've sinned. And I can't stop myself from sinning again."

"You're talking in circles. Please explain better, what it is that you are trying to tell me."

"She's already married," Eli blurted out.

"She's married? Oy vey, Eli, this is a sin. You must never tell her how you feel."

Eli nodded. "I wish it were so easy. I've already told her. I've made love to her."

"You did what?" Ari was shocked. "You had sex with a married woman? This is a terrible sin." Ari shook his head from side to side in anguish.

"I know."

"You must pray for forgiveness. Go and talk to the rabbi. Tell him what you did."

"I can't."

"Then talk to the man who is above the rabbi. Go and see the rebbe. He's the wisest man in town. He should have some advice for you. Make an effort to help yourself."

"I can't. I can't do that to her."

"You must. I know you don't want to tell him who the woman is, and I don't blame you. So, you won't tell him that. But you must tell him what you did and that you need help, so you don't do it again."

"Ari, all I can think of is how much I can't wait to do it again."

"This is terrible, Eli. Does she have children?" Ari asked.

"No, no children. She's newly married."

"Oy vey. Well, at least there are no children involved. Still, this is a big problem, my friend. You should end it now before it gets worse."

"I know you're right. But I also know I won't. I can't. She's my bashert. I can feel it when I look into her eyes. I feel my soul touch hers, and I will stay with her as long as she will let me. I will only leave her if she demands it of me."

"I don't know what I can say or do for you. But you can be sure that I will be here for you. No matter what you do or what you have done, you are my best friend, and you can always talk to me. You should know that. But I believe in my heart that you are making a terrible mistake. If her husband finds out, she will be shamed forever. And you will be shamed too."

"I don't care what anyone says about her and I certainly don't care what happens to me. I would marry her if her husband would give her a divorce."

"Does she want that?"

"No, she doesn't. He is a very successful man. And she's from a poor family. I am sure he helps her parents financially. That's why I must keep this whole thing a secret."

"I am worried about you," Ari said.

"I AM worried about me too. But I am more worried about her. That's what love is. When you care more about the other person than you care about yourself."

Ari shook his head, but he didn't say another word.

The next day Eli decided to take a job tutoring boys for their upcoming bar mitzvahs. He was willing to put off his constant studies, because he wanted to have a little money in order to buy a few gifts for Naomi. He also planned to put most of the money he earned away, so just in case they got caught and she wanted to leave the village, he would be able to afford to take her away and marry her. But in the meantime, he would buy her a few small things he knew would make her smile.

CHAPTER TEN

THEY MET THE FOLLOWING WEDNESDAY. SHE FELL INTO HIS ARMS, AND they made love slowly, devouring the seconds they were together, holding each other close for an hour. Naomi thought it was the most precious hour of her life thus far. After it was over, they lay side by side still breathless. He kissed her hand, and they began to talk. She told him a little about Herschel, the good and the bad. He told her about his parents and how they'd taken him in and given him a home when he was just a few days old.

"I was born in shame," he said. "My birth mother was the girl-friend of a married traveling salesman. This salesman knew the man who is now my father. From what my parents tell me, this salesman came to our neighborhood to sell my father sugar and flour for his store. My father, who is a kind and generous fellow, became friendly with him.

Somehow, this salesman learned that my parents could not conceive, and that more than anything, they wished for a child of their own. Finally, my birth father told my parents that his girlfriend was pregnant and thinking about trying to get rid of the baby. My father talked to my mother. They both agreed that they wanted to adopt the baby. So my father begged the salesman to ask his girlfriend if he and my mother could adopt me when I was born. From what my papa says, my birth parents decided that it was a good idea.

My birth mother came to live with my parents. She stayed in our neighborhood until I was born. Then she gave me away to my parents, who have been kind and wonderful to me all of my life. And she left. No one has ever seen or heard from her again. I was a lucky child. My papa, who raised me, is a brilliant man, and although he never had enough money to quit working and spend his days studying, he always wanted that for me."

"Don't your parents own the bakery in town?"

"Yes, but they own it in partnership with my uncle and his family. They do well enough, but not so well that my father can quit his job and study."

"I understand," she said.

"Your husband is a lawyer, and he owns several of the buildings in town, doesn't he?"

"Yes, he does," Naomi said.

"So, he earns a good living. That's why your father chose him to be your husband."

She nodded. "My parents are poor. My father is a handyman. He has always done odd jobs. But there was rarely enough money when I was growing up."

"Yes, I know."

"How do you know that?"

"In this small town everyone knows everything about each other," he said.

"That's true."

"Money." He sighed. "If I had a lot of money, I would buy you a castle and make you my princess."

Naomi laughed. "You do say the sweetest things." She was more comfortable with him than she had ever been with her husband. He was easy to talk to, easy to laugh with, easy to dream with.

"I mean it. I wish I could give you everything good in the world. But all I have to give you is myself, my heart, and my soul."

"After you told me that story about the twin souls, I read it in the

Talmud last week. I spent the entire afternoon reading it while Herschel was at work."

"It's a beautiful story, isn't it?"

"It is. And you have made me believe that it's true. You have made me believe that your soul is the other half of my own. All my life I have been searching for something, but I never knew what it was. I felt empty most of the time, and except for my twin sister, I haven't ever felt close to anyone. Miriam, that's my sister, is my best friend, and I have always felt fortunate to have her in my life. But it's different with you. My parents were never close to me or any of my siblings. My father was cold and distant, and my mother was over-whelmed with trying to keep her home and children together. So, although they knew me, they never really knew me. Not the way that you know me. So, I believe that you're right. Maybe it's true that our souls were one before we came to live here on earth."

"And when we are together, when we make love, our souls are joined again."

"Yes," she said. "Oh yes."

"You can feel it too?"

"Yes, I can feel it too."

They made love again. Afterward they walked hand in hand as they gathered a basket of wild mushrooms for her to carry back home with her.

"I hate for you to leave," he said.

"I know, but I must get home."

"I'll be thinking of you every single minute of every day until I see you again next week," he said, and his lips brushed hers. Then he took her in his arms and kissed her passionately. She almost dropped the basket of mushrooms. They both laughed.

"Goodbye until next week," she said and began walking back to the village.

Naomi and Eli continued to meet every week except for the weeks when she was unclean with her period. *I am such a hypocrite, I refuse to see him when I am having my period because I am unclean, and it is a sin to lie with a man when I am having my period. But the truth is I am unclean all the time now, because I am sharing myself with a man who is not my husband.*

When Eli and Naomi were together, she could forget everything. He filled her mind and body so completely that there was no room for guilt or thoughts of Herschel and her responsibilities to him. She had never been as happy before, not for a single day in her entire life, and she cherished the precious moments that she stole to spend with Eli. However, once she returned back home after being with Eli, and she heard sound of Herschel opening the front door as he returned home from work, she would take one look at her husband and her stomach would drop.

All the guilt fell upon her shoulders, and she was once again reminded of the sins she had committed and was continuing to commit. Often, during the week when she was alone, she would think of what she was doing and make a promise to herself that she was going to stop. She would tell herself that she was not going to return to the field to meet Eli the following week. But when the time to meet him came around, she found herself hurrying back into his arms again.

Winter arrived. It was too cold to meet outside, and there was no other safe place to meet. So, reluctantly Eli and Naomi agreed to stop seeing each other until the weather was warmer. A week passed, and Naomi fell into a deep depression. She had tasted the sweetness that life had to offer, and now the bitterness of her marriage was almost unbearable. When Herschel was at work, she did her chores as was expected of her, but her mind was always on Eli. She wondered what he did with his time now that they could not see each other. She cursed the frigid temperatures and the icy snow that kept them apart. *If he were my husband, the winter would be cozy. We would keep each other warm. But instead, I am here with a man I don't love, and he is at the yeshiva. Eli, I miss you so much. I wonder if he is studying all day? Perhaps he has forgotten me; perhaps he set his sights on someone else. I know it would be best, but I hope it is not true. I can't imagine spending the rest of my life without him. Is it even possible that he could think of me as often as I think of him? Hashem, forgive me. I am so weak.*

A month passed slowly. It seemed like a lifetime since she'd last seen Eli. Since her periods had always been regular, when she did not bleed that month she knew that she was pregnant. Although she'd been with Herschel as well as Eli, she was certain that Eli had given her the child. The pregnancy filled her with a million conflicting emotions. It was wrong to expect Herschel to raise another man's baby. Yet she dared not divorce him because of her family. She told him she was pregnant, and he was ecstatic. But he didn't hug or kiss her. Instead, he walked out of the house and went to the synagogue where he made a substantial donation. But there was no warmth in his feelings toward her. She felt like little more than a vessel that he was using to carry his child. And that made her miss Eli even more. She stopped praying, not because she stopped believing in God, but because she was ashamed to speak to Hashem after all that she'd done. She'd broken God's laws. How could she hope God would ever understand?

Her loneliness grew deeper, so deep that on the cold morning of the night before the Sabbath, near the end of February, she got out of bed and dressed warmly. Then she went into town to the marketplace in search of Eli. She had strategically planned to go on a Friday morning because she knew he would be shopping for food for Shabbat dinner that night. The cold wind penetrated her coat, which hid the small, rounded belly of her pregnancy. She passed the dry goods store; she passed the bakery that Eli's parents owned.

For a moment, she decided she wanted to walk inside. It suddenly felt very important to her to see the mother and father who had raised the man she loved. The two kind people who had so generously opened their home and their hearts to an unborn, illegitimate child. She wondered what they would think if they knew she carried their grandchild inside of her body. But she said nothing of this. Instead, she just smiled and bought a loaf of bread when his mother asked what she wanted. Naomi looked at the woman's hands as she wrapped the loaf, and a great tenderness came over her. *These hands wiped Eli's tears when he was a child. They helped him to get dressed in the morning. They prepared his meals.* If only she could put her arms around this stranger who had nurtured the man she loved. If only she could thank her. But she said nothing about it. She just paid for her purchase and left.

Back outside in the chilly winter weather, Naomi drew her scarf up around her throat and began to walk through the town shops searching everywhere for his dark hair, his winning smile, his gentle eyes. And then she saw him. He was in the butcher shop negotiating a deal with the butcher. She was so cold from the biting wind, but just looking at him made her feel warm all over. Naomi walked into the shop. She saw Eli's face light up with delight when he saw her. A smile formed on his lips, but she pretended not to notice him. He finished his purchase. Then she bought some soup bones and left as soon as she could. Eli was outside waiting for her. He was hiding between the two buildings.

"Naomi," he called in a soft voice.

She rushed to him. But he didn't touch her because they were outside, and even though they were hidden by the buildings, there was a good possibility they might be seen, and he knew she couldn't risk that. It was bad enough that they were speaking to each other and in a hiding place too.

"Eli," she said, her voice a little above a whisper.

"I'm so glad to see you."

"I am glad to see you too. But I also have something I must tell you."

"Tell me."

"I can't. I have to, but I can't. The words just won't come to me."

He laughed a little. "Please?"

"I'm pregnant," she blurted out the words. "The child is yours, I am sure of it. My grandmother told me in a dream, and I know it's true," she said, and then she looked down at the ground.

"Mine?" he said, surprised.

She nodded.

"Then, I am going to be a father?"

She nodded again.

"Oh, Naomi, I feel so blessed. How I wish I could hold you and kiss you."

"I know, but you mustn't."

He nodded. "I love you," he said. "I wish there was some way we could be together. I am going mad without you. Could I come to your home when your husband is at work?"

She longed to say yes. But that was too much of a sin. How could she let him make love to her in the room she shared with Herschel? It was beyond wrong. "No, it's bad enough what we are doing."

"It's not bad. I mean, you're right. Maybe it's a sin. But it is the most wonderful thing that has ever happened to me," he said.

She smiled, but at the same time she was crying. "Me too," she said.

CHAPTER ELEVEN

$\mathrm{I\!I}$

On a breezy morning in May, when the sky was a cloudless and bright robin's-egg blue, and the sun looked like a yellow ball of fire, Naomi went into labor. She and Herschel had been expecting it, and they'd already paid the town midwife in advance. Herschel had wanted Naomi to go into Warsaw to the hospital to have the baby, but she said she preferred to have a female midwife come to their home. "I want my child to be born the way my twin sister and I were born. We were born at home in our mother's bed. My children should be born here in my bed. It's the right way."

While Naomi was pregnant, Herschel was more indulgent than normal toward her. He wanted this birth to go smoothly, so he did whatever he could so as not to upset his wife. "I believe it's safer to give birth in the hospital," he said gently, "but if this is what you want, then I will agree to it. After all, I was born at home too."

She nodded and gave him a smile.

When Naomi told Herschel that the baby was coming, he said, "Lie down. I'll go across the street and ask if one of the women can stay with you while I go and pick up the midwife."

Across the street lived a family of four: a husband, a wife, a child, and the husband's mother. Herschel returned in a few minutes with the grandmother at his side. He left the old woman with Naomi and headed for the midwife's house.

"Don't worry, my dear. You'll be just fine," the old woman said. "You lie down and relax, and I'll be here with you until your husband returns with the midwife. I know how frightened you are. I remember my first birth. I was so young then, and I was afraid too," she said gently. Her face was so deeply lined that it was hard to see any evidence of the girl she had been when she was young.

"Thank you for coming," Naomi managed to say between intense labor pains. But she wished she could be alone with her fears. She had never felt such horrible pain, and she was suddenly afraid that God might punish her for her sins with Eli. The pain came upon her in tidal waves and although she was hot, her body was shivering. Her thoughts were of Eli. *How can I dare to pray for the safety of my child or myself after what I have done?* She longed to see Eli's face. *Somehow I know that if I could look into his eyes, I would not feel so frightened. I would remember that he is my bashert, and because of that, our love cannot be a sin.* But she didn't believe it. And she was terrified.

Herschel arrived with the midwife a half hour later. But Naomi labored the entire day and well into the night. Herschel grew worried, and because he was worried and unable to find a way to express himself, he grew angry. He couldn't bear to listen to Naomi crying out. So he went into the room where she was sweating and struggling. His emotions took over. "Why did you do it this way? I told you to go to the hospital and you refused. Now look at you. I could lose you both. You and the child could both die because this woman is incompetent in an emergency. If you were at the hospital, you would have a doctor taking care of you, and you would have the best care. Instead, you have this primitive, untrained woman who has put a knife underneath your bed to cut the pain. Naomi, you have made a mistake, and it could cost us both." Then he left, slamming the door behind him.

The midwife stared at Naomi in disbelief. "I have been delivering babies for twenty years, and I have never had a man walk in and say things like that while his wife was giving birth. I promise you, Naomi

Aizenberg, I may not be a doctor, but I will help you, and you will be all right."

Naomi nodded. She was so emotional that she couldn't stop crying. It wasn't as if she didn't know and understand Herschel's way of thinking. She did. She knew that whenever there was a problem, in order for him to feel in control, he must find someone else to blame. This was important to him. And since he had given her his permission to have the child at home, he had to make it clear that this was her fault and not his. But even knowing that he would respond this way didn't make it any easier to take. Between the intense pain and Herschel's cruel words, she was spent and reduced to weeping.

Gently the midwife examined her again. "The baby still has not turned. I don't think we should wait any longer. I am going to have to intervene and help the fetus."

Naomi nodded. *I am in trouble. I've heard of women dying when this happens, bleeding to death, or getting an infection after the birth. But if it is my destiny to die in childbirth, at least this waiting and constant pain will be over.* "All right. Go ahead and do what you have to do," she said.

The midwife nodded. "Brace yourself. This will hurt a little. Here." She handed Naomi the sheet from the bed that had been covering her. "Pull on this, it will help with the pain."

Naomi swallowed hard. And the midwife began. The pain was so agonizing that the room turned dark and began to spin. Naomi didn't know if she was crying out or not, but she was tugging on the sheet as hard as could. It felt wet between her legs. *I am bleeding*, she thought. *My baby is in danger.*

"All right, I know you're tired, but push as hard as you can when I tell you to."

Naomi nodded. Her eyes were wide; the sweat from her brow was dripping into them and it burned. She couldn't even tell if she was still crying or not.

"Ready?"

"Yes."

"Push."

Naomi pushed for the next forty-five minutes, and then she felt a rush of relief. The baby tore out of her body, leaving her exhausted. There was a lusty cry, and then the midwife said, "Mrs. Aizenberg, you have a little girl."

With trembling hands, Naomi took the infant and held her close. "Shoshana," she whispered.

"Am I bleeding?" Naomi asked the midwife.

"A little, but that rush of liquid you felt wasn't blood; it was your water. You're going to be fine, and the baby is perfect."

"Thank you so much for everything."

"You're welcome. Now I have to go and tell that husband of yours that he's a father."

She hates him, Naomi thought. *I don't blame her; sometimes so do I.*

Because Naomi was superstitious, nothing had been done to put together a nursery for the baby, before it was born. Therefore, as soon as Herschel was informed that he had a daughter, he went out and bought everything that they would need for their new child. And within a few hours, everything was delivered. After all, the furniture makers were well aware of this very superstition, which was very popular in their little village, and so they made sure to always have cribs on hand.

CHAPTER TWELVE

♊

IT WAS LESS THAN A WEEK AFTER SHOSHANA'S BIRTH THAT HERSCHEL went to the synagogue to make a donation and to arrange for his daughter's brit bat, or naming ceremony, when her Hebrew name, Shoshana Zahara, would be announced. He scheduled the special service for the following week, then stopped in town on his way to work where he purchased a dress for the baby to wear to her brit bat ceremony.

News of births, marriages, divorces, and deaths traveled quickly in this small village, where everyone knew everyone else. And it was less than an hour after Herschel Aizenberg left the synagogue that the rabbi's secretary spread the word about the Aizenbergs' new baby.

Eli and Ari were in the middle of a discussion when one of the young scholars told Eli and Ari the news about the Aizenberg baby. When Eli heard the news, his face turned white, then he asked, "How is the mother? How is the baby?"

Ari gave him a warning look as if to say, *You are appearing to be interested in this child's birth. For a single man, it looks suspicious.*

"Everyone is fine. Herschel Aizenberg made a nice donation to the shul. So, that's good for us, no?"

"Yes, very good," Ari said.

Eli's hands were trembling as he closed the book in front of him and asked, "So when is the brit bat?"

"Since when do you care so much about a brit bat?" the scholar asked.

"It's free food, no?" Ari made light of Eli's strange behavior. "And since the father is wealthy, the food should be exceptional. I want to attend. So does my friend here. Isn't that right, Eli?"

Eli nodded. "Yes, of course it's right," he managed to say. "Nu, so when is it?"

"Next week. I'll get you all the details."

CHAPTER THIRTEEN

EASTERN EUROPEAN JEWISH PEOPLE DO NOT NAME FOR THE LIVING. They name for those who they love who have passed on. In giving a child the name of a deceased loved one, it is believed that the loved one's soul will never die.

Shoshana Zahara was to be named for Herschel Aizenberg's paternal grandmother, who had adored and doted on Herschel when he was a small child. Naomi would have liked to name her daughter for her own grandmother, but Herschel was insistent, and as always he won.

On the day of the naming ceremony, as Naomi and Herschel walked up to present Shoshana to the rabbi, Naomi's eyes scanned the room. She saw Eli sitting with a group of other yeshiva scholars. His eyes met hers. His eyes were trying to communicate with her; they were deep and dark and filled with emotion. If only she could speak to him. If only it were not forbidden. But she knew he must not speak directly to her. He would be forced to congratulate Herschel. And that would be difficult for Eli, she was certain, because he knew that Shoshana was his child.

After the ceremony was over, pastries, coffee, and tea were served in the recreation room. The men and women were on separate sides.

Herschel took Shoshana to the men's side to show her to the crowd, while Naomi waited for him to return with the baby. As she waited, Eli and Ari walked past her on their way to the food, which was laid out on a long table. As Eli walked by Naomi, he slipped her a note. The paper burned in her hand as she looked around to make sure no one else saw what happened. Then she tucked the note into the pocket of her dress without reading it.

The reception, after the naming ceremony, seemed to take forever. Naomi tried to get away to read the note, but there were too many women surrounding her, and she was unable to escape them, until finally it was over, and the guests began to leave.

Once Naomi was at home, she took the note into the bathroom where she unfolded the small paper. Her hands trembled as she read.

Meet me tomorrow at eleven.

That was all it said. She knew where he expected her to meet him. And she also knew she would have to bring the baby with her. Still, she was excited to be seeing him, but a little disappointed too. She had hoped he would have written more. But she realized that he couldn't. In fact, it was best that he hadn't even signed his name. That way if Herschel somehow found the letter, she could tell him it was from Sarah or some other female friend. Naomi folded the letter and stuffed it back into her pocket.

Herschel had arranged to take the entire day off from work. He told Naomi that he hoped to have a relaxing afternoon reading and resting after the brit bat. However, he was not used to the needs of a newborn. She either needed to be fed or changed or carried around. When she took a nap, Naomi quickly cleaned the house while Herschel slept. But when the baby woke up crying, Herschel was clearly annoyed.

"It's easier to rest at work than it is here with this child," he said.

"I'm sorry she woke you."

"She doesn't sleep at night; she doesn't sleep during the day. Is this normal?"

"Yes, she's just a baby, Herschel. She'll get on a schedule. You just have to give her a chance."

"I'm sorry. I'm just tired. She wakes me up all hours of the night. I have to admit I wasn't expecting this."

"I know. And I realize that you have to work. That's why I would never expect you to get up with her during the night."

"Even so, she cries, and I can't get back to sleep."

"I'm sorry. It will get better. I promise."

The following day, Herschel seemed glad to leave for work. And Naomi was happy to see him go. Now she could get herself and Shoshana ready to meet with Eli.

It was a lovely spring day. Naomi gave the baby a quick sponge bath and clothed her in a dress she'd made for her to wear the first time she met Eli. Then Naomi put on a clean dress and scarf to cover her head. Next, she put Shoshana in the basket she used to collect mushrooms and began walking to the special place where she and Eli met.

As Naomi approached their meeting spot, she saw his tall, slender figure standing in the distance. *He is so handsome*, she thought, and her heart ached with love and desire for him.

A smile washed over his face that began at his lips and traveled to his eyes. "I have missed you," he said.

"I've missed you too."

"I was so worried about the birth, and I couldn't see you. I didn't know if you needed anything. It was terrible."

"I wanted you to be with me when I was giving birth. Believe me, you were on my mind."

"Naomi, we can't go on like this. You have to ask Herschel for a divorce. We have to be a real family. You can't imagine how I felt seeing another man claim my child as his own. This isn't right. Not for you, not for Shoshana, not for me, and not even for Herschel."

"I know," she said, and she turned away from him. "But I can't do anything to change it. This is all I have to give you. Please accept it."

He shook his head. "I should break this off. But I won't. I can't."

"I'm sorry," she said.

"I love you," he said, then he took the basket away from her and gently put it down on the grass. Shoshana had fallen asleep during the long walk from the house to the countryside and she was still slumbering. Eli took Naomi into his arms and kissed her. Then he held her tightly. "I love you, so I will accept whatever you can give me. Anything you can offer is better than a life without you."

The sweet fragrance of the wildflowers made her feel warm and overcome with emotion.

It was too soon to make love, but they were wrapped in each other's arms when Shoshana awakened and began to cry.

"Let me get her," Eli said.

Naomi nodded. "All right. But she doesn't know you, and she might start crying even harder. If she does, don't be offended. She'll get to know you."

Eli gently lifted his daughter out of the basket and held her against his naked chest. She stopped crying. "I can feel her little heart beating," he said.

"She likes you already."

"I love her."

"I know, so do I."

CHAPTER FOURTEEN

♊

THE FOLLOWING MORNING, NAOMI AWOKE WITH A START. HER HEART was throbbing in her chest. *Another dream. Another terrible dream,* she thought as she glanced over at Herschel. Desperate to talk to someone, she got out of her bed and sat down on the side of his bed. Then she gently nudged his arm. His eyes opened.

"Nu? What is it? What's the matter?" he said.

"I had another dream, Herschel. This time I dreamed of those same soldiers, the ones who had the flag with the black spider in the middle. They had taken control of everyone and everything. It was horrifying. But there is another part of it. I had twins, two little girls. And they wanted my twins for some reason. There was something they wanted from my twins. I felt like they might hurt my daughters." She was in a panic.

Herschel looked at her like she was out of her mind. "You don't have twins," he said.

"But I did in the dream."

It was just another dream, Naomi. Nu? For this you woke me up? A dream about crazy soldiers with spider flags and twins we don't have? What's the matter with you? I didn't think mental problems ran in your family."

"How can you be so cold?"

"Because you're acting crazy. I work hard. I need my sleep. You wake me up for no reason, and now I'll have trouble falling back to sleep. I don't know what's wrong with you. Are you meshugah?"

"I am not meshugah. I had a very bad dream, and I am afraid it was a premonition."

"It wasn't. I promise you that. The only thing real about all of this is that I am not going to get enough rest tonight." He shook his head. "I have to go back to sleep now."

She got up, defeated, still frightened, and walked back to her bed where she lay awake. *It's Monday. I only have two days until I can speak to Eli. I'll tell him my dream. I don't know if he can help me, but I know at least he will listen.*

It seemed like a lifetime until Naomi and Eli would meet that Wednesday. She tried to keep herself busy, but no matter how much work she did, she couldn't shed the foreboding feelings that were smothering her.

Finally, Wednesday arrived, and she went to see Eli. He was waiting for her, and he smiled when she approached. But then he saw the worry on her face and he stopped smiling. "What's wrong, my love?" he said, his voice filled with genuine concern.

"I had a terrible dream."

"Oh?"

"You see, there is a curse that runs in my family."

"What do you mean?" he asked.

"Well, twins run in my family, but one of the twins has always had dreams, and often those dreams were premonitions."

"That's not a curse. It's a gift."

"Every gift is a curse; every curse is a gift sometimes. When the dreams are bad, it feels like a curse. Anyway, I have a twin sister. But I am the one who has these dreams. So I am the one who feels cursed."

"I see," he said. "Do you want to tell me what you dreamt? You don't have to if you don't want to."

"I want to. I need to talk to someone. I dreamt I had twin girls and that a group of soldiers were trying to take them away. They were just small children, but I knew that the soldiers wanted to hurt them. But there was nothing I could do to stop them. They had all three of my daughters. Shoshana too. And I was so scared, Eli. I was terrified."

"It's all right." He soothed her and took her into his arms.

"This isn't the first time I've dreamt of these soldiers. They have a red-and-black flag with a black spider in the center. They are very dangerous. And I believe that they are coming."

"Don't be afraid. Please, don't be afraid. No matter what happens, I will protect you and Shoshana. And if you have more children, I will protect them too. I love you. I will always love you, and no matter what happens, I will give my life, if need be, to keep you safe. Do you believe me?"

"I believe you," she said.

Then lay your head on my shoulder, and let me be your comforter. Let me make you feel secure and safe."

She did as he asked and she felt comforted.

CHAPTER FIFTEEN

THINGS WERE EASY FOR ELI AND NAOMI FOR THE NEXT FEW YEARS. Shoshana was too young to speak or understand what was going on between her mother and Eli. But things changed when, at three and a half, Shoshana began to speak in full sentences, and one day she said something to Herschel about Mama's man friend. That day, Naomi knew that she was going to have to stop bringing Shoshana when she met with Eli. There was no doubt in her mind that Eli was going to be upset about not being able to see his daughter. Over the last three years, they had grown very close, but Naomi knew that children could and would say anything that came to their minds. And Shoshana had no way of knowing that the relationship between Eli and her mother was not supposed to be. The time had come to separate them.

At first, when Naomi told Eli that she was not going to bring Shoshana to see him anymore, Eli was furious. She'd never seen him so angry. He told her that he was tired of playing these games and that he was done with her. She had taken his heart, and now she was taking his child away from him. "The price of your love is just too high for me to bear," he said, then he walked away, leaving her standing in the middle of the field alone.

For the next two weeks, she went through the motions of living, but inside, she felt as if she had died that day that Eli walked away from her. If Herschel noticed that she hardly ate, and got very little sleep, he didn't mention it. He was busy working on a case with a non-Jewish business owner in the city, which he didn't bother to discuss with his wife.

Shoshana kept Naomi busy; she was an active and curious child. Naomi was grateful that she didn't have much time to think about how miserable she was. However, in the middle of the night when Shoshana was asleep, and she should have been getting her badly needed rest, Naomi was crying softly in her bed.

One morning, on her way to the market, Eli came out from behind one of the houses on the road. "I have been waiting here all week trying to see you," he said.

She was hurt and angry. "Well, now you see me, don't you?"

"Please don't be cold. I can't live without you."

"You hurt me. You left me standing all alone."

"I know. I wanted to try and say goodbye. But I can't. I hope you will forgive me and help me, at the very least, to see Shoshana at the market for a few minutes each week."

"I'll do it," she said. "I'll bring her with me. I come almost every other day. I can't guarantee which days I will be here. But I always come on Friday morning to buy food for the Sabbath that night."

Then I'll be here every Friday. And I'll at least be able to watch her grow even if it is only from afar."

For the next five years, Naomi and Eli continued to see each other. However, their relationship changed in many ways. Not because they chose for it to change, but because now it was difficult for Naomi to get away. She had Shoshana with her all day, and that meant that she couldn't go to her lover. Once in a while, Naomi was able to make up a story to her sister Miriam or her friend Sarah about desperately needing some time to sleep. "She doesn't sleep well," Naomi lied. "I can't remember the last time I slept through the night. When their own lives permitted it, Miriam and Sarah each did what they could to watch Shoshana for an hour or two, so Naomi could get the badly needed rest she told them she was lacking. During those infrequent times, Naomi would arrange to meet with Eli in the same place they had been meeting. Once they were together, they made desperate, passionate love to each other. There was no loss of feeling between them.

On Friday mornings, Naomi brought Shoshana with her to the market. Eli was always there doing his own shopping. Each week he would manage to find a way to look at his daughter. Naomi saw the love in Eli's eyes when he looked at Shoshana, and it upset her because she knew he would be good father. Not that Herschel was a bad father—he wasn't. He provided for Naomi and their daughter, and he never denied them anything they needed. But he didn't have the warmth within in him to share. He had never been able to show Naomi any warmth, so how could she expect him to show it to Shoshana. It was a relief that her little girl didn't remember Eli at all even though Naomi knew it hurt him. *I am horribly selfish*, she thought, *but I love him so much that I can't bear to let him go, even though it would be best for him.*

As Shoshana grew older, she became a good sleeper. And Naomi knew that the excuse she had given to Miriam and Sarah in the past would no longer work. Since Sarah's daughter, Neta, was the same age, Naomi began to use that as an excuse to leave Shoshana with Sarah and Neta. But now that she could no longer use exhaustion as an excuse, she had to find more clever ways to ask her sister to watch her child.

Sarah complained that it was too hard for her to keep an eye on both children and clean her house too. But Naomi knew that it wasn't Sarah who didn't want Shoshana around—it was Sarah's husband. So she stopped bringing Shoshana to visit with Neta. The only time she saw Sarah and Neta was when they took their daughters for walks together, or to the park.

Miriam's house was the only place she could safely and comfortably leave Shoshana while she went to see Eli. But her excuses were growing more and more lame, until one day her sister confronted her. They were alone in Miriam's kitchen. Miriam had just made fresh dough, and she was braiding it for challah. Shoshana was contented to be playing on the floor in the living room.

"What's going on with you? You ask me to watch Shoshana while you run here or there, to buy some flour, or to get some fabric. These are places you could easily take Shoshana. I don't know why you always want to leave her behind. She's a good girl; she behaves. Now, you know I love Shoshana as if she were my own, but I must admit I am worried about you. I feel something isn't right with you and Shoshana. Why do you still need to be away from her? You must tell me so I can help you."

"Do you promise me that if I tell you everything, you won't tell anyone?"

"Do you even have to ask me that? You know I would never say a word."

Naomi looked away, then she sighed. "I don't know how to tell you this, but I have a lover."

"It's worse than I thought," Miriam said, her hand flying up to her throat. "Oy vey, Naomi. What are you doing? Who is he?"

"You know him."

"I know him?" Miriam threw her hands up. "I know him?"

"Yes, you know him. It's Eli."

"Oy vey. What have you done?"

"He is Shoshana's father."

"What? What are you saying?"

"I am saying that Herschel is not Shoshana's father. My lover fathered Shoshana."

"This is terrible. And, of course, Herschel doesn't know?"

"No. He doesn't know."

"Oy, this is worse than terrible."

"I know. I can't end it with my lover though. I have really tried. But I love him."

"Love? Love isn't a part of our world. And things like this are the reason why." Miriam said. She was reprimanding her sister as if Naomi were a child.

"I know that too. But the difference between us, is that you feel something when you're with Aram. I know he makes you feel like you have value?"

"He does. He's a good man. He's kind to me. And I suppose if you want to use the goisha word 'love,' you could say I love him. Is Herschel unkind to you? Does he hit you?"

"No, and I feel fortunate for that. I know that Neta's husband hits her, and that is the worst thing any woman can endure. I am lucky to have a man who is a good provider and who isn't violent. I know all of this. But I have to stress to you that there is something missing with Herschel and me. I feel like I am alone, even when he and I are together."

"What do you mean?"

"He never talks to me. He never shows me any affection or appreciation."

"A lot of men are quiet like that. That's just their way. Mama always said that."

"I understand that. And I would never have gone looking for a lover, but when I met Eli, something just happened, and now it's like a snowball. I can't stop it."

"Now I am part of all of this, and I don't know what to do. You realize that you are bringing me into your sin. Because I am watching Shoshana while you spend time with your lover. I, too, am sinning, now that I know."

"I understand. And I understand that you can't watch the baby for me anymore. It's just that I don't know what I am going to do. Maybe I will just run away with Eli and Shoshana. Maybe that's my only choice."

"Don't do anything rash. I didn't say I wouldn't watch her for you. I wish you would stop this. But you're my sister, my twin. And you know that, no matter what, I can't say no to you. And I can't let you run away from your home and your husband, and me and our parents."

"Then I won't ask you."

"But I have to do something. I can't just ignore this. I can see how much this man means to you, and so I'll do it. I'll watch Shoshana for you."

Naomi looked away from her sister. She felt terrible that she'd pulled Miriam into all of this. And yet, she longed to go to Eli. The draw to him was so magnetizing that she couldn't resist. So she pushed the guilt out of her mind, and she accepted Miriam's offer to watch Shoshana. Then she arranged to be with the man she loved as often as she possibly could.

Early one hot summer afternoon, Naomi had made arrangements for Miriam to watch Shoshana for a few hours. Once she was dressed and ready to go, she went outside to wait for Miriam's arrival.

"Look up, Mama," Shoshana said. "Look at the clouds. That one looks like an elephant."

Naomi picked her daughter up and held her in her arms. Then she glanced up at the sky. There were billowing clouds that looked like cotton candy in all kinds of shapes. "Yes, it does, sweetie. And that one looks like a dragon."

"And that one looks like the face of wise old woman," Shoshana said as she pointed to a particular cloud.

Naomi stared at the cloud for a few moments. In the face, she saw a very close resemblance to her grandmother who had passed away when Naomi was young. The old woman seemed to be looking down on her, and Naomi imagined that she saw a tear her grandmother's eye. *She had such high hopes for me when I was small. She loved me so much, and now she knows that I am acting in a sinful way and bringing shame to our family, in the eyes of God. What am I doing, and why can't I stop?* A wave of guilt came over her; she felt as if she might begin to weep.

"Mama, what's wrong?" Shoshana said, touching her mother's face. Naomi looked at her daughter. She could see Shoshana was scared.

"Oh, nothing, I was just remembering my grandmother. I miss her so much."

"You look so sad."

"Well, yes, I am sad that she is not here to see you. But I know she is watching over you. I am sure of it."

"What was her name?"

"Devorah."

"So why didn't you name me for her?"

"Because I promised your father to name you for his side of the family."

"So, you'll name the next baby you have for your grandmother?"

"I would like that."

Maybe I should stay home with my daughter today. Maybe I shouldn't go to Eli, she thought, but when she imagined him holding her in his arms, her face grew hot, and she knew she would go. She pushed her guilt aside and tried her best not to think about it. For Naomi, Eli was like a magnet. When she was away from him, she was consumed with thoughts of him and the next time they would be together.

Miriam was waving and calling out to her as she walked up the street, carrying a bag of toys she'd recently purchased for her niece. "Naomi, Shoshana, I'm here."

Shoshana ran to her Aunt Miriam and put her arms around her.

"Did your mother tell you that I'm going to watch you this afternoon? That's because your mother has some business to attend to," Miriam said.

Shoshana, who was just turning six years old at the time, looked up at Miriam, and said, "I am so glad you're here. I always love spending time with you, Auntie Miriam. And you know what, I am glad you don't have any children because that means you can give all of your love to me."

"That's not nice," Naomi said. "You shouldn't say things like that."

"It's all right," Miriam said, and she smiled at Shoshana, but Naomi knew that the remark cut Miriam deeply. She knew how much her sister longed for a baby.

"I'm so sorry, Miriam. Children sometimes say the most terrible things. They just don't think before they speak," Naomi said. "She is just a child. And she loves you. She doesn't understand how much it would mean to you to have a child."

"I know," Miriam said, "and I love her. Don't even give it another thought."

Naomi hugged her sister. "I'm leaving. I'll be back before Herschel gets home."

Miriam nodded, and Naomi could see the disapproval and worry in her sister's eyes. It bothered her. But neither of them said a word about it.

"There's some cheese in the kitchen, and a challah if you get hungry," Naomi told her.

Miriam nodded.

Naomi left the house and walked as quickly as she could without drawing any attention to herself. But when she passed Frieda's house, Frieda came running outside.

"Where are you going in such a hurry?" Frieda said as she approached Naomi. "You are all dressed up. I would have to say that you certainly look pretty today."

Naomi glanced at Frieda. Her compliments were never really compliments. They were actually digs. "Thank you," Naomi said, but she was unnerved by Frieda noticing that she had taken extra care with her appearance.

"Nu, so where is the baby? A mother should never leave her baby. You run around a lot for a new mother. I see you sometimes in the market without the little one. You don't seem to have that strong motherly instinct that so many of us are blessed with. I am sure Herschel must worry that you are aren't the motherly type. Do you ever feel that you should be devoting more of yourself to your family than you do, Naomi?" Frieda continued before Naomi had a chance to answer. "Well, I suppose this is what happens when a man marries a woman who is just too pretty for her own good. She is busy showing off for the whole town, running around wearing fancy dresses, lipstick, and rouge instead of doing her wifely duties." Frieda clicked her tongue.

"What I do is none of your business. Shouldn't you be working? Why are you at home?"

"You're so on edge. There is no reason for you to be so angry at me, Naomi. I came to help you by hemming your husband's pants one day. And after that, you have been so cold toward me. I thought we were friends."

"Friends?"

"Yes, you and me and Herschel. We have always been friends. Now, as far as why I am home so early, Herschel sent me to pick up some things for him. Then he told me to go home early. He thought I needed the rest. I work very hard for your husband. It is because of how hard I work that you are so rich. Think about that sometime. It's the tremendous workload that I carry that gives you the good life you and your children have."

"I never asked you to do anything for me. You don't work with my husband because you want to give me a good life. You do it because you want to be around Herschel as much as you can. Don't lie to me."

"You are very wrong. And you are a very bitter woman. You should go and talk to the rabbi or someone to help you get rid of all your jealousy."

"I have to go."

"I am sure you do. And I can't imagine where you are headed in such a hurry."

Naomi was unnerved by this meeting. She knew she couldn't trust Frieda. Even when they were friends, she'd never been able to trust her. There had been many times when Frieda had betrayed her behind her back, and she knew that given the chance, Frieda would do it again. Quickly, she glanced behind her to see if she was being followed. *It would be just like her to follow me*, she thought, but she saw no one. So she continued on her way.

The conversation between Naomi and Frieda had made Naomi late. When she arrived at the open field, where she knew Eli would be waiting for her, she saw that he was distraught.

"I was worried," he said. "You're very late."

"I know. I am sorry. One of my neighbors stopped me, and I was afraid to brush her off."

"You did the right thing. I was just worried. If anything ever happened to you, it would kill me," he said.

"I'm sorry. You know I hate to worry you."

"I know. It's all right. By the way, you look beautiful," he said, then he smiled. "I brought you a gift."

"For me? But why?"

"Of course, for you. And why? It's because you are the woman I love. A man gives his heart and soul to the woman he loves. And if he can, he enjoys giving her gifts. When you smile, it lights up the whole world for me," he said.

She laughed a little and then touched his cheek. "That's the sweetest thing anyone has ever said to me."

"You are my world. You should know that. Now, do you want to see your gift?"

"Of course, I do. Nu, so what did you bring me?"

He took a small box out of his pocket and handed it to her. She opened it. Inside she saw a small gold heart in two pieces hanging on a gold chain.

"We are two parts of the same heart of the same soul," he said. "Do you like it?"

"It's beautiful and I love it. But I can't wear this. You know that. What would I tell Herschel when he saw it?"

"I know you can't wear it. But you can keep it somewhere secret. Somewhere safe. And when you look at it, you'll know that each half represents our hearts. And that my heart is always with you no matter where you are."

"You spent a lot of money on this. A student doesn't have money to waste on jewelry. I don't like to see you spend your money on me."

"First of all, it was not a waste. I wanted to give you something, something of meaning from me to you. And second of all, I got a job tutoring boys for their bar mitzvahs, so I have a little bit extra each month."

She kissed him. "You are so kind to me."

"How else could I be? I love you. You know that. I want to give you everything beautiful in the world. I want to share every part of my life with you."

"And a day doesn't go by that I don't wish that we could do just that. But then I look at my husband and my child, and I am reminded that I have responsibilities."

"Your husband is not the right man for you. And Shoshana is my daughter too. It is only because I love you, and I don't want to cause you any shame that I don't tell the world that she is mine. But every time I see her, I wish that you and I had a home together and that the three of us were a family."

"Don't, please stop. Let it be. There is nothing I can do to change things. The consequences would be horrible. My parents would sit shiva for me, as if I were dead, if I left Herschel. They would never take me back into their lives. And I couldn't live with the guilt of seeing them as they enter into their old age without any help or comfort from me. I just can't do it, Eli. And as for you, can you imagine the shame you would bring to the rabbi? He has chosen you as a favorite. The whole town would look at him and think he was a terrible judge of character. It would be bad for him too. This is what we have, Eli, a few hours a week if we are lucky. And we must be happy with these few stolen moments we share. Anything else would bring disaster to us and to the people we love. Not to mention the stigma our relationship would put on Shoshana if everyone in town found out you are her real father. Just imagine what would happen when she gets to marriageable age. It would be so difficult to make a match for her. Everyone in town would say she was born to a crazy mother, who had an adulterous affair. They would call her bastard, born out of wedlock. My shame would become hers. You know how they would talk. And they would ruin her."

"Yes, unfortunately I do know. And that is why I don't say a word. I just watch you and Shoshana from afar. And I take these moments with you as a gift, and I savor them greedily because even a few moments with you is heaven."

They spent the afternoon in each other's arms. Then a half hour before Naomi had to leave, they walked through the field and collected the mushrooms together for Naomi to bring home with her.

CHAPTER SIXTEEN

WHEN NAOMI ARRIVED BACK AT HOME, MIRIAM WAS SITTING IN THE living room. She was nervous and distraught. Her face was flushed, and her voice was strained. "You were gone a long time," she said.

"What happened? You look upset. Is Shoshana all right?"

"She's fine. She's taking a nap. But something happened while you were gone, and quite frankly, I am worried."

Naomi sat down beside her sister on the sofa. "Tell me what happened."

"While you were gone, Frieda Bergstein came here to see Herschel. I told her Herschel was at work. And since she works with him, she should know that. Nu, so why did she come? The truth is, I don't really think she came to see him at all. I think it was an excuse. I think she came to check up on you. Maybe he sent her."

"That's odd. Very odd. You're right. She is his secretary, so she would know where he was."

"Perhaps he sent her to spy on you?" She brought him a box of mandelbrot; it's on the kitchen table. I am assuming she baked it for him."

"Hmmm, well, she's done that before. But never during a work-day. Usually, she comes by in the early evening."

"She said Herschel left work early, and she thought that he went home. So, she finished her work and left for the day. Then she went home to get the cookies and brought them here, thinking he would be home."

"If it is true, where is he?" Naomi asked.

"I don't think it's true. I think he sent her to spy on you. She was so curious as to where you were and why you weren't at home. She asked a lot of prying questions. Like why I was here watching Shoshana. You know how bold and nosy she is. She wanted to know why you couldn't take Shoshana with you wherever you went."

Naomi chewed on her lower lip. Then she said, "So, what did you tell her?"

"I told her that you went to see a doctor."

"A doctor? Why?"

"She asked me why, but I told her that it was personal."

"What am I ever going to tell Herschel? Why would I have gone to see a doctor?"

"Fainting spells? Tell him you get dizzy, and you feel faint sometimes, so you went to see the doctor."

Naomi nodded. "That's a good idea. I'll tell him that if he asks."

"I'm sure he'll ask. I'm sure Frieda will run back and tell him that you were not home and that I said you were seeing a doctor. Oh, Naomi, this is getting so dangerous. What if Herschel has someone follow you and they see you and Eli together? What then?"

"I don't know. I don't know," Naomi said as she was holding her head. "I should give Eli up, but I can't. Except for Shoshana, he is the brightest light in my life. I love him, and my love for him makes this marriage bearable. Without him, I don't know how I could live through each day and night with Herschel."

But Herschel never asked about the doctor or why Miriam was watching Shoshana. If Frieda told him anything about her coming over and finding Naomi gone, he never mentioned a word of it to Naomi.

That was five years ago. Five years since, Naomi and Eli said goodbye. Yet it still hurt her as much as the day they parted.

CHAPTER SEVENTEEN

THAT NIGHT, WHICH WAS THE SECOND NIGHT OF HANUKKAH, THE TWINS sat on the floor while twelve-year-old Shoshana helped her mother clean up the kitchen after dinner so the family could light the menorahs.

The twins were engrossed in a game of dreidel. They played with a dreidel that had been in the family for years. In fact, Naomi and her sister Miriam had played with it in the exact same way when they were just little children. Naomi glanced at her two daughters and thought, *I must remember to always be grateful to Hashem for giving me such wonderful and healthy children. I must not think about Eli and what could have been. I must be happy with what I have, even if my husband is not the man I wish he was.*

"Dreidel, dreidel, dreidel, I made you out of clay, and when you're dry and ready, oh, dreidel I will play." The twin girls sang the old familiar Hanukkah song, giggling. Bluma was an expert at spinning the dreidel. She held it carefully by the top and then set it into motion. The little top spun perfectly while Perle watched with admiration.

"You're so good at this," Perle whispered into her sister's ear. "The truth is you're so good at everything. You're not like me. I can't get anything right."

"You want me to show you again how to do it?" Bluma asked. "Here, watch"—she held the dreidel—"like this."

"It doesn't matter; it won't help. You've shown me a hundred times, and I still can't do it. So, how about this, you can do it for both of us," Perle said. Then she added, still whispering, "By the way, I know what our parents got us for Hanukkah."

"How do you know?"

"A dream," Perle said.

"When?"

"Last night."

"So, what did they get us?"

"Guess," Perle said.

"Socks?"

"Yes, socks, but also something really good."

"What . . ." Bluma asked, frustrated. "I can't guess."

"A wooden rocking horse big enough for us to sit on it and rock like we were riding a real horse," Perle whispered.

"Are you sure? I can't imagine Papa spending that much money on us," Bluma said. "You know how he hates to spend money unless he is making a donation that everyone in town knows about."

"I know he is always saving it, just in case he needs it. Or so he says. But he did spend the money."

"You saw it in a dream?" Bluma asked skeptically.

"I did. It's painted blue and white with a brown mane," Perle admitted.

"If you saw it in a dream, then it's for sure. Your dreams are never wrong. So it looks like we're getting a wooden rocking horse," Bluma said excitedly. "I've always wanted one."

"Me too," Perle said, "but I am a little afraid to get on. I think this one might be kind of tall for us. Papa might have to lift us up to get on."

"I'll get on," Bluma said. "Even if I have to climb on a chair."

Bluma believed in Perle. She believed in her heart that her sister's dreams were always accurate. Once, a few months ago, their mother had misplaced a soup ladle. She and Shoshana had searched the entire house, but the soup spoon was nowhere to be found. Finally, there was nothing to do but give up the search. They were all quite sure she would never find it. But then one night, a few weeks later, Perle had a dream in which she saw the soup ladle. She saw that her mother had left the utensil in the kitchen at the synagogue. And although Naomi did not remember ever taking the ladle to the synagogue, she went to check. And to her surprise and delight, the ladle was there.

Another time, there was a very strange incident in the village. A fourteen-year-old boy went missing. His parents were distraught. They didn't know what had become of him. The rabbi called everyone to the synagogue, where a search party was formed. The town's people searched everywhere but found nothing. Panic and chaos ensued. People began to talk as if the boy were dead. "Perhaps he was taken by one of the salesmen who came to our town. Maybe they did him harm. They could have easily killed him. After all, there are bad people out there in the world. That's why we like to stay here in the safety of our small village," someone said.

Then the old beggar woman, who lived alone, said, "What if he was taken by a dybbuk, an evil spirit? What if that spirit returns and wants more of our children?" This accelerated the panic that had already begun in town. There were no children out on the street. Their parents refused to allow them out of their sight for a minute, and even Naomi refused to allow her daughters to leave the house alone.

At the Friday night service, the rabbi explained that the boy's mother had become ill and was unable to get out of bed, and his father had stopped going to work. The rabbi asked the congregation, "Whoever is able to offer any time or provisions to help to this family, I would implore you to do so. They are suffering a terrible loss. And although I know that many of you have lost children, too, this poor mother and father desperately need their community right now."

In the women's section of the temple, because men and women did not sit together, Naomi saw a young mother hold her small child close to her breast and spit on the floor three times to ward off the evil eye. People were afraid that something sinister had come to their village. They weren't sure if it was human or monster, but they were frightened.

A few days passed, and then one night, Perle had a dream. In her dream, she saw the missing boy playing with a dog. She didn't tell her parents about her dream because she didn't know what to say except that she believed he was all right. However, she had no idea where to tell them to look for the boy. She trusted her twin sister, so in the morning, she told Bluma about her dream. Bluma listened carefully, and when Perle was done, she said she was certain the boy was alive.

Weeks passed, and the boy was still missing. But the shock died down, and although parents were still cautious, life began to slowly go back to normal. Then, about two months later, the boy returned to the neighborhood. He was unharmed. When the rabbi asked him where he had been, he said he'd run away with a traveling salesman. He said that his parents were arranging a marriage for him, and he quite simply did not want to get married. Not now or ever. He refused to say anything more, but the strange thing was, that he brought a small dog back with him.

"That's the dog I saw in the dream," Perle whispered to Bluma.

The following Sunday night, Naomi and her family went to Miriam's house for dinner. While everyone was in the living room eating dessert, which was rugalach that Miriam had baked, Miriam and Naomi were in the kitchen talking.

"I think that boy that was missing is a faygehleh, a boy who likes other boys instead of girls, and that's why he doesn't want to get married. He was afraid to tell his parents. I am sure of it," Miriam said.

"He always was feminine," Naomi agreed. "I feel bad for him. His life will be hard."

"Yes, especially here in our neighborhood. Maybe he should have stayed away from here. He would probably have done better in the outside world," Miriam said.

"Maybe he should have. But can you imagine how difficult it must be to live out there? I wouldn't know how," Naomi said. "Everyone who is born and raised here in our village is taught to live a certain way. I don't think we are equipped to live outside of here."

"Me neither," Miriam said, picking at a piece of rugalach. "I think I put too much cinnamon in these." Then she cleared her throat and whispered, "Do you still think about Eli?"

Miriam was the only person who knew about what had happened between Naomi and Eli. And except for the couple, she was also the only person who knew how and why the affair had finally ended five years ago. It wasn't because Naomi had wanted her sister to know or be a part of it all, but as it turned out, Miriam's feelings had also figured into the painful sacrifice that Naomi had made to finally release the love of her life. Naomi and Miriam were so close that even now, whenever they passed Eli at the market, Miriam could see the love and pain in her sister's face.

"Nu, so do you?" Miriam asked gently again.

"Do I what?"

"Still think about Eli?"

Naomi shrugged. "No."

"Liar. I feel so guilty that you had to end it. It bothers me all the time."

"So, you're right, I am a liar. Of course I think about him. How could I not? But I know it's hopeless. I know because of what happened that it was not God's will for us to be together, and our love was not bashert, as Eli thought it was."

Miriam hugged her sister.

CHAPTER EIGHTEEN

$$\text{Ⅱ}$$

ON THE THIRD NIGHT OF HANUKKAH, THE TWINS SAT ON THE BED IN their room. Perle was brushing Bluma's hair. Their parents thought the twins were asleep, so they were talking quietly in their room. But Perle and Bluma overheard them.

"I'm surprised the twins get along as well as they do," Herschel said to Naomi. "Bluma is so capable. She learns fast; she's good with her hands. She's healthy, strong, and smart. And even though they are identical, she's prettier. Perle is weaker and tends to get sick more often. Daily tasks come harder to her. I'm sure you've noticed."

"Perle has her own good attributes. She has a beautiful soul," Naomi said.

"Well, as you know, when there are twins, one of them is always stronger, healthier, just more vibrant. I'm sure your father told you and Miriam that, between the two of you, you are the prettier one. That's why I chose you, when your father came to talk to my father to make the match for us."

"You're just saying that because you're my husband."

"That's not true. I know that you and Miriam are supposed to be identical, but you're not, really. You are prettier, more vivacious. More soft and delicate than your sister. And that's why I chose you and not

Miriam. Now, tell me; did your being prettier ever cause jealousy between the two of you?" Herschel asked.

"Never. My sister and I have always been the best of friends. We still are," Naomi said.

"I wonder if Miriam feels the same way," Herschel said. "I wonder if she isn't secretly jealous of you."

Bluma looked at Perle. She wished that they hadn't overheard this conversation between their parents because she saw Perle's face fall. She turned away from Bluma, but she looked as if she was going to cry. "You are much prettier than I am," Bluma said.

"Please don't feel bad. Please don't listen to Papa. You are so pretty. I know you will make a better match than I will. You're delicate and sweet. Besides that, you have the gift. I wish I had it."

"No, you don't," Perle said, taking Bluma's hand. "It can be very scary. Sometimes I have nightmares, like the time I had that dream that Shoshana was going to fall and hurt her knee. And then two days later, she did. I know you remember that."

"I do. And I know that sometimes the things you dream scare you, but you must like being able to see the future. It makes you special. I'm not special. I'm like every other girl. But you? You are different. You have a gift. Even Mama says so."

"I would much rather be like you," Perle said.

"Please don't tell me you are jealous of me."

"I'm not. I couldn't be because I love you too much. I just wish I were more like you."

"You look like me, and you think like me . . ."

"But I am weaker, and I don't look exactly like you. Even worse, I can't do everything you can do."

"Yes, you can. I have confidence in you."

"I can't carry heavy things like you can. And I am so clumsy. I can't run fast or catch a ball."

"None of that matters. Mama is right, Perle." Bluma squeezed Perle's hand. "You have the most beautiful soul of anyone I have ever met," Bluma said as she was whispering, trying hard to convince her sister of all of the good qualities she possessed. "When we were learning about souls in our religious class, I thought about you and how your soul must be old because you are so good and kind. I wish I were more like you." A few minutes passed, and neither of them said a word. So to break the uncomfortable silence, Bluma tried to change the subject. "I'm excited about the rocking horse we're getting. I am assuming we'll get it on the eighth night of Hanukkah."

"I know. I'm excited too. It's our big gift this year, so you're right; we won't get it until the last day of Hanukkah," Perle said. "Tomorrow night, we'll get socks and nightgowns."

"What are you two little princesses whispering about?" their mother asked as she opened the door. "I thought you were both fast asleep."

"We are going to sleep," Perle said.

"Good. You should be sleeping already. It's late," Naomi said.

"Yes, Mama."

"You're such good girls." Naomi walked into the room and tucked each of the twins into their beds. Then she kissed them good night.

And sure enough, the following night, the girls received socks and nightgowns.

CHAPTER NINETEEN

♊

HERSCHEL WON THE BIG, IMPORTANT CASE HE HAD BEEN WORKING ON. He was quite elated. It not only meant more money, but his reputation would be even better than it was now. And, of course, that meant more and better clients. He hummed softly to himself as he walked into work that day. His attitude was bright, and everything seemed to be going his way.

"Good morning," Frieda said.

"Good morning," Herschel answered. Even she couldn't get on his nerves today. Everything he had worked for seemed to be falling into place. Herschel Aizenberg was on his way to becoming an important man. *I am on my way. I will be a well-respected lawyer. Not just in the Jewish community, but also among the goyim, the non-Jews, in Warsaw.* All of his life, Herschel had wanted to be accepted by the non-Jewish community. He had always seen them as a step above, and now, finally, he was on his way.

"I was wondering if maybe we could go and have a cup of coffee or a drink after work to discuss the case you won," Frieda said boldly.

Why not? I am not some backward Jew that doesn't have anything to do with women who are not married to him. I am a modern man. And besides, I would love to hear what Frieda has to say about this case. She is ugly, that's for sure. But the one thing she has is that she's so insightful, that her thoughts can be worth a fortune. "Sure, why not?" he said.

She was beaming. Her face was pale, and her smile was a wide grin. Her eyes were hooded, but he could see that she was delighted.

Herschel was in a wonderful mood the entire day. And after work, as he had promised, he took Frieda to a tavern. *I would never take Naomi to such a place,* he thought. *But Frieda is more like another man than like a woman. She doesn't appeal to me at all. So it's easy to sit here with her and feel no desire.*

She told him everything he wanted to hear.

"You are the best lawyer in Warsaw. And everyone is about to discover you. You are brilliant, generous, and very successful."

His head swelled. He was enjoying this, so he allowed her to continue.

"You should have seen the faces on the jury when you gave your final argument. They were riveted. Glued to their seats. You were so fantastic. I was so proud of you."

This continued for an hour, then Herschel said, "I'm sorry, but I should get home. It's Hanukkah, and the children will be waiting for their father."

"Yes, of course," Frieda said. Then she stammered, "A-a-and since it's Hanukkah, I brought you a gift."

"For me? But Hanukkah is for children," he said.

"I brought a gift for you. I hope you like it," she said, handing him a black box. He cocked his head, then opened the box.

"My goodness, Frieda. This had to cost you a fortune," he said, taking the watch out of the box.

"It did." She smiled. "Do you like it?"

"Yes, I do. Very much. But I don't have a gift for you," he said, but he thought, *This is a very expensive and inappropriate gift for a boss from his secretary. I know she wants more from me. But I don't want it from her. What do I say? What do I do?*

"Oh, that's all right. You give me a gift everyday by just allowing me to work with you."

He smiled. He was uncomfortable again. She always had a way of making him feel uncomfortable. "Well, thank you," he said as he put a couple of bills down on the table. "I've got to get home. You know, as I said, the children are waiting for me. Thank you again, for the watch."

She smiled. He could see from the way she was looking at him that she wanted to kiss him.

That would make me even more uncomfortable, he thought as he rushed out of the restaurant and headed home.

CHAPTER TWENTY

ON THE SEVENTH DAY OF HANUKKAH, SHOSHANA TOOK HER SISTERS TO the market to buy a fish for the gefilte fish dinner her mother was planning to prepare. Naomi had promised Herschel that she would prepare gefilte fish for him. And since this was his favorite dish, it was very important that Shoshana pick the perfect fish. As Shoshana and the twins walked down the old familiar road, which led to the marketplace, Albert Hendler, the butcher's son, was walking the opposite way. He was only a few years older than Shoshana, and she knew that her parents hoped to make a shidduch between him and herself. Albert glanced at her, then he quickly looked down at the ground as he passed the girls. But once he'd passed them, he quickly glanced up at Shoshana. She blushed when their eyes met. Then she hurried her sisters along toward the shop of the fishmonger.

As they walked, Shoshana wondered why she didn't feel excited by the prospect of marrying Albert. *He's handsome; there is no doubt about that. And Neta tells me she would give anything if he were to be her betrothed. But she says she doubts that he would he want her because her family doesn't offer much of a dowry. I know my father will offer a substantial dowry, so there is a good chance he will accept my father's proposal. I should be glad about that, and yet, for some reason, I am not. He bores me.*

The idea of being married and having babies bores me. I want to do exciting things. Yet I know the only way that would ever be possible is if I run away from our village and go off on my own to live in the city. And if I did such a thing, I know that Papa would never accept me back. I could never see Mama or my sisters again. Even Neta would be forbidden to see me. I would be an outcast, and I would have no one to turn to. I am not strong enough to give up everyone I love. So if my father decides I must marry Albert, then I must.

Neta was Shoshana's best friend. They had been friends for their entire lives. Even though Shoshana's family was much better off financially, there had never been even a small flicker of jealousy between them, at least not that Shoshana was aware of. Not only that, but everyone in town considered Shoshana a beauty, while Neta was referred to as a plain-looking girl. It was true that Neta was a little too plump and her frizzy red-brown hair was unruly. But Shoshana loved her friend. She thought Neta was beautiful because she had a warm and wonderful smile. In fact, when the girls were only eight years old they made a secret pact, in which they decided to be sisters even though they were not biologically related.

When Shoshana and the twins arrived at the shop of the fishmonger, Bluma demanded, "I want to wait outside." She turned up her nose. "It smells terrible in there."

"It's just the smell of fish and the odor from the smokehouse," Shoshana insisted. "Come on in with me. Mama would be furious if she found out I left you alone outside."

"Perle will stay out here with me. Won't you, Perle?"

"Perle nodded. "I'll stay with Bluma."

"I'm sorry, Bluma. But Mama would not want you and Perle standing outside alone. She would say you are too young, and I agree. Now, come in with me."

"Please, Shoshana," Bluma said. "I promise you that Perle and I will wait right here for you. You will be able to watch us through the window. Please don't make me go in there. I'll vomit. I know I will."

"Bluma, you can be so dramatic," Shoshana said, shaking her

head. "All right. But you must stay right here where I can see you. Don't move at all. Do you understand me?"

"I promise we will stay right here. Won't we, Perle?"

"Of course, Bluma."

Shoshana went into the fish store and got in line. There were two women ahead of her. Each made their way to the front of the line in turn. But they both seemed to take a long time when choosing their fish. And Shoshana was growing impatient.

While she was waiting, she tried not to tap her foot or do anything else that might be considered rude. Instead, she gazed out the window and watched her sisters, who were sitting very close to each other on the sidewalk. *I wonder what it is like for the twins. I can't imagine how it would be to have another person who was so much like you that you could almost read their thoughts.* The twins had always been connected to each other, almost as if they were one person. They knew what the other was thinking; they finished each other's sentences, and they trusted each other implicitly. But even though they looked almost exactly alike, their personalities were mirror opposites. Even so, they complimented one another. And were never seen apart.

"Next," the fishmonger said, interrupting Shoshana's thoughts.

Shoshana stepped up to the counter and looked over the fish that lay on ice in the case. Her mother had given her strict instructions, and she didn't want to disappoint her. "Now, here's how you pick the perfect fish. Are you listening?" Naomi asked Shoshana before she left for the market.

Shoshana nodded.

"Make sure the eyes are clear, not glassy. Make sure the scales are shiny and not dull." This was the first time Shoshana had been sent alone to buy fish. And she had thought it would be easy, but now that she was here at the fish store, she found that it was not.

"Hurry up," an old woman who was in line behind Shoshana said, "We don't have all day. Some of us have to go home and cook. Nu? You are young you have time to waste? No?"

Shoshana nodded. "I'm sorry. I'm trying," she answered the

woman. Then she looked over the fish again nervously. "That one, I think," she said to the fishmonger, who pointed to the fish she had indicated.

"Are you sure this is the one you want? I need to know for sure before I start cleaning it," the proprietor said.

"I think so." Then Shoshana nodded. Then she asked him, "Does it look all right to you?"

"They all look good to me, or I wouldn't sell them," he said matter-of-factly. "So is that the one you want?"

Shoshana nodded. "Yes, I'll take that one."

"I assume you want me to clean it?"

"Yes, please."

"For gefilte fish?"

"Yes. And my mother said to tell you to be careful to take out all of the bones."

He nodded. "But, of course." Then he began to clean the fish. Shoshana glanced out the window. To her horror, she saw a man of about fifty standing next to Bluma and Perle. He was talking to her sisters. A shot of fear traveled through Shoshana. *Who is this man?* She had never seen him in town before. He was definitely an outsider. Probably a salesman. She could tell by his clothes. He not did wear a payot, and his head was uncovered. He wore a suit in a bright blue color, which she had never seen any man wear before. She stood there for a moment watching. Then she shivered when she saw the man handing Bluma something. The twins were sitting close together on the sidewalk. When the man said something to them, they leaned against each other, calmly giggling. It made Shoshana nervous to see her sisters speaking so easily and casually with a strange man. She knew her mother would never approve.

"I'll be right back to pay you and pick up my fish," Shoshana said to the fishmonger.

"Don't you leave here without paying," he said. "If you do, I'll have to sell this fish to someone else. I am running a business here. You can't run in and out."

"Please. I am not leaving. I'll be right back. I promise you."

The old woman who was waiting in line behind Shoshana said, "The young people in our community have no respect these days."

"Put your money down on the counter, and I will finish cleaning and wrapping your fish," the fishmonger said.

"I can't do that. My mother would be very upset if I paid you before you finished. She would never allow me to do that," Shoshana said. She was almost in tears. "Please, just finish packaging my fish. I promise you; I'll be right back." She couldn't wait a second longer. Shoshana felt her heart racing as she watched her sisters talking to the stranger. She saw Bluma stand up. Now she couldn't wait for even a second. Her heart was pounding so hard it might explode in her chest. She was afraid if she hesitated, her sisters might walk away with the man and be gone forever.

Her parents had always stressed how dangerous outsiders could be. They warned their children that there were bad people in the outside world who stole children. What if this stranger was one of them? What if he stole her sisters and she never saw them again? Shoshana ran to the door.

"Do you want this fish or not? I can't keep the line waiting for you," the shopkeeper complained. Then he clicked his tongue. "Never mind. I don't have all day for you, young lady. I am running a business here. So I am going to take the next person in line. You'll have to go to the end when you come back. That is, if you come back." He shook his head, then he said, "Next."

"I'll take that fish. The one you were cleaning for that young girl. It looks like the best one you've got," the old woman who had been behind Shoshana said.

But Shoshana didn't hear them talking. She was too frantic. *What are my sisters doing talking to a stranger, like that?* she thought as she ran out the door.

"What's going on here?" Shoshana said to the strange man who was standing in front of Bluma.

"I was just giving your sisters a piece of candy. It's not every day you see such a beautiful zwillinge. Beautiful twins like these are rare." He smiled.

Shoshana's heart was racing. "Go away, please. Leave us alone." Then she turned to Bluma. "You give him back that candy right now. It's not kosher anyway. So, you can't eat it."

"But Shoshana, it's all right. He means no harm," Perle said calmly. "I can see it in his eyes. He is a nice man."

"I don't want to hear that. Just do as I say. Give the candy back to him, right now." Shoshana was nervous and angry, and her sisters knew it by the sound of her voice.

Bluma took Perle's piece of candy and then handed both pieces back to the man.

"I'm sorry," the man said to Shoshana. "I didn't mean to frighten you. I am a traveling salesman. I was on my way to the dry goods store when I saw these two beautiful twins, and since I had some candy . . ."

"Yes, I understand," Shoshana said to the man, cutting him off mid-sentence. "But we don't talk to strangers, do we?" She was red faced when she turned and spoke angrily to her sisters.

"I'm sorry," Perle said to her big sister. "Bluma and I didn't mean to upset you."

"Just go away and leave us alone," Shoshana said to the salesman. "Please."

He shrugged his shoulders, then walked away. "You both should know better." Shoshana turned to the girls. Mama and Papa have told you a million times not to talk to strangers and never to take anything from them. What were you thinking?" She didn't wait for either of her sisters to answer. She grabbed Bluma's hand and then she grabbed Perle's and pulled her upright. "Like it or not, you're coming into the fishmonger's with me. I can't trust you outside without an adult."

"And you're an adult? You're only twelve," Bluma said. Now, she was angry too.

"I'm more of an adult than you are. And Mama left me in charge, so you're coming in with me, like it or not."

In the shadows, unseen, Frieda stood listening. She had come to the market to purchase a vinegar raisin strudel for Herschel. He'd expressed his desire for one, and she knew that he loved the strudel that came from the bakery in their village. He also mentioned that Naomi refused to go to the bakery to buy him the strudel. She always insisted on baking her own. And, although he liked his wife's baking, he remembered this particular strudel from his childhood and he craved it. So she had gone back to the village during her lunch hour in order to surprise him. She always loved the look on his face when she brought him something special that she knew he wanted. But she had been stopped in her tracks when she saw Herschel's twins talking to a strange man outside of the fishmonger's shop. She had hidden in the alleyway to listen. Now, she hurried back to the office but not before stopping at the bakery to pick up the strudel. She was excited. She had information that would make Naomi look like the poorly suited wife that she was.

"I know I am a little bit late, but I brought you a vinegar raisin strudel," Frieda said when she arrived back at the office.

"You went all the way back to our neighborhood, or did you buy it in the city?" Herschel asked.

"I went all the way back, because I know you like the strudel from Mrs. Silberberg's bakery. And I know Naomi thinks her strudel is the best so she won't go to the bakery to get it for you."

He smiled. "I do like it," he said. "Cut me a piece."

She did as he asked. Then she placed the strudel in front of him at his desk and sat down opposite him.

He took a bite. "Mmmm, always the best." He smiled.

She smiled. *I am so good to him*, she thought. "I have something to tell you," she said, trying to sound sympathetic. "I saw your twins today. They were outside the fishmonger's store. And they were all alone talking to a strange man. Shoshana was inside the store. But she left the two little ones outside alone. It seems to me that Naomi doesn't have good judgment, allowing Shoshana to take the girls into town. You and I both know that Naomi is always a little bit distracted."

He frowned.

"Now, I don't mean to speak badly about your wife. But the truth is, she is very immature and not really a good wife or mother. I don't know why, but it's true. It always seems to me that she is busy doing something other than what she should be doing. I suppose what I am trying to say, is that a man like you, Herschel, deserves better."

He looked at her, stunned. "The twins were talking to a strange man?"

"Yes, a salesman, I think. That's very dangerous."

"You're right. It certainly can be. I would think Shoshana would be more mature and not so irresponsible. Why would she not take the girls into the store with her?"

"She's a lot like her mother. She's lax," Frieda said.

He put the strudel down. He'd lost his appetite.

"You should get back to your desk," he said. "There's work to be done."

Frieda went back to her desk, but for the rest of the day, she watched him out of the corner of her eye. He was distraught. She could clearly see that. And as she watched him, she felt satisfied that she'd pushed him a little further away from his wife. *Sooner or later, he is going to realize how much better I am for him than Naomi is.*

CHAPTER TWENTY-ONE

WHEN THE TWINS CAME HOME CRYING, AND SHOSHANA WAS DISTRESSED, Naomi asked what happened, and Shoshana told her mother about the girls and the candy and the salesman.

"I can't tell your father. If I do he'll be furious at all of you, but especially at Shoshana. You must promise me never to do anything so reckless again," Naomi pleaded.

"But we didn't do anything. We just took candy . . ." Bluma said.

"That was reckless. I've told you girls time and again that you must never talk to strangers. Now, you must promise me that you won't do it again."

"I promise, Mama," Perle said.

"I promise too," Bluma said.

"And as for you, Shoshana, you must never leave the girls alone like that. Anything could happen. I shiver to think," Naomi said.

"Yes, Mama. It was a mistake. I promise I won't do it again."

"All right, all of you go and get cleaned up for dinner. Your father will be home very soon," Naomi said.

Herschel walked into the house in a sour mood. He slammed the door behind him and glared at Naomi. "Frieda had some interesting information for me today," he said.

Naomi was stunned and trying to hide her trembling hands in her apron pockets, but for a moment she was transported back to the day she had run into Frieda before meeting with Eli. *Could she have followed me? Did she see me with Eli? Does she know? I hate her and her meddling. She is always trying to destroy me, always putting her nose where it doesn't belong. She's a yenta, a busybody. What will happen to me? What will happen to Eli?* Naomi took a breath and tried to calm herself, and asked, "Information? What kind of information?"

"Is there anything you want to tell me about a man?" Herschel said.

Naomi's face turned white, and a bead of sweat formed on her brow. "A man?" she asked, trying to sound as calm as possible.

Herschel let out a sigh of disappointment. "Frieda was in town today. She saw something happen with the twins and a salesman. Perhaps Shoshana is not mature enough to take the girls to the market with her." Then he proceeded to tell Naomi what happened. But she already knew.

"Shoshana," Herschel called. "Get in here right now."

Shoshana came out of her room and walked into the kitchen. "Yes, Papa," she said in a soft voice.

"You are in trouble, young lady. You made a terrible mistake today." He reprimanded Shoshana until she cried.

CHAPTER TWENTY-TWO

THAT EVENING AFTER HERSCHEL LIT THE SEVEN HANUKKAH CANDLES, as well as the shamash, he and Naomi sat down on the sofa. Bluma and Perle sat close to each other on the floor. Shoshana was standing in the corner of the room with her arms wrapped around her chest. She knew her sisters were excited because they were anticipating their Hanukkah gift. For a moment she felt bad because she knew what was coming. Instead of receiving any gifts, they were reprimanded by their father for talking to the strange man that afternoon. Perle, who was highly sensitive, was so upset by her father's strict and angry lecture that when he was finished, she got up and went to her room. Bluma followed her sister who was softly crying.

"Better you should cry, then we should cry," Herschel yelled after them.

"I'm sorry. I had to tell you what happened. I feel bad because Perle is crying, and I know it's my fault," Shoshana said. "But the very thought that something could have happened to them terrifies me."

"I know," Naomi said, and she put her arm around Shoshana. "You did the right thing."

"Do you think they'll ever forgive me?"

"Of course. I know they will. You protected them."

CHAPTER TWENTY-THREE

BLUMA AND PERLE WERE SITTING IN THEIR ROOM HOPING THEIR FATHER would not come in and continue yelling at them about talking to strangers. He didn't. But there was a knock on the door.

"Who is it?" Bluma asked.

"It's me, Shoshana."

"Go away," Bluma said.

"Please let me come in and talk to you both," Shoshana said.

Bluma looked at Perle. Perle nodded, then Bluma said, "All right. Come in."

Shoshana walked in. "I'm sorry. I had to tell them what happened."

"No, you didn't. You didn't have to tell them," Bluma said.

"I did. What happened today could have been very dangerous."

"I don't think so," Perle said. "You know how I just know things sometimes?"

"Of course, I know that you have the same gift as mama and that you sometimes know things. But what if you were wrong this time? Do you realize what could have happened to the two of you. I shudder to think about it," Shoshana answered.

"Well, I knew that man wasn't going to hurt us. I could tell. I saw it in his eyes."

"But maybe Papa is right. You could have been wrong this time. You were taking a big chance." Shoshana said.

"I don't think so. I think he was just a lonely salesman. I know that he meant us no harm."

Shoshana shook her head. "Well, all I can say is please don't do it again. Mama and Papa and I love you girls so much. We would be heartbroken if anything happened to you."

Bluma glared at Shoshana. "You still didn't have to tell them."

"I did what I thought was right. But even so, I am sorry. I want you both to know that I would never do anything to purposely hurt you." Then she added, "Can you ever forgive me?"

Perle said, "I forgive you."

Bluma just nodded. "Yes, I suppose I do too."

CHAPTER TWENTY-FOUR

♊

Shoshana and Neta sat at the kitchen table in Neta's house. It was midmorning, and they were busy plucking the feathers off a chicken that one of the neighbors had given Neta's mother early that morning. It was rare for the family to have meat of any kind. In fact, they only had such a luxury when someone in the neighborhood felt charitable and brought them a gift. Sarah walked into the kitchen and stopped. "I didn't know Shoshana was here helping you," she said.

"Yes, Mother, I hope it's all right."

"Nu? Of course it's all right. Why wouldn't it be? You know you're always welcome here, Shoshana."

"Thank you," Shoshana said.

"I'm not surprised you two girls are best friends," Sarah said, sitting down at the table. "Did you know that before either of you were born, Shoshana's mother and I had been best friends for years? We carried you in our bellies at the same time. And then can you imagine how excited we were when you two girls were born only a month apart. And you were both girls. We knew you would be good friends."

But, of course, in a small village such as this one, there was always talk. And Shoshana had heard most of it. She heard people say that her mother was much prettier than Neta's mother. It was true. And everyone knew that was why Naomi was more fortunate too. Shoshana's father was more prosperous and very well respected, and although he was strict, he was not known to be physically abusive like Shlomie, Neta's father. Shlomie ruled his family with an iron fist. And the town's people told many stories about the times they remembered when the screaming that came from Neta's house was so loud and terrifying that some of the neighbors had to go over to the house to intervene. More often than not, when Sarah came into town, which she rarely did, she had bruises on her face. To make matters worse, they were dirt poor. Everyone would click their tongues when they mentioned Shlomie and Sarah. They would say that it was a terrible rachmones, a pity, how little they had. But everyone also said that Shlomie was lazy; he never wanted to work. In fact, he avoided it in every way he possibly could. He even told the rabbi that he was not physically capable of working in order to receive as much charity for his family as possible. People felt sorry for Neta, and she told Shoshana that the pity made her ashamed. But everyone could see that Neta never had a new dress, and when she went to market with Shoshana, she never had enough money to buy fish or meat. Sometimes when Shoshana and Neta went to the market together, Naomi would give Shoshana a little extra money to give to Neta. A few times Shoshana would give Neta one of her dresses. But when she did, it seemed to hurt Neta to accept it. So Shoshana stopped.

Still, even though Sarah and Naomi lived very different lives, they remained friends. But now that they were older and had homes and children to care for, they hardly ever had time to spend with each other.

"Well, if you girls don't need me for anything, I am going to go and do the wash," Sarah said.

"We're all right, Mother," Neta answered.

After Neta's mother left the kitchen, leaving Neta and Shoshana to finish their work alone, Shoshana told her friend what had happened the other day outside the fishmonger's shop, with her sisters and the salesman.

"That had to be so scary for you," Neta said.

"It was. I was responsible for them."

"You did right by telling your parents."

"I have a family secret to tell you," Shoshana said.

"You know you can tell me."

"I know. All right, I'll tell you. My mother and my aunt, her twin sister, are certain that Perle has this gift of being a seer. My mother's supposed to have this same gift. My mother says that she and Perle have had some dreams that they believe predict the future. I'm not supposed to tell anyone. My parents think it will hurt our chances of making a good match."

"Really? Dreams that predict the future?"

"Yes, that's what my mother says anyway. My father isn't convinced. He thinks it's all nonsense. You know how practical he is."

"Yes, I know."

"And, although I would never say this to my mother, I don't know what to believe. It's sort of scary in a way. I mean, there were times in my life when I've had nightmares, and I've also had dreams that felt so real, I was surprised to wake up and find they weren't. But none of my dreams ever came true. They were just dreams."

"Yes, me too. I've had dreams like that where they seem so real you can't believe it when you wake up to find that they weren't. But what about Perle? Have any of her dreams ever come true?"

"So far, Perle's had a couple of dreams with premonitions that came to pass. But my father says that it was only coincidence. I don't know what to think. Bluma believes completely in everything Perle predicts. But they are just little children, and because Perle is Bluma's twin, they are so close they are like one. Sometimes, I don't know if that's a good thing. To tell you the truth, I worry that one day Perle will tell Bluma she has seen something in her dream, and then because Bluma believes in her so strongly, the two of them will get into some kind of trouble. Or make a terrible mistake."

"You mean, a mistake like going with a stranger? You mean a mistake like that?"

"Yes, like that, or who knows what else. When Perle says something, it's as if Bluma forgets to think for herself. Do you know what I mean? She just believes her sister."

"That is something to worry about," Neta said, plucking a feather from the chicken.

"Bluma is the stronger one, at least physically. And I know she's smart too. But she blindly follows whatever Perle says." Shoshana sighed. Then she went on. "I know that if I hadn't been there to stop them, they would have gone with that man. And then who knows what would have happened. Maybe they would have disappeared forever."

"Did he try to take them somewhere?" Neta asked.

"I don't know. They say no. They say he just gave them candy. But I can't be sure. I mean, why would a stranger, an outsider, someone who is here in our community to sell things, give two little girls candy if he didn't mean to do something bad like kidnap them. Candy is hard to come by. No one just gives it away for no reason. Do they?"

Neta shivered. "I don't know. Perhaps he was just being nice."

"Perhaps. But it scared me."

"Well, was he a Jew?"

"I think so. But I couldn't tell. He wasn't one of us. I mean he might have been a secular Jew, but he was most certainly not a real Jew, like we are. If he was actually Jewish, then he was one of those Jews that live like the goyim. He was dressed like a goy. A bright blue suit, no payot." Shoshana shivered.

"Well, it's over now. Your sisters are safe," Neta said. "Praise Hashem that you saw what was happening, and you were able to protect your sisters."

"I hope he's left our town. I hope we never see him again."

"I hope so too," Neta said.

"And you know what the worst part of it is? Frieda saw everything. My father said she was going to the bakery when she saw the twins talking to that man. Then she ran back to work to tell him everything.

She is the biggest yenta in our town. I can't believe she works with my father, and she watches our family constantly. I can't stand her," Shoshana said.

"I know. You've told me about other things she did in the past. I don't like her either," Neta said.

There were a few moments of silence. Then Shoshana sighed. "Neta," she said, "I love my sisters. I really do. But for as long as I can remember, my parents have given me the responsibility of protecting and taking care of them. Sometimes I think my parents forget that I am only twelve, and I am not capable of making them listen to me all the time. Sometimes they do; other times they treat me like I am just another child. I am doing the best I can, but my parents expect so much of me. And, well, sometimes, I just wish I could be a child and not have to be so responsible. There are times when I get caught up in other things, like lying in the grass and thinking about pretty clothes, or wondering who will be betrothed to who, and I forget what's important. But then I remember my responsibilities, and I am angry with myself for daydreaming."

"And looking at the boys too?" Neta said, giggling. Then she winked at Shoshana and patted her hand.

"Yes, I like to look at the boys. But there are so many other things that occupy my mind too. Sometimes I just get lost in daydreaming about what life is like in the outside world. I mean, yes, I wonder who my father will choose for me. But sometimes I wish that I didn't have to get married. I just have so much curiosity about the world. I find myself getting lost in wondering what it's like out there, out in the cities away from our little neighborhood. It's scary in a way, but even so, I would love to know. In fact, I could never admit this to anyone but you, but I would love to leave here for a while. I'd love to run away and see the world," Shoshana said. "Do you ever wonder what it's like out there in the big cities?"

"I never wonder. I know that it's not as good out there as it is here in our village. First of all, the goyim hate us, and they are dangerous. They can't be trusted. And as far as the Jews who live in the cities, they are a lot like the goyim. They are not like us. They are all like the salesmen who come here to our village. They are fast talking and not to be trusted. They don't know the proper Jewish laws. And if they do know them, they don't follow them. From what I hear, and what I've seen of the ones who have come through here, most of them don't even keep kosher. I saw a salesman who was eating cheese with a sausage. I thought I would throw up. And would you believe, I heard him talking to Mr. Straumberger from the bakery, and he told Mr. Straumberger that he was a Jew. Some Jew, huh?"

"But what do they do all day out there in the world? Do they pluck chickens or cut vegetables? Do they bake bread? What are their lives like? Haven't you ever wondered? I have. I wonder about it all the time. I have also wondered if the girls' fathers make the shidduch with the matchmakers. Or, as I have read, are the girls really allowed to find their own husbands?" Shoshana asked.

"I don't know the answer to any of your questions," Neta said, "but what I do know is that you should stop reading those goyish books. If you are going to read, you should be reading your religious books. You are so lucky that your father allowed you to learn to read. My father forbids it. But if your parents find out that you are reading goyish books, they'll be furious. Where did you ever get your hands on books with those goyish love stories in them? Books about goyish girls who chose their own husbands?" Neta clicked her tongue. "Oy vey, if your parents knew, they would be furious. I am sure of it."

"I got the books from one of the traveling salesmen who came through here last year," Shoshana said. "I secretly traded him my gold mezuzah that my aunt gave me for three books."

"Oy vey! You have always been such a bold one. I would never have had the nerve. And what did you tell your parents when they saw that your mezuzah was gone?"

"I lied. I told them I lost it."

"Lying is a sin, Shoshana. You know that."

Shoshana hung her head. "I know. But I am so hungry for knowledge. I want to know about the world. We are hidden away here. We live as our parents and grandparents did. I know it's scary out there, but I can't see how you don't want to know how they live?"

"No, I don't. I know our way of life is best. We are the true Jewish people. We are Hashem's chosen people."

Neta's mother walked into the kitchen. "I'm glad you two girls are so quiet. Neta's papa is asleep, and he isn't feeling well."

"I hope he feels better soon," Shoshana said. But she knew that Shlomie was not sick. Neta had told her in secret that her father drank to excess and then spent the next day sleeping it off.

Then Sarah turned to Shoshana. "It was very nice of you come to help Neta make soup. She hates to pluck the chicken. I know it. But she must learn, yes?"

"I am learning, Mama," Neta said quietly.

"Good, good. I know you are trying, my love. And it's good, so you'll know how to do it when you get married," her mother said, then she turned to Shoshana. "Nu, so you'll take a little soup home with you for your family? And you'll tell your mother I said hello?"

"No, please. I insist that you keep the soup," Shoshana said, not wanting to take anything away from Neta's family, who was so needy.

"Don't insult me. Take a bissell, a little bit. Bring it for your mother, will you, please? It would mean a lot to me," Sarah said.

"Of course I will, and my mother will appreciate it," Shoshana said, not wanting to hurt Sarah's pride.

"Of course. Of course. And you'll stay and have some sauerkraut and rye bread for lunch with us? The baker's wife gave me a nice rye bread yesterday. It's one day old, but it's not stale."

"Please, stay for lunch, won't you?" Neta asked.

"All right," Shoshana said, then she turned to Sarah. "I will stay. And thank you for inviting me."

Shoshana was glad that Neta's father did not come to the table for lunch. She was afraid of him and relieved not to see him. Sarah made up a bowl of soup and cut a few slices of rye bread, which she brought to her husband in the bedroom. Then she came back out and sat down at the table with the two girls.

After they finished eating lunch, Shoshana made up a small pot of soup to take home to her family. She was careful not to take any of the chicken. In fact, she took mostly broth with a couple of carrots.

Then she thanked Sarah and Neta for lunch and began to walk home. She thought about Neta as she walked carefully to not spill the pot of hot liquid. *Neta has always been such a good girl. She's so obedient. I don't know how she does it. She never wonders about things outside of this neighborhood. She believes only in the things we have been taught. I don't know how she can be so sure that our life, here in the neighborhood, is the best possible life. But she is certain. I wish I were.*

Naomi was waiting for Shoshana in the kitchen when she arrived home.

"I brought soup," Shoshana said.

"You're very late. I thought you would be home earlier." Naomi sounded angry.

"I'm sorry. Neta's mother asked me to stay for lunch, and I couldn't refuse her."

"I hate to take food out of their mouths. They have so little, and we have so much. Next time you and Neta go to the market, I'll give you some extra money to buy them some bread."

"That would be nice, Mother."

"So, what kind of soup did you bring? Chicken soup?"

"Yes. Neta and I made a pot. So her mother gave me some to bring home for us."

"That was very nice of her," Naomi said.

"I only took broth. I didn't want to take any of the chicken."

"That was good," Naomi said. "Now that you're home, I need you to wash some clothes. I've been busy cleaning all morning, and you have been wasting time at your friend's house."

"I'm sorry, Mama. It's just that Neta's mother asked me to stay for lunch and then Neta asked me. And . . ."

"It's all right. I'm not angry at you. But I do need your help around here. There is so much to do," her mother said, her anger gone. That was what Shoshana liked most about her mother; she never stayed angry for long. "I was a young girl once too. I know how you can get lost in talking and daydreaming. Neta's mother and I used to get lost in talking, and my mother used to be so angry. I miss those times. I'll have to make time to go and see Sarah soon. She and I are both so busy these days. So, I understand. Still, my dear child, you should remember, idle hands are not a good thing. You must never neglect your work."

"Yes, Mama," Shoshana said, "but we weren't idle. We were plucking a chicken most of the morning."

"I've always hated that. Plucking chickens. Killing them is even worse. I really hate that. Every time I go to the butcher shop, I am grateful to Hashem that we have a butcher in our town," Naomi said, giggling a little.

"Me too," Shoshana answered. "And Neta hates it too."

Naomi put her arms around Shoshana's shoulders and hugged her. And Shoshana knew her mother not only loved her but that she understood her as well.

CHAPTER TWENTY-FIVE

THAT NIGHT, PERLE WAS ON EDGE. SHE WAS QUIET, BUT JUMPY. EVERY noise made her turn her head. Bluma sat at her sister's side. But when Shoshana asked Perle what was wrong, Perle said nothing. She said she was fine. But she was unable to eat any of her dinner. It was the eighth, and final night of Hanukkah, and when the family said the prayers and lit the eight Hanukkah candles, Perle's eyes were darting around. It seemed she was distracted by some unknown noise that no one else could hear. Bluma held tight to her sister's hand. She didn't need to ask what was bothering Perle. She knew that eventually, when she and her twin were alone, Perle would tell her everything.

Tonight was the night the Aizenberg children waited for all year. It was the night they would receive the one big gift that they had been anticipating. It was always this way. On the first seven nights of Hanukkah, they received practical gifts: socks, scarves their mother knitted, nightgowns, and underclothes. And sometimes they received candy too.

Shoshana was given her gift first. Her mother handed her a black sweater with mother-of-pearl buttons that ran down the front. Shoshana slipped the sweater on and buttoned it. It fit her perfectly.

"Do you like it?" her mother asked.

"Yes, Mother, it's beautiful," Shoshana said, wishing that she'd received a book, a goyish book filled with stories of life and love in the outside world. But, of course, she knew that would never happen. Her parents forbade her from reading such things, so why would they ever give her such a book?

Herschel Aizenberg stood up and stretched. "You will all have to excuse me, because, I am going to have to go outside," he said, winking at the twins. Then clearing his throat he added, "I think I must have left something important out in our backyard."

Bluma giggled. This was the way their father always gave them their big gifts. He pretended to leave something outside and disappeared for a minute. When he returned, he would present them with the special gift of that season. It was several minutes before Herschel returned, struggling, carrying a heavy wooden rocking horse. He'd even purchased a white ribbon to make a bow around the horse's neck.

"For us?" Bluma said.

"Yes, for you and Perle," their father answered.

Bluma turned to Perle and whispered in her ear, "Shall we give the ribbon to Shoshana for her hair? She would love that."

"Of course. Yes, let's give it to her," Perle agreed.

Bluma carefully took the ribbon off the horse's neck and then brought it over to Shoshana. "This is for you to wear in your hair. It's a gift for you from Perle and me."

"Oh, how thoughtful," Shoshana said. "I love it."

Bluma smiled, then she immediately climbed up on the horse and began to rock. She smiled at Perle who returned her smile, but Bluma could see that Perle seemed to have no interest in the new toy. Perle hadn't eaten a single potato latke that night, and she wasn't interested in playing with the dreidel either.

"Do you want to get on the horse?" Bluma asked. "I'll get off and let you try it. I'll even help you get on if you would like." Bluma knew that Perle would always allow her to play with any new things they received, first.

"No, you go ahead. I'll play with it later." Perle sat down on the sofa and gazed out the window. It was dark outside and cold. The newly fallen snow was like a white blanket covering the ground and dusting the tops of the bare trees. It was a beautiful night, even if it was terribly cold.

Herschel had gone to sit in his easy chair and read his law books, while Naomi had gone to the kitchen to prepare herself a cup of tea.

"Do you want to go out and look at the stars?" Bluma asked, walking over to Perle.

"No, it's too cold."

This is not like Perle. She always loves to look at the sky. But not tonight, Bluma thought as she was becoming concerned about her sister.

"Do you feel all right?" Bluma asked. "Are you sick?"

Perle shrugged. "I don't know. I don't feel right. If you know what I mean."

"I don't know what that means. Are you sick? Should I tell Mama? Maybe we need to get a doctor right away." Bluma was worried. She loved her sister more than anything in the world. And for the most part, she understood her. But when Perle got into these strange moods of hers, Bluma felt lost, alone, abandoned, and frightened.

"No, please don't say anything to Mama. I don't know what's wrong. I just feel strange. I wasn't hungry for dinner. And I am very cold. I don't feel right. I am shaking a little bit. Do you know what I mean?"

Bluma shook her head. "I don't know what's wrong," she said. Then she took her sister's hand. "Let me get you a blanket. Your hands are freezing."

"I know. I am so cold," Perle said. "A blanket would be nice."

Bluma took the blanket off her bed and put it around her sister's shoulders. Then their mother walked in to the room. "Nu? What's this, Perle? Why are you wrapped up in a blanket? Tell me, are you feeling all right?"

"Yes, I'm fine, Mama."

"You didn't eat any of your dinner. And you love latkes. Now you're not playing with your new rocking horse. I think, if you're not feeling better by morning, maybe we should see the doctor."

"Nu, Naomi, again with the doctor? That doctor is a gonif, a thief, I tell you. He takes all of our money. The child is fine. It's cold outside. So she's got a little chill. She'll be all right," Herschel said.

This is so like him, Shoshana thought. *He is always thinking about money and how much everything costs. He is so worried about it that he forgets what is important. And it's not like he is poor. We have plenty. But he is so greedy that he would rather put Perle at risk than pay a doctor. Sometimes Papa makes me so angry.*

It was getting later. And because Perle wasn't feeling well, Bluma lost interest in the rocking horse. She sat beside her sister with her arm around her trying to warm her. Naomi made them all cups of hot tea. Perle trembled as she sipped hers. Once she'd finished, she said, "I'm tired. I want to go to bed now."

"I'll come with you," Bluma said.

Bluma put her blanket and Perle's blanket on top of Perle. Then she got in bed beside her sister and held her close trying to warm her until both little girls fell asleep.

Just before dawn the following morning, Bluma heard Perle struggling to breathe. The sound woke her up, and she turned over in bed and opened her eyes. Perle was awake, but her face was bathed in sweat. Bluma touched her sister's forehead. It was hot. "Perle?" Bluma whispered softly. She gently ran her fingers over Perle's cheek. "Perle?" Bluma said, her voice filled with fear and desperation. "Please answer me." But Perle didn't answer. Bluma began to panic. She shook Perle frantically. Perle lay still with her eyes wide open. "Perle. Please say something, anything. You're making me so scared. Please don't be dead." Bluma was crying now. But Perle still didn't respond. *I need help*, Bluma thought. She was wide awake now; she jumped out of bed and ran to Shoshana's room, where she found Shoshana laying curled up on her side and still asleep. Bluma began shaking her big sister's shoulder. "Wake up." Through her tears, Bluma said, "Perle is sick. Please wake up, Shoshana. I'm scared. Perle needs help. Her eyes are open but she won't talk to me. I am afraid she is dead."

Shoshana stirred awake. "What's going on? What's wrong, Bluma?" she asked, "You look frantic."

"I don't know what's going on, but I need help. I was lying in bed next to Perle because she was so cold last night. Remember? But then I heard her breathing funny, and when I woke up, I felt how hot her body was next to mine. She's really hot, and her face is all red and sweating. I am so scared. You have to help her."

"Shhhh, it's all right. I'm coming." Shoshana got out of bed. She walked past the white ribbon on her dresser that her sisters had given her the night before and quickly followed behind Bluma to the room the twins shared.

Perle was awake now. Her eyes were open wide and very glassy.

"Perle," Shoshana said, shaking her sister gently. "Perle."

"I had a dream," Perle said, and she trembled as a shiver ran through her. "In my dream there was this man. He was a dark-haired man with very sharp white teeth. His teeth reminded me of the teeth of a creature from some terrible place. There was a big dark space between his front teeth, and when he smiled, his lips were dripping with blood."

"Perle, you have to wake up, and you have to listen to me. It was just a dream. That's all. It meant nothing. You had a bad nightmare."

"He had blood dripping down his chin. It was dark red and flowing like a river. There was so much blood . . . so much blood."

"Perle, please, you must stop thinking about the dream."

"Perle, please, stop talking about this man with the blood and the teeth. You have to be all right. Please be all right," Bluma said. Shoshana heard the desperation in Bluma's voice, and it hurt her heart. Bluma was weeping softly. She picked up Perle's hand and held it tightly for a moment. Then she kissed it.

Perle did not respond. She was still staring glassy eyed into space as if she were seeing things that neither Shoshana nor Bluma could see. Then Perle turned to Shoshana and looked directly at her. "Do you remember when we were visiting Neta, and we saw pictures of hyenas in that book that Neta had? They had killed another animal and they were covered in blood? Do you remember?" Perle asked.

"Yes. Of course, I remember. So you had a dream about a hyena and a scary man," Shoshana said, putting her hand on Perle's forehead to see if she was still hot. She was burning up. "But you're all right. You have to be all right," Shoshana said, tears forming in her eyes.

"Does she have a fever?" Bluma asked.

"She's very warm. She might have a fever. I think we should wake Mama," Shoshana said as she looked into Bluma's worried eyes.

Perle's eyes were still glassed over. "The man with the white smile and bloody teeth had the look of that hyena. But he wasn't a hyena; he was a man. Not one of the men who live in our village; this man was a stranger. His hair was black and straight. And he kept smiling. But it wasn't a warm, kind smile; it was an evil smile. A dangerous smile. Then suddenly, Bluma and I were standing in front of a big building with a flag hanging from the top. The flag was red, and in the center was a big, black spider. We stood there side by side, wearing the same nightgowns that we are wearing right now. We were both so scared, Shoshana. Then the man with the bloody teeth appeared again. He took two pieces of candy out of the pocket of his coat and handed one to Bluma and one to me." Perle said, her breath ragged. Then she took Shoshana's hand and said, "This is when you appeared in my dream. I don't know where you came from, but you were standing beside me, and you were crying. But you said that even though we didn't want to, and we knew he meant to hurt us, Bluma and I had to listen to this man with the wicked smile. You said that we had to do whatever he told us to do, or he would kill us," Perle told Shoshana.

"It was just a dream," Shoshana said gently. "Sometimes we have bad dreams that really scare us. Then we wake up, and we realize that we were only dreaming and it's all better."

"No, this was more than a bad dream. It was so real. I felt the soft skin of the evil man's hand when he gave us the candy. It was like touching something that was burning. I imagine it was like touching the blacksmith's hot horseshoe. It's what I think it would feel like. His voice was soft, and he tried very hard to seem nice. But I saw through him. I felt evil coming at us, and it all came from him. I was afraid of him. Very afraid. I told Bluma we should try to run away. But you heard me, and you said we shouldn't. Not yet. Shoshana, you said we couldn't get away. If we tried to run, the man would kill us. You said you would try to think of a plan."

"Well, as I said before, this was only a dream. And you know me, so you know that in reality, I would never tell you to listen to a strange man. Isn't that right, Bluma?" Shoshana tried to sound as casual as she could, but the dream Perle had unnerved Shoshana.

"Yes, of course it's right. You would never tell us to listen to a strange man," Bluma said.

"And I would never tell you girls that we should stay there with him. Now, would I? You know that I would say we should run away from such a man. So, because I wouldn't do that, this couldn't be anything but a nightmare. Nothing more," Shoshana insisted. "Now, let me get a wet rag, so Bluma can wipe your face. Then I am going to wake Mama. You might need a doctor."

"No, you must not bring a doctor. I'll do anything, but you must not bring a doctor." Perle was shaking. She grabbed Shoshana's hand. "You must promise me you won't bring a doctor here. The man in my dream, the one with the bloody teeth . . ." Perle trembled. "He was a doctor. An evil doctor. You must be sure that you do not bring him here . . ."

"I am not going to bring anyone evil here. We will see Dr. Blumenthal about this. He is kind and good. You have known him your entire life. Was he the man in your dream?"

"No, the evil man in my dream wasn't Dr. Blumenthal. It was another doctor. A horrible doctor."

"It was a just a nightmare, Perle. You're burning up with fever. I need to ask Mama what to do. I'll be back," Shoshana said.

"Don't go yet. I have more to tell you." Perle grabbed Shoshana's hand, stopping her from leaving the bedside. "This man. The doctor. His smile was the scariest thing about him because he was hiding behind it. While he was only pretending to be nice, he was making plans to hurt us." Perle was shaking so hard, her teeth were chattering. "He wanted to hurt me and Bluma. And, Shoshana, you tried, but you couldn't save us. You wanted to very badly. But you couldn't because you were his prisoner too."

"It's all right. You are safe. You had this terrible dream because of what happened the other day when you and Bluma were talking to that traveling salesman. That's all this was. I promise you. There is no meaning to it. None at all."

"You're wrong, Shoshana. This dream was more than just a dream. Much more. In fact, I wish I could die here and now in our little neighborhood before this darkness comes to swallow us all."

"Don't talk like that. It's a sin. Hashem's greatest gift is life. You must appreciate it. You must be grateful," Shoshana said, gently prying her hand away from Perle. Then she reached up and touched Perle's cheek. "Bluma will stay with you. And I'll be right back. I'm going to get Mama."

CHAPTER TWENTY-SIX

"Mama . . ." Shoshana shook her mother gently. Naomi awakened immediately. Even with all of the hard work she did each day, she still slept very lightly. After Shoshana was born, she had never again fallen into a deep sleep.

"What is it?" Naomi whispered, not wanting to wake her husband.

"It's Perle. She's had another one of her dreams. And this time it's a bad one. She's sweating, and her skin is hot. I'm afraid she is ill."

Naomi got out of bed quickly. She didn't say another word. There was no need. Shoshana followed her mother into the twins' room.

"Should I go and get a cool, wet rag to wash her face?" Shoshana asked her mother.

"Yes, please, and hurry," Naomi said.

Shoshana left. Naomi knelt beside Perle's bed and looked at her daughter. "How are you feeling?" she asked.

Perle smiled. There was no trace of the sweat that had been there only moments before. "I feel fine, Mama," Perle said, her eyes now clear, and she seemed perfectly normal.

Naomi touched Perle's face. It was cool, with no trace of sweat. "Did you have another one of those dreams?"

"Yes, this time it was a bad one. But I can't remember much about it. Only a man with black hair and a big gap between his front teeth. And blood. I think he turned into a hyena and tried to eat me and Bluma."

"It was only dream," Naomi said, trying to comfort her daughter. She knew how frightening these dreams could be and she felt sorry for Perle. She also knew that once the dream passed, Perle would be fine. Because that was how it had always been for her. Some of Naomi's dreams turned out to be premonitions. But some didn't. She could still remember how she'd seen her husband's face in a dream long before she'd ever met him. And she remembered that she had seen Eli's face, too, in another dream. She remembered the first time she'd looked into Eli's eyes and realized that he would play a big part in her destiny. But at the time she had no idea what that would mean.

Perle took her mother's hand. "I'm all right Mama. I can't even remember the whole dream. All I can remember are bits and pieces of it and that it really scared me. Naomi nodded as she recalled the reoccurring dream she still had of the smoking chimneys. It had come to her for the first time when she was only six years old, and still, to this day, it made no sense at all. But she could count at least five times that she'd had the same nightmare. And the most recent time had been as little as two months ago.

Most of her dreams lingered only in bits and pieces, but this nightmare of the chimneys was different. And it was still vivid in her mind. In this dream there was always a row of chimneys belching smoke. And within the smoke she'd seen dying butterflies. They fell to the ground soundlessly and they made her cry. She couldn't explain why, but that always frightened her terribly. Even now, when-ever she had it, she'd awaken, weeping. That first time she dreamed about the chimneys, she'd woken up, and her mother had held her and rocked her until she could regain her composure. But later her family became used to her having the same nightmare, and they stopped taking it seriously. Although, her sister Miriam never made light of it. She believed in Naomi, and she was afraid that someday the dream would have a deeper meaning.

Even now as Naomi was remembering her dream, the very

thought of it sent a shiver up her spine. Yet she had no idea why. It didn't make sense. Naomi had told her daughters and her husband that she had the gift of sight, like Perle. But she'd never told anyone but her mother and her twin sister about the dream of the chimneys.

"It's all right." Naomi took her daughter Perle into her arms, remembering how her mother had done the same for her. Then she slowly rocked Perle while Shoshana and Bluma stood by watching.

"I told you I am fine." Perle smiled. Then her face went dark again. "I just remembered something else about the dream," Perle said. "The evil doctor told Bluma and I that we must call him uncle. Do we have an uncle that we don't know about? An evil uncle?"

"No, we don't have an uncle like that." Naomi gently ran her fingers over Perle's forehead, soothing her.

"I'm glad," Perle said. She closed her eyes for a moment. But then she opened them wide. "There was another very strange thing in my dream."

"Oh?" Naomi said softly. "Like what?"

"Well, there were flags. Red-and-black flags. In the center of the flags there was a black spider. When I saw the flags I was very scared. Even though it wasn't a real spider, I felt it crawling across my chest."

Naomi felt her heart stop for a moment. She couldn't speak. Her face turned white, so white that she had to get up and turn away from the girls so they wouldn't see her terror. *I have seen that same flag. I have never mentioned it to Perle. Now she has seen it too. This is more than just a nightmare. Much more. But I don't know what to do about it. Is there anything that I can do?*

Outside the window, a black crow squawked.

CHAPTER TWENTY-SEVEN

♊

ONCE NAOMI KNEW THAT PERLE WAS FINE, SHE LEFT HER THREE daughters in the twins' room and went to the kitchen to begin her daily chores. Although she didn't say anything to Herschel when he came into the kitchen for breakfast, Perle's dream had left Naomi shaken. She watched her husband as he ate the food she'd prepared for him, and she envied the fact that very little upset or bothered him as long as his family was well behaved and people spoke of him with respect and admiration. Most of all, as he was able to earn a good living, he never thought much about anything spiritual or deep.

Most mornings, Herschel woke up crabby. He hardly spoke until later in the day. Over the years of living with him, Naomi had grown used to this. He ate and then left for work, without so much as a word. He never once had said thank you to her for preparing his food. However, long ago, before the children were born, when they were newlyweds, she had felt bold one day and asked him, "Why don't you ever thank me for getting up and preparing your breakfast each morning?"

She knew he was not happy with her for bothering him with such a question because his eyes narrowed when he answered her: "Why don't you thank me for going out to work and providing for you each day? You know why? I'll tell you why. It's because there is no need for thanks between a husband and wife. This is what we are supposed to expect from each other," he said curtly.

So, although his harsh words had hurt her feelings, she just nodded in agreement because she couldn't speak. Then she quickly turned away so he could not see her lower lip trembling. There was nothing more to say. She was his wife, and if she wanted to have a peaceful home, she had to accept him as he was. Naomi had learned this from her mother from the time she was very young. "A woman accepts her husband the way he is and makes the best of it. Look for his good qualities and try to remember them when he hurts your feelings." Her mother had said this more times than she could count. *I was just hoping for more. I somehow thought that my life and my marriage would be better than my mother's. It's not. It turns out my husband is so much like my father that it's almost frightening. So, Herschel is not appreciative, and he can be unkind. But unlike my father, he is a good provider, and for that I should remember always to be grateful.*

For a while in the early days, when they were still newly married, each time Herschel made her feel bad, Naomi went to her room and closed the door. She lay down on the bed and cried. Herschel never once came after her. He let her be alone to sort things out on her own. But that was when she was a young bride and her heart was still so tender. Over the years, she grew harder as she came to understand him better and accept this marriage as her destiny. When he was cruel, instead of crying, she told herself this is just his way. And as time passed, no matter what he said or did, he couldn't hurt her anymore. And she never again expected gratitude from him for anything she did for him.

After Herschel left to go into the city to work, Naomi began to clean the kitchen. Once the kitchen was spotless, she planned to put on the soup she was going to prepare for dinner. As she washed and scrubbed, her mind drifted, and she thought about some of the dreams she'd had that she had almost forgotten.

There was one such dream that she remembered. It had occurred several times during her pregnancy with Shoshana. She and Sarah were still very close at the time. They were both carrying babies. The dream was about their unborn children It had shocked and upset Naomi, so she had never told anyone about this dream, especially not Sarah.

She liked Sarah from the day they first met. She still remembered that day when Sarah's family had moved into their neighborhood from Russia. Naomi was nine and Sarah was eight. And from the day they met in the front of Sarah's home, the girls became fast friends who did everything together. It was as if Naomi was a triplet instead of a twin. When anyone saw Naomi, they could expect to see Miriam and Sarah with her.

Both Sarah and Naomi's mothers taught the three of them how to sew and cook. They learned the best way to make a kugel, a noodle pudding, at Naomi's house, and how to braid a challah at Sarah's home. Those were days that still filled Naomi with fond memories. Then when all three had come to be of marriageable age, they were betrothed within a few weeks of each other. It seemed as if they were meant to be best friends forever. That was until after they were married.

Shlomie, Sarah's husband, was the problem. He decided that his wife wasn't doing enough around the house and that she was spending too much time with her friends. So he only allowed her to see Naomi and Miriam once a week. The three girls relished those hours they spent together. They took long walks and talked about their lives. Then when Naomi and Sarah both became pregnant within a month of each other, it was an exciting time for all three of them. And even though Naomi knew that her sister Miriam felt left out, Miriam was excited for her sister and her friend. Both Naomi and Sarah tried their best to assure Miriam that she would conceive soon. But somehow Naomi knew deep in her gut that it was not to be. She was certain that Miriam would not have a child until much later in life. It made her feel bad for her sister, but even so, nothing could overshadow the joy she felt carrying life within her body. And when combined with the love she felt for Eli, and their secret affair, Naomi was the happiest she'd been since the day she and Herschel had been married.

One night, Naomi had a dream that she and Sarah would both give birth to daughters, and their daughters would grow up to be best friends like they were. In the dream, Naomi was glad and excited. She told Sarah and Miriam about the dream, and the three of them shared the joy of it. They loved talking about their future children, but Sarah thought it was just a dream, because she didn't know that Naomi's dreams were often premonitions.

Then one night, a few months later, Naomi had another dream; this time it was not a joyous one. It was a dark nightmare. And this was the one she did not share with her friend or her sister. She dreamt that her daughter and Sarah's daughter became enemies. She knew something happened that came between the friendship, but she didn't know what it was. All she knew was that it was something dark and ugly. Try as she might, Naomi couldn't determine what it was that would pull the two girls apart. But she felt uneasy when she thought about it.

During the day, Naomi found happiness and beauty in everything around her. Her love for Eli helped her to cope with how miserable she was in her marriage. But meanwhile at night, her dreams were increasing. One night she woke up in a cold sweat. She'd had a nightmare about a snake that coiled itself around her baby's neck. Naomi tried to pull the snake off, but she couldn't as she wasn't strong enough. It was choking the life out of her child. She screamed for Herschel, then for Eli, but no one came to help her. In the background she heard Frieda Bergstein laughing. And when she turned to look at her, she saw that Frieda was naked and she had wrapped herself around Herschel like a snake, and blood dripped from her lips. Naomi was trembling when she awoke. The dream had unnerved her, and for the next few weeks she thought about it constantly. She began to forget, but whenever Frieda came to visit

Herschel, Naomi looked into Frieda's eyes, and she remembered the dream.

After Shoshana was born, Naomi found that she was so busy between caring for her child and keeping house that she saw less and less of Sarah. Between Shlomie's constant complaining and the added work, it was difficult to make time for each other. This was not so with Miriam. Instead of waiting for Naomi to have time for her, when she wasn't working part time at the Hebrew school, Miriam went to Naomi's house and helped her with the cooking and cleaning. And because she was around so much, Miriam took on the role of second mother to little Shoshana.

The days seemed to fly by. Early on Friday afternoons, when everyone went to the market to purchase food for their Sabbath dinners that evening, Naomi and Sarah would sometimes run into each other. Then it was just as it had been when they were young girls. They would laugh and talk and giggle, and then they would make plans to spend a few hours together again, but this time they would bring the babies. If she was off from work, Miriam would join them. They would place the two little girls on blankets on the floor and watch them play. And even though the children were still very young, Shoshana and Neta began to form a bond.

Herschel wanted more children. He wanted them as soon as possible. "She should grow up with a sibling," he said. "Maybe it will be a brother, yes?"

Naomi nodded.

They tried desperately to have more children. But as time passed, they began to feel as if there might be a dark cloud over them because Naomi miscarried three times early in her pregnancies. Then she became pregnant, and it looked as if she would carry the baby full term. Careful not to do too much physically, Naomi depended upon her sister for help. Miriam always came through. On her days off, she would help Naomi with the housework and play with Shoshana, so Naomi, who was always very tired, could rest. While she was pregnant, Naomi and Eli did not make love. In the stolen moments when they were together, they lay quietly in each other's arms.

All of Naomi's caution was for naught. In her eight month of pregnancy, she gave birth to a little girl who was stillborn. This was the greatest tragedy she had ever faced. She'd come so close to having this baby. She'd begun to believe that everything would be all right. When Naomi saw the tiny blue body of her unborn child in the arms of the midwife, with Naomi's umbilical cord wrapped around the baby's neck, Naomi shivered. She wept uncontrollably as she remembered her nightmare of the snake. *I didn't realize it at the time, but the snake was my own umbilical cord. I killed my child.* She was so horrified that for a while she could not bear for Herschel to touch her. Depression set in, and she talked to Eli about her feelings. He begged her not to blame herself. But no matter what he said, she was certain that this was her fault.

Naomi lay in bed unable to eat. She was so distraught that she did not even go to see Eli. Miriam took time off from her job to care for her sister. She arrived at the house early each morning and stayed until Herschel returned from work. Never having taken care of himself let alone a young toddler, Herschel was overwhelmed. He didn't know what to do. His clothes were not clean or pressed. Most days he didn't eat unless Miriam prepared something for him. And worst of all, he found himself being annoyed with Shoshana who needed constant attention.

Finally, not knowing where else to turn, Herschel went to speak with the rabbi. The rabbi told him to be patient with his wife. And Herschel tried. But Naomi was unresponsive to his attempts at kindness. Then unable to cope, he went into the bedroom where she lay on the bed in the darkness staring blankly at the wall. Looking at her, he clenched his fists. Then he lost his temper. He knocked her favorite vase to the floor. The glass shattered. Naomi trembled, but she didn't move. "You will listen to me now," he said. "You will get out of that bed and make yourself useful. This month you will go to the mikvah, after your menses cycle and you will get clean," he roared, breaking the silence in the house. "And when you return we will try again to have another child. I don't want to hear anything else from you. I've had enough of your laziness. You've lain around here for over a month. Enough is enough. Do you understand me?"

She looked away.

"I said, do you understand me, Naomi?"

"Yes."

Shoshana had been asleep in her crib. Herschel's yelling woke her, and now she was wailing.

"Get out of that bed and take care of that child. And don't you forget that I want a decent meal for dinner tonight too."

Naomi got out of bed. Her legs felt weak from lying still for so long. She walked into Shoshana's bedroom and picked the baby up out of her crib. Holding Shoshana close to her made Naomi feel alive again. Tears ran down her cheeks as she sat down in the rocking chair and rocked her child gently. The door slammed, and she breathed a sigh of relief. Herschel had left for work.

When Miriam arrived an hour later, Naomi was still in the rocking chair with Shoshana asleep in her arms.

"Where's Herschel?" Miriam asked.

"He left for work early."

"I'm glad to see you are out of bed."

"Yes, I am trying to get better. Herschel was angry at me this morning. And I suppose he was right. Shoshana needs me. And he deserves better."

"I'll tell you what. I'll put up a stew for your dinner tonight. All you have to do today is sit up with me and Shoshana and have tea. How does that sound?"

"I think I can manage it," Naomi said and smiled at her sister.

That month after she was clean of blood for seven days following her period, Naomi went to the mikvah, the ritual bath. When she returned home, she was deemed pure and ready for her husband. But when he came to her and tried to have sex, she went cold. Taking his arm, she looked into his eyes and begged him to wait. "I am doing my best. I've been preparing your meals again. And I am not lying in bed. But I am not ready for this yet," she said. He nodded and accepted her refusal. But the following month, he was not as accommodating when she tried to beg off from having sex with him. He said he could not wait any longer, and he demanded that she fulfill her wifely duties, or he threatened to ask for a "get," a Jewish divorce. "How can we have children if you won't allow me to touch you?" he said and walked out of the room.

CHAPTER TWENTY-EIGHT

♊

FOR YEARS, HERSCHEL'S WIFE, NAOMI, HAD BEEN FRIEDA'S NEMESIS. Frieda believed that Naomi, with her youth and beauty, had stolen her chance of making a match with Herschel. Many times, when Frieda was young, she had heard her parents say that when the time came, Frieda and Herschel would marry. But then Frieda met Naomi. At first, they were friends. But that only lasted a few months because something happened that set Frieda reeling.

One afternoon as Frieda and Naomi were taking a walk by the park, Frieda saw Herschel and smiled at him. When she saw the look on his face when he first laid eyes on Naomi, Frieda knew he was smitten with Naomi. And why wouldn't he be? She was a beautiful girl, a few years younger than Frieda. She was slender and delicate, with long, thick dark hair, while Frieda had frizzy, unruly hair, was heavyset, and big boned. Not only that, but Naomi had the face of an angel. Her eyes were soft; her skin was creamy, and she had heart-shaped red lips. After Herschel began to show an interest in Naomi, the friendship between Naomi and Frieda turned into something else, a competition. However, only Frieda was competing because Naomi had no interest in Herschel. In fact, Naomi was hurt that Frieda had seemed to turn on her. But Frieda didn't care. The more she saw Herschel watching Naomi like a puppy in love, the more she hated Naomi.

But Frieda still had hope, until she found out that Naomi and Herschel were betrothed. Then she was furious. But there was no one she could talk to about it except her mother, who was even angrier than she was. Frieda's family was not wealthy. However, they were a little better off than Naomi's parents, and they would certainly have cherished a son-in-law like Herschel, who had plenty of financial resources. Frieda and her mother blamed Naomi for taking Herschel away from Frieda and ruining her chances for a prosperous marriage.

Every time Frieda saw Naomi walking through town, she felt the fury rise within her. *Naomi is not his intellectual equal. She's just a boring little nothing. But she makes a good impression; she is pretty and sweet. And Herschel has always cared deeply about what people thought of him. However, he is too smart for her, and I know as time goes by, he will grow bored of her. So I will go to school in Warsaw where I will learn to type and to take dictation. He's a lawyer. He's apprenticing under a goy in Warsaw. Once he has learned enough from this goy, he says he will open his own practice. I will be ready and be there to assist him. I will learn as much as I can about law and I will stimulate him intellectually. Herschel Aizenberg will see my value. I will win him over. He will divorce her, I'll make sure of it.*

So, although Frieda's father brought home several marriage prospects, Frieda did not marry. She did little things which discouraged each of the boys that her father brought home. Sometimes she spoke out of turn, giving her opinions on things that were reserved for men only. Other times, she asked too many personal questions that made the prospective grooms uncomfortable. And consequently she did not receive any proposals for marriage. Frieda had a plan, and for the most part it worked. At least sort of, anyway. As she predicted, as time passed, Herschel lost interest in Naomi. He was living a bigger life, a life outside of the small village where they had grown up, and he was meeting with people who had more varied interests. This changed him. At first when Frieda brought a kosher lunch, which she prepared for Herschel each day, he appreciated it. They ate together, and she was happy. But these last few months, he'd refused the food she brought.

It began a few months ago when he had several clients who asked him to meet them at restaurants. Slowly, he stopped keeping kosher. Frieda would have gladly given up anything, including keeping kosher, if he would have taken her with him to these lunches. But he never asked her. She told him that she would love to accompany him and that afterward, they could discuss strategies. He refused.

Frieda tried to get close to him, but he pushed her away. He stopped discussing his cases with her. When he'd first opened his practice, he had talked everything over with her as if she were a partner. But now he treated her like she was just his secretary. She didn't know what to do. She was growing older, and the marriage prospects had stopped coming around. Frieda had put all of her hope into a future with a man who was not interested. But then tragedy struck the Aizenbergs. Naomi began to have one miscarriage after another. Frieda assumed that Herschel, like every man, wanted a son. Perhaps this was her opportunity. She had always been bold, and now was the time to use her greatest gift to lure the man she wanted.

One afternoon, a week after Naomi had given birth to a stillborn baby, Frieda went into Herschel's office. He was busy writing something.

"I need to speak to you," she said.

"What is it?" he asked curtly.

She closed the door. "It must be hard on you."

"What?"

"The babies. I know it must be difficult," Frieda said, trying to sound sympathetic. He was so closed off. She wished he would make it easier to talk to him. The words caught in her throat.

"It's difficult, but it's all right, we'll try again."

Frieda had never been with a man. She'd saved herself for marriage, and the only husband she'd ever wanted was Herschel Aizenberg. Now, as she stood before him, trembling, she had no idea how to seduce him—what to say, what to do. She sucked in her breath, then she looked away. She couldn't say what she was about to say if she was looking directly at him. "I could give you a healthy son. I am strong and healthy."

Herschel put his pen down. "Frieda, what's the matter with you? What are you trying to say?"

"I'm offering myself to you."

He shook his head. "No, you and I are friends. We are working together. No."

"I have always wanted to be your wife." Her voice was cracking, and the tears were welling up in her eyes.

"I am married. You know that."

"Yes, but you aren't happy. You could ask for a divorce, a get. Your wife can't give you a healthy heir. I could give you a boy to carry on your name."

"I don't want to talk about this with you. Go to your desk and do your work."

She'd walked out of his office feeling rejected and ashamed. Humiliated, she returned home. For the first time since Frieda had started working for Herschel, she considered quitting. But she realized she had nowhere else to go. She had spent her entire life trying to link her future to his; she had known that she was taking a risk. However, she had never met anyone else who she wanted as badly as she had wanted him. Convinced that if she could only make herself so necessary in his life, he would naturally turn to her. However, he was a stubborn man, and nothing with him had turned out the way she had hoped it would. But she knew that the relationship between Herschel and his wife and gone sour.

CHAPTER TWENTY-NINE

HERSCHEL COULD NOT EVEN LOOK AT HIS WIFE. HE LEFT THE HOUSE early in the morning and went into work. When Frieda arrived, he sent her to a restaurant to get him some breakfast.

"But it's not kosher," she said. "I could go home and make you something and then bring it back with me."

"Just go to the restaurant," Herschel said. He was in a terrible mood.

Frieda did as he asked, and when she returned, she put the food down on his desk. Then she said softly, "I can see something is wrong. Do you want to talk?"

He did want to talk. It was unusual for him to want to talk to anyone, but he needed to get his feelings out. So he told Frieda everything. She listened quietly. When he was done, she said, "You are right about everything you say. You are always right. Naomi should not deny you. You are her husband. If you were my husband, I would never deny you anything."

He looked at her. It was good to have someone agree with him. "Thank you," he said. He knew he was not often kind or tender toward her. And because of this, at this moment when he was treating her as if she mattered to him, she was hanging on to his every word.

He knew how much she wanted him. She'd never made a secret of it. And it had been a long time since he'd had a woman. *Why not?* he thought. *She's better than nothing.*

Herschel stopped eating and stood up. He wiped the grease off his fingers on his handkerchief and walked over to Frieda. Then he took her into his arms. She didn't resist. Not at all. In fact, she fell into his embrace with such desire that he knew she would comply with everything. He took her. Not lovingly, but hard and forcefully. He was man fulfilling a need. For a moment, he felt bad when he saw that she bled. *She was a virgin*, he thought. But it had gone too far. He couldn't stop now. He moved faster to get it over with quickly. And once he was finished, he was disgusted with himself.

"You had better go back to your desk," he said. "We have a case coming up. There's work to do."

She looked hurt. He knew she wanted him to cuddle her and say kind things, but he couldn't. He couldn't even bear to look at her.

CHAPTER THIRTY

Naomi would have loved nothing more than a divorce from Herschel. *But my parents would be horrified if it happened,* she thought *They would never forgive me for shaming them in the eyes of their friends and their community. My father has grown used to the financial help that Herschel provides. He would be livid if he had to give that up. And my life would be hard here in this little village if I were a young, divorced woman with a child. Everyone would shun me. They would say I was damaged goods. No matter what caused the divorce, people would blame me. They would look at me and say I was a bad wife and a woman that no sane man should ever take a chance on. I know Eli would stand up to all of them. He would turn his back on his friends and his community. He would even turn his back on the rabbi if he had to in order to marry me, but it would not be fair to him to take him away from the synagogue and the life he loves. I love him too much to do that to him.*

For a moment she put away all thoughts of herself and thought only of Eli and how all of this would affect him. *If he married me after Herschel divorced me for being unfaithful, not only would Eli suffer, but the parents who had adopted him would suffer the humiliation as well. People would look down on them for the terrible thing Eli had done. How can I allow that to happen after they had been kind enough to take Eli in. He was just a child who no one wanted. His adoptive parents did a mitzva and took him in. Then they raised him as their own. Marriage to me would ruin him. It would destroy the respect everyone in the community has for him. I would rather die than cause that.*

The only alternative would be for me to take Shoshana and move back in with my parents and become a burden on them. When she thought of living each day with her father, she felt sick to her stomach because she knew he would make her miserable for having divorced Herschel. And what about my other two girls. I know that Herschel would forbid me to see them. It would destroy me to be separated from my children. But more importantly, it would hurt them terribly. Girls need a mother when they are growing up. And the older they get, the more they will need me. Herschel is not the kind of man who can offer his girls warmth or comfort. No, I can't allow this to happen.

Therefore, I must make things right with Herschel. When I finish my menses this month, and after the seven clean days have passed, I will go to the mikvah and make myself ready to be a proper wife to Herschel. The idea was abhorrent to her. But she followed her plan. And when she'd been thoroughly inspected and declared clean at the mikvah, she walked home slowly, dreading the night ahead.

Naomi walked in the door. Miriam was on the floor playing with Shoshana. Naomi knew that what she was about to say should be said in private. But she didn't care. *Let Miriam hear what I have to say.* She looked at Herschel, and in a resigned tone of voice, she said, "I'm ready to be a wife to you. There is no need for a 'get.' I've been to the mikvah, and I am clean."

He nodded.

Later that night, after Miriam had gone home and Shoshana was asleep, Herschel turned to her. "Shall we go to bed?"

She nodded. She felt sick to her stomach, but she followed him into the bedroom. Herschel began to remove his clothes. She didn't remove hers. She just lay down on the bed and waited. It had been so long since he'd been with her that he was overeager and more than a little rough. He didn't say a word, not a kind word, not a word of encouragement. In fact, he was so lost in his own physical satisfaction that he never noticed the tear that fell down her cheek.

When it was over, she got up and went into the bathroom. Hot tears burned her eyes as she wept while she washed her body clean of him. But to her surprise, that first time she was with him, she became pregnant again. She was happy and excited, but she also secretly terrified that she would miscarry, or worse, she would see that snake strangle her child again. Her dreams grew more vivid. They were haunting and terrible. And to make matters worse, they now came every night. In her nightmares she heard voices. The voices were calling her a sinner and telling her that the death of her unborn children was evidence of God's wrath at what she had done with Eli.

Naomi didn't sleep well. Dark circles formed under her eyes. She thought about Miriam and how, because she'd needed her help, Miriam had become a part of her sin. This made Naomi feel even guiltier. *Will my sister suffer because of what she'd done to help me?* This pregnancy was very hard on her. She couldn't keep anything down. Every time she tried to eat, she vomited. Her body felt weak, achy, and tired. She didn't talk to Herschel about how she felt. But she told Eli everything. He didn't try to convince her that everything was fine the way he had in the past. Instead, he just held her in his arms, gently rocking her and trying to comfort her. She didn't ask him, but she wondered if he, too, was afraid that she was losing the babies because God was angry that they'd sinned.

Herschel didn't notice that Naomi was not sleeping or eating. He was oblivious to her needs. Happy about the pregnancy, he sang to himself and drummed his fingers on the table while looking out the window after work each day. If he had any fears that she would lose this baby, he hid them very well. And, of course, Naomi knew better than to tell Herschel her dreams or share her fears.

In the past, whenever she mentioned her dreams, he refused to give them any credibility. He called them bubbe-meise, old wives' tales, superstitions. Maybe they were, but she didn't think so. She had to smile, though, because she'd often heard him say that she shouldn't mention her nightmares, because doing so was giving their good luck a kenahora, which was an opportunity for the evil eye to set its sights upon them. She believed in being careful not to attract the evil eye. But she also thought that if he believed her dreams were bubbe-meise, wasn't a kenahora the same thing? Wasn't it possible that a kenahora was just another form of bubbe-meise?

Herschel was like this. He was practical and didn't believe in dreams, yet he was wholeheartedly afraid of the evil eye. It seemed to Naomi that Herschel was always contradicting himself, but if she brought it to his attention, he became furious. So she told no one except Eli of her fears, not her sister, not Sarah, not her mother. No one. Instead, she bore her fears alone, or with Eli, praying daily, begging God to forgive her and to grant her this one wish.

I will do anything. I will give you anything. She prayed. Then one afternoon, she saw a spot of blood on her underwear. She was sure she was going to miscarry again. Panicked, she began to pray. *Please, I beg you to forgive me for what I did with Eli. I know it was wrong and that I was weak. But I will let him go if you will only give me a healthy child. I know that Shoshana is not Herschel's daughter, and I am sick with guilt over it. I owe it to Herschel to give him a baby of his own.* It had been years since she prayed. She'd stopped because she'd been ashamed to talk to God because of what she'd done with Eli. But she needed God's understanding, so she wept as she begged for forgiveness.

The death of all of my unborn children is on my hands for what I have done with Eli. I promise you that I will never see him again if you will only grant me this one wish. Please let this baby be born healthy and alive, and please forgive my sister for her part in my sin. It was not her fault. It was mine. Then, like a true miracle, Naomi gave birth to two little twins who came into the world healthy and beautiful. And when Naomi saw the two tiny girls, with their perfect little fingers and toes, her heart swelled with love and . . . the dream of the snake was forgotten.

CHAPTER THIRTY-ONE

AT FIRST, NAOMI TRIED TO AVOID MEETING WITH ELI. SHE TRIED TO control the strong desire that burned with her. *I must not go to him again. I promised God that I would end this thing Eli and I have, and I must keep my vow.* But when she didn't show up for their weekly meeting, Eli boldly sent one of the young students at the yeshiva to her home with a note for her:

> *I waited for you. Are you all right? I am so worried. Please come next week. I have to see you.*

The letter was not addressed nor was it signed. But he had taken a tremendous risk sending it, and it unnerved her.

Naomi was shaking when there was another knock on her door. She was certain that the delivery boy had forgotten to give her something. Pulling the door open she was about to ask what he wanted, when she saw that it wasn't the delivery boy at all. It was Frieda. She scrunched the letter in her hand but not before Frieda noticed it.

"So, what did the yeshiva boy want?" Frieda asked.

"Nothing. What do you want?" Naomi said.

"Just to visit with you. I brought some mandel brot for Herschel."

Naomi didn't take the plate. The letter felt like it was burning a hole into her hand. Frieda kept her eyes on the paper.

"So, what's that? Did the yeshiva student give you a note?"

"Yes, it's a letter from the rabbi. I am thinking about working at the shul part time. Not that it's any of your business," Naomi lied.

"Oh, very nice," Frieda said, ignoring the insult. "So, can I come in?"

"Not now. I have too much to do." Naomi put the letter into her dress pocket, then she took the plate and put it down on the table. "Well, thank you. I'm sure Herschel will enjoy it," she said coldly, and then she closed the door with Frieda standing there.

Her heart beat wildly as she reread the letter. Standing far enough away from the window, she watched as Frieda walk away. Once she was certain Frieda was gone, Naomi tore the letter into small pieces. Then she slipped out the back door and buried the pieces of the letter in her yard. Then on the following Wednesday she went to see him. *This will be the last time,* she told herself. *I owe him an explanation. And I will give him one. I will tell him the truth.*

But when she saw him standing there waiting for her, looking so vulnerable and alone, she felt her heart ache with love. *One more time,* she thought, *just one more time.* She fell into his arms, and neither of them said a word. He kissed her tenderly and gently made love to her.

She'd broken the vow she'd made to God, and it haunted her. *What would be the consequences?* She knew she should break it off with Eli. And each week when they met, she told herself that it would be the last time. But she couldn't say goodbye. She'd told Miriam about the promise, and Miriam warned her to stop seeing Eli, but Naomi begged her not to judge her. She pleaded with Miriam to continue to babysit. "I can't give him up. I feel like if I don't have him in my life, I'll die of sadness. Herschel makes me feel so alone. And somehow I can't seem to get rid of Frieda. She is here all the time," Naomi told Miriam.

"I should refuse to babysit for you," Miriam said.

"But you won't. Will you?"

"You know I won't. I wouldn't do that to you. I know how hard your marriage is on you, and I know what Eli means to you. But, Naomi, you made a promise to God. And you continue to break it. I am scared for you."

"I will try to give him up. I will . . ."

"I wish I could believe you," Miriam said, but even so she came each week as she promised to watch Naomi's children.

And Naomi was as happy as she could be. Her babies filled her with a special kind of joy that only a mother could experience. And Eli filled her empty heart with the love Herschel had never supplied. So she put the vow she made out of her mind and hoped that God would understand.

CHAPTER THIRTY-TWO

THEN A LITTLE OVER A MONTH LATER, NAOMI'S FATHER BECAME ILL. HER mother sent for her and for Miriam. Miriam left right away to go to her mother's house. But Naomi had to wait for Herschel to return home to watch the children, so she could go to their father's bedside. By the time Naomi arrived, it was too late. Her father was already gone. He had died within a few hours of showing symptoms. Naomi returned home because of her children, but Miriam stayed with their mother to help her prepare for their father's shiva and burial.

The following day, Miriam knocked at Naomi's door. Naomi opened it, holding Bluma in her arms.

"Sit down," Miriam said. Her face was a pale gray. Her eyes were sunken in. Naomi sat down on the sofa. Shoshana was on the floor playing with Perle who lay on a blanket. "Mama didn't wake up this morning. I came as soon as I could."

"What are you saying?" Naomi asked her sister in disbelief.

"I'm saying that Mama died during the night."

"Died? Mama? From what? Why? She was fine yesterday." Naomi was too shocked to cry. Her hands were shaking so badly that she was afraid she would drop the baby, so she put Bluma down on the blanket beside Perle.

"I don't know from what. I only know that I stayed the night at Mama's house so that she wouldn't be alone. This morning I made her breakfast, but she didn't come out of her room. So, I waited for an hour thinking she was tired from everything. Still, she didn't come out. So, I went in. And . . . I found her."

Naomi's shoulders dropped. She put her head in her hands. "I blame myself," she whispered. "This is my fault."

Her parents were old, and they had been sick, but Naomi was certain that this was her punishment for breaking her vow.

"I'm going to go home now. I need to rest. I'll let you know when we are going to bury them both, and I'll tell you all the details about the shiva as soon as I have them," Miriam said coldly. Then she stood up and walked out of Naomi's house. Naomi stared at the wall for a long time until Bluma started to cry. The sound of the baby brought her out of her daze, and she picked Bluma up and held her close.

Naomi and her sister buried their parents, then they went back to the house where they had grown up to sit shiva for the next seven days. Naomi was sick over what had happened. She couldn't eat or sleep, but somehow she couldn't cry either. All she could do was sit on one of the boxes that had been prepared for the mourners and stare out into space. Deep in her heart, she feared that she had caused her parents' deaths. And although she knew she couldn't tell Herschel how she felt, she decided that she would find a time to talk to Miriam about it. The neighbors who had known Naomi all of her life, were kind and generous. They helped to prepare for the shiva in every way. They brought food and sweets to the house. Mrs. Saltzsky who had been Naomi's mother's best friend, covered the mirrors and set out the water and towels in front of the house so that those who returned from the graveyard could symbolically wash the death off their hands.

Most of the time, Miriam seemed to be too busy to talk. But Naomi thought it was unintentional. She just assumed Miriam was trying to occupy herself so she didn't have to face her grief. On the fourth day of the shiva, Miriam was alone in the kitchen. She was trying to keep busy by arranging a plate of cookies to put out on the table for the visitors. One of the neighbors had brought it from the bakery. Naomi went into the kitchen to speak to her sister. Miriam's hands were shaking as she placed the cookies on her mother's favorite serving tray. Her hair was uncombed. Her eyes were red from crying. And it was easy to see that she was grieving. But what Naomi had not anticipated was that, in her grief, Miriam was not herself. She was filled with anger toward her sister.

"Can I talk to you?" Naomi asked.

Miriam whirled around and looked directly into Naomi's eyes. For the first time in their lives Miriam lashed out at Naomi, and her rage made her cruel. In a deep, angry, guttural voice, she said, "You made a promise to Hashem and then you broke it? How could you do that? This is all your fault. I told you to stop it with Eli, but you wouldn't. And you made me feel guilty if I refused to help you, so I suppose this is my fault too. I have been indulging you since we were children because you were always the delicate one, the one who needed more attention. The prettier one . . . the better one . . ."

Naomi shook her head. "It's not true. I am not prettier or better. I am weaker. And I am so weak when it comes to Eli." She began to cry. "I know I have been wrong . . ."

"Wrong? Is that all you have to say for yourself? Let me tell you what you are, Naomi. You are a vain and selfish girl who thinks only of your own needs," Miriam said. "I am done with you. I never want to speak to you again. Go away. Get out of my sight."

Naomi was devastated by her sister's words. It felt as if she had been punched in the stomach and all of the wind was knocked out of her. She stood staring at Miriam for a few moments, hoping Miriam would say something to make things better. But Miriam did not speak. Picking up the platter of cookies, she walked out of the room leaving Naomi alone.

Naomi stayed away from Miriam for the rest of the shiva, hoping every day that Miriam would try to speak to her. She didn't.

And now, Naomi was absolutely certain that unless she made good on her promise to God, more death and destruction would follow. Losing Miriam was the hardest thing she had ever had to bear.

But she understood how Miriam felt, and she also knew that even if she went to Miriam's home and stood outside her door begging to be let in, Miriam would send her away.

My sister can be stubborn, and the loss of our parents has made her hard and cold. She blames me for everything and she's right. Naomi was feeling lost and alone, and facing the end with Eli was more than she could bear. She had no one to talk to. Herschel was busy with work. He expected her to recover quickly from her parents' deaths but she couldn't. Naomi considered suicide. *I have made such a mess of everything. Maybe it would be best if I were dead. I wouldn't have to say goodbye to Eli and see the hurt in his eyes. I wouldn't have to get up in the morning each day and know that my sister hates me.*

She thought about Shoshana and the twins. *If I am dead, who will raise my daughter, especially now that Miriam wants no part of me. I can't count on her anymore to take my children. Maybe she wants no part of my family either. And if Eli took Shoshana, she would bear the stigma of my sins. Everyone in town would know that she was born out of wedlock. When she was of marriageable age, she would have to accept one of the men who were the least desirable for her husband: a sick boy, or a boy with mental illness in his family. Her husband would be poor, and she would struggle forever.*

If Herschel learned the truth, he would reject Shoshana too. And that would be terrible for her because she has never known any other father. She only knows Eli to be a family friend. And my twins, what would become of my twins? Would Herschel think that they belonged to someone else too? Would he send all of my children to an orphanage? He can be very cold hearted. Tears welled in her eyes. Death was not an option. She had to break things off with Eli and somehow make things right for her daughters. Naomi doubted it, but she hoped that in time Miriam would find it in her heart to forgive her. She was alone in her house, broken and abandoned. That was when she fell to her knees and begged God for forgiveness.

CHAPTER THIRTY-THREE

NAOMI KNEW THAT SHE MUST BREAK UP WITH ELI. THE PAIN SHE FELT in her chest, as she walked to the field to meet him, was so deep that she had to stop and lean against a tree to steady herself. She held her chest and wept. *This is the last time. I can never meet him like this again. I cannot let him touch me today. I must not look at his eyes. I have caused too much pain and death to those I love. Miriam is right, I am selfish. And until I make things right, the worst will come to those I care for. If I continue this, something terrible could happen to my children, and it would be my fault. I couldn't bear that. I must do this. I must have courage and strength. I will always love Eli. I will go to my grave with my heart filled with love for him. But I can't continue to sin. Hashem is angry with me, and I must stop this and hope that I will be forgiven.*

When Naomi arrived, Eli went to take her in his arms. She wanted to push him away, but he said, "I heard about your parents. I am so sorry, my love. What can I do to help you?"

She let him hold her for a moment. And she felt his strength course through her. Then she began to cry because she knew that she would never feel that strength again. The ache in her chest was growing stronger. "I have to end our relationship. I made a vow to

God," she said in a broken voice. "I will always love you. But our love is tainted. I think we are being tested."

"Goodbye? Why? I don't want to say goodbye." He was trembling. "Tested? What do you mean?"

"I have lost so many children, miscarriages, a stillborn with my own cord wrapped around her throat." She shivered. "And now my parents. We must end this."

"No, no, it's not because of our love. How can love be a bad thing? Love is a gift from God."

"Not when one of the people who is in love is married to someone else. Then it's a sin."

Eli fell to his knees and took both of her hands in his. "I beg you. Please don't do this, Naomi."

He said her name, and it felt as if he were speaking directly to her soul.

"I must do this. It's hard for me too. You can't imagine how hard. I want to change my mind, but I can't because, as I told you, I made a promise to God. I said that I would stop committing this sin if he would only grant me a healthy child. And he did. He forgave me and gave me two beautiful little twin girls. But I didn't stop. I couldn't stop. I was . . . I am, and I always will be, so in love with you. I was selfish. I ignored my promise. I knew I was doing wrong. But I couldn't stop myself. So I have been punished. But not only me, my sister too. Hashem took my parents away from us. And now my sister refuses to forgive me. She says I am selfish, and she's right."

"Your parents were old. They were both ill. It was bound to happen at some time. Old people pass away," he said gently.

"How can you say that?"

"Because it's true. No one lives forever. You know that. I don't believe that you are being punished."

"I know I am. The miscarriages, the stillborn, my parents' deaths. Can't you see it? I must make this right. Please, Eli. I am begging you not to make this breakup any harder than it already is."

He stood and walked away from her. "I'm sorry. I would never do anything to make your life more difficult. You should know that."

ROBERTA KAGAN

She could hear the pain in his voice. "I know," she said, wishing she could put her arms around him and hold him close to her heart.

"I will stay away from you. If this is what you want . . ."

"It's not what I want. It's what must be done."

He nodded. "I will say this only one more time, then I promise you, I will never try to be with you again." He cleared his throat. Then he looked directly into her eyes, and in a soft voice, barely above a whisper, he said, "I love you. I would do anything in this world for you. I will always love you, and I know that whatever happens in the future, that will never change. You can always come to me if you need anything, and I will do whatever I can to help you."

The fragrance of wildflowers traveled through the breeze. The scent hit her like a train in the night. A phantom train. One where she couldn't see the track but knew it was coming and was powerless to stop it. It was an aroma of secrecy and forbidden love, of sweet forbidden fruit, of a secret garden. It was the scent that would always bring to mind the love that they had once shared.

She nodded. She wanted to say so many things, but there was no point. She had to let him go. Her throat was so dry that she couldn't speak.

"Goodbye," he said.

Tears ran down her cheeks as she turned away from him and left him standing alone under the oak tree.

CHAPTER THIRTY-FOUR

THREE LONELY MONTHS PASSED. NAOMI LOVED HER CHILDREN, BUT SHE missed Eli and Miriam terribly. She considered going to see Sarah, but she knew that even though she cared for Sarah, she couldn't talk to her about everything that had happened, and the truth was that there was no one, except Eli, who could ever take the place of her twin sister.

Then one afternoon, Naomi had the twins in a carriage and Shoshana at her side while she was purchasing a bunch of carrots and a bag of potatoes from the vegetable vendor. When she looked up, she saw Miriam coming out of the fishmonger's store. Their eyes met. Miriam turned away, and Naomi felt her heart sink. She put the vegetables she'd purchased into her basket and began to walk toward home. Then to her surprise, Miriam came running up to her. She was carrying a package wrapped in brown paper that smelled of fish.

"How are you?" Miriam said.

"I'm all right. How are you?" Naomi asked carefully.

"All right, I guess. But I've missed you," Miriam admitted in a small voice.

"I have missed you too."

"I guess we're twins, so nothing can separate us for too long," Miriam said. "I can't stay mad at you."

Naomi dropped her basket and grabbed Miriam and hugged her sister tightly. "I'm so glad you have forgiven me."

"Did I say I forgave you? All I said was that I am not mad at you anymore," Miriam said. But her tone of voice let Naomi know she was joking. Miriam let out a short laugh.

Then Naomi laughed a little too.

They were both quiet for several moments. Miriam bent down and picked up Naomi's basket. She handed it to Naomi.

"I ended it with Eli," Naomi whispered in Miriam's ear.

"Why don't you send the twins home with Shoshana so we can talk while we walk," Miriam said.

"Good idea," Naomi answered. Then she turned to Shoshana. "Why don't you go on ahead with your sisters. Your aunt and I will follow."

"Yes, Mama," Shoshana said and took her sisters' hands.

Miriam and Naomi waited until Shoshana and the twins were far enough ahead that they couldn't hear. Then the two began walking slowly.

Miriam reached for her sister's hand and squeezed it gently. "I know how hard it had to be for you to give up Eli."

"Perhaps the hardest thing I've ever done."

Miriam nodded.

"I really loved him. I will always love him. But I knew by the things that were happening in my life that Hashem did not approve. I was breaking a sacred commandment. And I had to find the strength in myself to let him go."

"I know."

"And to make things worse, I didn't have you to talk to. I felt so alone."

"You never told anyone else about you and Eli?"

"Never."

"That's good. It's better that no one else knows. You can trust me.

But you can never be sure of other people. Sometimes friends turn into enemies. People you trust can sometimes turn on you."

"Are you talking about Sarah? She's my only other friend."

"Well, yes. Not that I think she would ever turn on you. But why take the chance. I mean she has so little in life and you have so much."

"I don't know what you mean."

"Sure you do. You are beautiful. She is plain. Your husband is a good provider. Hers is not. Sometimes people become jealous."

"I don't think she has a jealous bone in her body."

"But why give her fuel for the fire? You did a good thing not sharing this secret with her."

"I suppose."

There was a long silence. "Miriam, you haven't ever been jealous of me, have you? I mean, some of the things you said when you were angry scared me. I am not prettier; you and I look alike. And well, to be quite honest, I've always thought you were the prettier of the two of us. But . . . well . . . I mean . . . have you been jealous of my husband's income?"

"Sometimes, but I love you, and so my love overcame any jealous feelings I ever had. You're my sister. Even more than a sister, you're my twin. We are like one person. What you have, I have. What I have, you have. You've always been kind and generous with my husband and me."

"I love you too," Naomi said.

"And . . . by the way, you were always the prettier one. You know that. Everyone, even Mama and Papa always said so. Only my husband thinks I am the prettier of the two of us. And I suppose he is the only one who should matter to me," Miriam said.

"I've really missed you." Naomi grabbed her sister and held her in a bear hug for a long time.

"I know. Me too," Miriam said.

CHAPTER THIRTY-FIVE

AND SO IT WAS THAT FIVE YEARS PASSED DURING WHICH NAOMI AND ELI didn't speak a single word to each other. Occasionally, they saw each other in the market or at the synagogue. But when they did, Eli always walked away quickly.

Shoshana was just turning twelve, and Naomi could already see that she was growing into a beautiful young girl. But sometimes Naomi would detect traces of Eli's rebellious streak in Shoshana. Unlike her twin sisters and her mother, Shoshana had the courage to disagree with her father if she believed in something strongly enough. He made it clear that he didn't appreciate it when Shoshana questioned him or stood up to him in any way. That didn't stop her.

Bright and intelligent, like Eli, Shoshana had a burning desire to ask questions. A desire she could not seem to control. And although Herschel was always kind to Shoshana, their relationship was strained. Naomi sometimes wondered if Herschel questioned whether Shoshana was his daughter, because they were just so different. *Could it be that Herschel knew about her affair with Eli? Had someone seen them and told him, and had he just chosen never to mention it to her?* These questions ran through her mind. But she never said a word to Herschel, and she was relieved that he never asked her any questions.

Herschel was not an understanding man. He didn't often consider the feelings of others, so he did nothing to hide the fact that out of all of his children, he favored Bluma. Although Shoshana and Perle seemed to accept this without questioning it, Naomi wondered if they secretly felt badly. Bluma was a lot like her father: strong, athletic, and capable. And as they grew, each of the girls' personalities became more defined.

At five years old, Bluma, unlike her sisters, was already showing that she had a hard exterior, which shielded her from hurt. No one, except Perle, was able to penetrate the wall she had built around her. Perle was the complete opposite of Bluma. She was more like her mother: introspective, with deep thoughts and feelings, tender hearted, caring for everyone and concerning herself with the well-being of everything around her. But most of all, she and her mother shared the strange experience of having those prophetic dreams.

Daily life in the shtetl, where Shoshana was growing up, was not enough for her. The menial tasks of baking, cooking, sewing, and tending to a garden left her unfulfilled and often bored and restless. She wanted more out of life, and it was becoming more and more obvious. Naomi mentioned it to Herschel, explaining that she was worried about Shoshana. But he didn't seem to be concerned. All he said was "Soon she'll be married, and she won't have so much time on her hands to sit around and worry about what she thinks she's missed in life."

Naomi knew that Shoshana's restless streak came from Eli, her real father. Eli was a seeker, and so was his daughter. Miriam knew that Shoshana's difficult personality, which didn't fit in among her peers in the shtetl, was no fault of her own. And because of this, Shoshana and her father were like boiling water and ice. Miriam felt sorry for her eldest. She could see that Herschel ignored her. So her Aunt Miriam brought her niece special gifts and spent time combing and styling Shoshana's hair. They didn't discuss anything serious, but there was a closeness between them. And since Miriam had been so much a part of Shoshana's life, watching her for Naomi when she was just baby, Shoshana became Miriam's favorite of the three girls.

It was a week after Hanukkah. A week after Naomi had seen Eli at the poorhouse when he brought the bread from the rabbi. Her thoughts had been clouded by him ever since. It was always this way whenever she happened to see him. They had not so much as shared a single word in the last five years. But every so often they ran into each other in passing. Each time this happened, their entire relationship replayed in Naomi's mind, and it always took several days for her to get over the pain of reopening the wound.

It was Friday night. Miriam and Aram were coming for dinner to celebrate the Sabbath with the Aizenbergs. Naomi had spent the day preparing food and getting ready.

They arrived early, and Miriam helped her sister set the table and get ready for the Sabbath. As always, the Sabbath dinner was special. The candle lighting, the prayers, the beauty of the Sabbath. And . . . of course, the luscious food. When everyone had finished eating, Herschel and Aram went into the living room to have an after-dinner drink, and Naomi and Miriam began to clear the table.

"Can I help you clean up?" Shoshana asked.

"No, not tonight. You help your mama every night. Tonight, I will help her. Why don't you go and entertain your little sisters?"

"Are you sure, Aunt Miriam?"

"Absolutely."

While Miriam and Naomi were stacking the dirty dishes, Miriam said, "I have something that I must speak with you about."

"Of course," Naomi said, and she stopped cleaning for a moment. Then she turned to look at her sister. "Go on. What is it?"

"Well, I know this is going to be hard for you. I know, because it's hard for me." Miriam chewed on her lip.

Naomi put the dishrag down and asked in a nervous voice, "Tell me already; what is it?"

"I am pregnant," Miriam said. "I am finally pregnant. I am so happy. Aram is so happy."

"Oy! What a blessing. I am so happy too." Naomi pulled her sister into a tight hug.

"Yes, it is a blessing," Miriam said, "But with the blessing came a curse."

"What is it? Are you ill?"

"No, I'm fine. But Aram received a letter from his cousin Hymie in Lithuania. Hymie is a bookkeeper. I think I told you that."

"Yes, you told me that a long time ago. Please, tell me already; what is it? What's wrong?"

"Hymie is sick."

"Nu, so I am sorry about that. I feel bad for Aram, but we don't even know this man. Let's be happy about the baby that is coming, no?"

"I am happy. But there is more to this. Hymie wants Aram and I to move to Lithuania. He wants Aram to take over his accounts. He says it is a very good business, and he will train Aram to be a bookkeeper so long as Aram promises to take care of his wife, Esther, after he passes away. Hymie is old; all his children are grown and gone. They were girls anyway. So, they got married and left home. Apparently, his sons-in-law have trades and are doing well, so they don't want the business. Hymie says he has no one else to turn to. Aram will make good money, and he won't have to do such dangerous work anymore."

"And so? You are moving away?" Naomi said. Her hand went to her heart. She sank down onto a chair.

"Yes. I am afraid I have to go. I tried to convince Aram that we should stay here. I begged him. I told him I would die if we left here. I told him I couldn't bear to leave you. But he wouldn't listen. He said that this is a wonderful opportunity for us, and he insists that we go. Especially now that I am pregnant. Aram wants to give our child a better life. I do, too, but not this way. But no matter what I have said to him, he refuses to listen. In fact, I have never seen him so adamant about anything. He says we will go to Lithuania, and that's that. Aram says he has had enough of tough and dangerous manual labor. He wants a job where he can earn decent money working inside instead of out in the weather. I know he's right. But it's breaking my heart to leave you. And I know that there is no way Herschel would leave here. He has a good law business in Warsaw."

"You're right. Herschel wouldn't leave." Naomi felt tears welling up in her eyes. "So, if you move, then when would I see you?"

"We would have to make plans to visit each other."

"You can't go," Naomi said, and she began to cry.

"I can't stay. I must do as my husband commands."

The two sisters hugged each other.

"When are you leaving?" Naomi asked.

"The end of next month."

CHAPTER THIRTY-SIX

♊

PERLE WOKE UP ONE MORNING AND SAT UP IN BED. SHE TURNED TO Bluma who was just awakening. "I had another dream," she said.

Bluma's eyes flew open. "Are you feeling all right?"

"Yes, don't worry, I am all right."

"That's good. What was this one about?" Bluma yawned.

"About Shoshana and a boy."

"Was it Albert?" Bluma asked excitedly.

"No, silly."

"But I overheard Shoshana and Neta talking one day, and they both think that Shoshana is going to be betrothed to Albert," Bluma said.

"It wasn't Albert. In fact, it was someone I have never met before. He wasn't from our neighborhood."

"What did he look like? Was he handsome?"

"No, not really. And he seemed like one of them. But at the same time he seemed to be nice," Perle said.

"One of who? A goy? Or a secular Jew?"

"No, something else. But I don't know what."

"That's so strange. Was Shoshana betrothed to him??" Bluma sat up and leaned her back against the wall.

"I don't know. All I know is that the other doctor, the evil one, was in the dream too."

"So was the evil doctor a friend of Shoshana's betrothed?"

"I didn't say that they were betrothed. I just said that they met."

"I don't understand. What happened when they met?"

"The evil doctor had us as prisoners, and he saved one of us from dying. But I don't know if it was you or me," Perle said.

"One of us was sick?"

"No . . . not sick."

"Perle, you aren't making any sense."

"I know. But I can't remember much more. All I know is that we were in a big stone building with a flag flying on a pole at the top of it. It was a red-and-black flag. And there was a lot of smoke. It smelled bad too."

"At first, I thought this was a good dream, but now I can't tell. Was it a good dream or a bad dream?"

"I don't know. I am confused. In a way it was good, but in a way it was bad, and it was also scary. So, I'm not sure."

CHAPTER THIRTY-SEVEN

Naomi spent every spare second she had with her sister. She knew the time was coming when they would have to part. They prepared meals together, splitting the food in half so they could feed both households. They helped each other clean, going from one home to the other. But time slipped through their fingers, and soon the day arrived that Miriam was scheduled to leave. Naomi felt as if her heart was being ripped out of her chest. She wished she could take her daughters and go with her sister, leaving Herschel behind. But, of course, that was not possible. She couldn't just go, and expect Aram and his cousin to support her and her daughters. And she knew Herschel would never leave Poland, no matter how much she begged. In the end, Herschel was the man of the house, and that made him the boss, just as Aram was the boss of her sister.

Naomi and Miriam wept; they held on to each other; they prayed that by some miracle, Aram would change his mind. But he didn't. At the end of the month, Miriam and Aram left the little town where they had lived their entire lives and headed toward a new beginning in a big city in Lithuania.

After they left, Naomi was broken. She went about her daily chores in a robotic fashion. There was work to be done, and she knew that Herschel would not understand if his house was dirty; his clothes had to be washed, and his dinner must be prepared. So, she did what must be done. And she grew silent. She was too depressed to speak.

One afternoon she went to the butcher shop to buy a chicken for soup. As she stood in line, she overheard two women speaking to each other.

"Mazel tov on your daughter's engagement. A friend of mine told me that your Rachel is getting married," one of them said.

"Yes she is. And I thank you for your congratulations. My husband and I are very proud to say that the chassan, the groom, is a scholar, no less. Favored by the rabbi for his brilliant mind."

"Nu, such nachas," the first one said. "When is the wedding?"

"Next month."

"Such nachas for you."

"Yes, it's true. He is a lot older than her. But, like I said, it's all right because he's a scholar. You might know him, his name is Eli Silberberg."

"Oy, yes, I know who he is. He's a handsome man, and it's true that the rabbi likes him."

"Yes, it's true. He is quite handsome, and he is in very good standing with the rabbi."

"That's funny. You see, I heard that he was also a bit of a rebel."

"He is, I suppose. He doesn't always follow the rules. I mean, he is almost thirty, and he's still unmarried. But the rabbi says he has a brilliant mind. And I believe that he respects Eli for this."

"Well, I am happy for you."

The women were still talking when the butcher said "Next," calling Naomi up to the counter. "How can I help you, young lady?" he said.

"I would like a fresh chicken."

"Ahhh, some lucky man is going to have chicken soup tonight. Am I right?"

Naomi nodded. Any other day she would give him a smile, but after what she'd just overheard, she was shaking inside. *Eli is getting married*, she thought. *My Eli is getting married to another woman. Her name is Rachel, and she is younger than he is.*

"Here you go," the butcher said handing Naomi a package wrapped in white paper.

"Thank you," Naomi said. She took the package and walked outside. *Who is this Rachel. I don't know her. I've never seen her. Is she pretty? Prettier than me? I am so much older now. I wonder how young she is. I feel sick to my stomach. I can't believe that my Eli will lie with her and put his babies into her belly.*

"Hello, Naomi." It was Frieda calling to her from across the street. She couldn't bear to see Frieda, not now. Frieda crossed the street and walked toward her. "How are you?"

"All right," Naomi said, but she stared blankly in front of her. She was far from all right. Her heart was aching, and she couldn't bear this woman, not today. Not after the news she'd just heard.

"I'm all right too. I can't complain. It wouldn't do me any good anyway. This is my life. I have to face it. It could be worse. Oy, well, anyway, you look terrible. Did somebody die? Look at that long face. Something is wrong."

"I'm fine. I am just tired. If you don't mind, I would prefer to walk home alone."

"Oy, so that tells me something is wrong. You don't want to walk with me?"

Naomi was so broken inside that she didn't have the strength to fight. It had been years since she and Eli were together for the last time, yet the pain was still as deep as when they'd first said goodbye. She felt like vomiting. And for a moment she thought about vomiting on Frieda. The very idea of it made her giggle. She began to laugh hysterically.

"Something is funny? I think maybe you are going crazy," Frieda said.

"Leave me alone. Please, just go away. I don't feel like talking to you right now. I am tired and not feeling well."

"You laugh when you're not feeling well. Gott im himmel, I was right. You've lost your mind."

Tears stung Naomi's eyes and covered her cheeks. She ran away from Frieda as fast as she could. *The last person I wanted to see today was that awful woman.* Naomi was breathing heavily as she opened the door to her house. Once she closed the door and was finally alone, she sat down on the sofa and wrapped her arms around her shoulders. Then she rocked slowly, back and forth, back and forth. It took her several minutes to calm down. *My Eli is getting married. I should be happy for him. He deserves to have a life, a wife of his own, children too. All the things I can't give him. Yet when I think of another woman lying beneath him, carrying his child in her belly, I wish the earth would open up and swallow me . . .*

Of course, I have no right to feel this way. He should have a home and a family. It's only right, and I can't give him that. I will never be able to give him that. God forgive me, I've often thought that if something happened to Herschel, then Eli and I could be together. But I don't want to see anything bad happen to Herschel. He isn't a bad person. He's just distant. Like most men. Eli is not like other men. He's one in a million. And I was fortunate to have his love, if only for a short time. The memory of it will be with me for the rest of my life, and I will have to find joy in the memory. Because that is all I have left.

Ohhh, if fate had been different, he would have been mine. I would not have cared if we didn't have any money. I would have been happy to live on bread and water if I was his wife. But it wasn't our destiny. Our love brought God's wrath upon us. It was tainted. So I must accept that he will be another woman's husband, and I must find it in my heart to wish them both happiness. I love him, and that means I must not think only of myself. Instead, I must wish him and his new wife a wonderful marriage even if it cuts me through the heart.

She sat staring out the window for almost a full half hour before she was able to think straight. *I'm glad that Shoshana and the girls are visiting Neta. I wouldn't want them to see me this way.*

CHAPTER THIRTY-EIGHT

The following morning, Naomi dragged herself out of bed and went into the kitchen to prepare Herschel's breakfast. He walked in just as she was putting his plate on the table. He ate in silence. Once he'd finished, he stood up and stretched. Then he took his coat off the rack. "I'll see you tonight," he said and walked out the door.

She prepared breakfast for Shoshana and the twins, but she couldn't eat a bite. Naomi sat down on the sofa and waited for Shoshana to wake up. It wasn't a long wait. Shoshana came into the kitchen a half hour later. Naomi looked at her daughter. Shoshana had started menstruating two weeks ago. *She is a woman now,* Naomi thought, *and she is already so beautiful. Her marriage prospects will be lining up soon.*

"I prepared breakfast for you and your sisters. I have to run to the market. Can you watch the girls for me?"

"Of course, Mother," Shoshana said.

"Thank you. I'll be back very soon."

Naomi left the house. She didn't go to the market. Looking around her as she went, trying to avoid prying eyes, she made her way to the synagogue, where she stood outside. Trying to look inconspicuous, she hid on the side of the building where no one walking by would notice her. It was cold, and the wind was whipping across her face. *I wish I could go in there and ask to speak to him. But I know better. A woman asking to speak like that to a man, is forbidden. Still, I must find a way to talk to him.*

A group of yeshiva boys walked by her without even taking notice that she was standing there in the shadows. She overheard them having a heated discussion on some religious law. *Why did I even come here? How was I planning to see him anyway? I am just not thinking straight. I should go home and start dinner. I suppose I should stop at the market first. After all, I can't come home empty handed. I told Shoshana I needed to buy something for dinner. If I come home without anything, she'll wonder where I went.* There was no point in standing out in the cold any longer. Naomi turned to walk away from the synagogue and head toward the market. That's when she heard his voice. Eli called her name.

"Naomi?"

She whipped around. Her scarf fell, revealing her hair. Her heart raced, and her palms grew sweaty. There he stood, so handsome. His hair had begun to gray just a little at the temples. *He's only thirty*, she thought, *and already he looks distinguished.* "Eli. I need to speak to you."

Snow began to fall. It dusted her hair and the shoulders of her dark coat. She looked at him. The she looked across the snow-covered ground. When she finally was able to look directly at him, she could see the deep, dark depths of his eyes. He didn't say a word, but he nodded to her. Then he quickly glanced around to see if anyone was watching. They were alone. He walked closer to her and said, "Meet me at our place tomorrow morning. We can talk more freely there."

She nodded. "What time?"

"Early, eight o'clock. All right?"

"Yes. Herschel leaves at about seven. So, I'll be there."

These were the first words they'd spoken to each other since they broke up. The sound of his voice made her tremble. She felt tears well up in her eyes and freeze on her eyelashes.

He turned and walked away, entering the synagogue and leaving her standing alone in the snow.

She stood there for a moment gathering herself together. Then she walked quickly to the market and went into the shop of the fishmonger. "I don't have many fish today," he said. "The weather is bad. There are not too many fish that are available right now."

She nodded. Then she said, "I understand. Do you have anything that I can use to make gefilte fish. It's my husband's favorite."

The fishmonger nodded. "I can help you," he said and began cleaning a fish for her while she waited.

I am going to make Herschel's favorite food, because I feel guilty that I still love Eli.

"Here's your fish," the fishmonger said.

Naomi paid him and left. Then she walked back out into the cold. The snow was falling harder now as she made her way home.

"What did you buy, Mama?" Bluma asked. "Shoshana said you went to the market."

"I bought a fish. I am going to make gefilte fish tonight."

"I hate gefilte fish," Bluma said. "Perle hates it too."

"Then I'll make soup, too, and you two girls can eat the soup."

CHAPTER THIRTY-NINE

THE FOLLOWING DAY, NAOMI REPEATED THE SAME THING SHE DID THE day before. She got up early and was ready to leave the house when Shoshana came out of her bedroom. But this time Shoshana seemed suspicious. "Mama, why are you going to the market again? You went yesterday. If you needed something, you should have bought it when you were there yesterday."

"You're right. But I am going to see Sarah. I want to bring some of the gefilte fish I made."

"I could go for you," Shoshana said.

"No, I need to get out and walk. I'll be back soon." She packed up some of the fish and then left.

Naomi handed Eli the fish when she saw him. "I made gefilte fish. I brought you some."

"How nice of you," he said, and she thought he sounded cold. "Thank you."

"I heard you're getting married," she said.

He nodded. "Yes, I am."

"Who's the lucky girl?"

"Rachel Feinstein."

Naomi was stunned. Why didn't she recognize Mrs. Feinstein, Rachel's mother? Now that she knew who Rachel's mother was, she realized that she knew Rachel too. They had never spoken, but she'd seen her at the market a few times, and she remembered thinking that Rachel was very pretty. "I think I've seen her around town." Naomi choked out the words. "She's a pretty one with long, dark hair, sort of like mine."

"Sort of, yes," he said, holding the wrapped package of fish in his hand.

"But, unlike me, she has rich parents who can support a son-in-law who is a scholar."

"Naomi, why are you doing this? Why are we here talking like this?"

She shook her head and began to cry. "I'm sorry. It's just hard for me. The real reason I wanted to see you was to wish you well. But I guess my jealousy is getting the better of me."

"I understand. And thank you for your good wishes."

"Please stop acting so formal. Please stop talking to me like we don't even know each other." Naomi's voice broke.

"We haven't spoken for five years. How am I supposed to speak to you?"

"Like I am your bashert." Her eyes became watery.

"Don't do that. You and I both know that we had something special and beautiful, but you ended it. I waited for five years for you to change your mind. I would have done anything you wanted, anything at all. But you never came around. And now I have to get on with my life. I want a wife and a home. And I want children. Children I can call my own. I don't have any of that now. All I have left are memories of you, of us . . ."

"Eli."

"Naomi, listen to me. I should tell you that after we get married, Rachel and I are leaving this shtetl. We are going to England. She has family there. There is a shul that needs a rabbi. Maybe they will consider me."

"Do you speak English?"

"I do. I actually speak it very well. I studied it. But I am sure most of the congregants there will speak Yiddish."

"It's hard for me to believe that you are really leaving here. I'll never see you again."

"Probably not. But I can't say for sure. That's in God's hands, not ours."

She was silent for a moment. Then in a small voice, she said, "Let me look at you one last time. Let me memorize the shape of your face, the look in your eyes. Let me have one last moment of loving you. Then I will go home and leave you with best wishes for a good marriage and a long and happy life."

A gust of wind blew across the landscape. A blanket of white virgin snow covered the earth, but when she closed her eyes she could still see the brilliant colors of the wildflowers that would return in the spring. For the rest of her life, wildflowers, their color, their sweet aroma, and the heady feeling they gave her, would remind her of Eli. She put her hands on his shoulders and studied him for several moments. He was trembling. His voice was soft as he said, "I love you, Naomi. I will always love you. But this is goodbye." He leaned down and kissed her softly, then he turned and walked away. She watched him go, leaving his footprints in the newly fallen snow.

The icy wind bit at Naomi's face. But she couldn't move. It felt like as long as she didn't leave, there was a chance he would return. *I know this is what is best. I know that he is doing the right thing. So why I can't I just let him go? What was I thinking when I came here today? I told myself that I was planning to say goodbye and wish him well. But was I? Was I really? Or did I secretly hope that he would tell me he couldn't marry her because he loves me. It's true. Miriam is right. I am a horrible, selfish person. It's been years since we spoke, years since we touched. That is until today. And when I heard his voice, and then felt his kiss, I knew that if he asked me, I would lie with him again. And what dark and terrible things would that sin bring to both of us? I know that I should go home. I must go home and never again return to this place and the memories it brings. I should hurry. Shoshana will wonder where I am.*

Naomi walked away slowly.

CHAPTER FORTY

When Eli returned to the yeshiva, the rabbi was waiting for him outside the room that Eli shared with his roommate. "Shalom, Eli," the rabbi said.

"Shalom, Rabbi Geldman."

"You look like you've been out walking in the snow?"

"Yes, I have."

"Do you have a moment? I would like to speak with you," the rabbi said.

It was a rare thing for Rabbi Geldman to be waiting for Eli by the door to his dormitory room.

"I was just on my way to the classroom. I have an appointment with a pupil. You know I have been tutoring boys for their bar mitzvahs."

"Yes, I know this. But I also know that you are wearing your coat. And it's wet from snow, which tells me that you were outside for quite a while. Nu, Eli? I think you should take a few minutes and come into my office so we can talk."

There was nothing else for Eli to do but follow the rabbi's request. He walked behind the rabbi up the stairs and into the main sanctuary. Then he followed the rabbi into his office.

"Take off your coat and sit down, please." The old man sighed.

Eli did as he was told.

"Eli," Rabbi Geldman said as he rubbed his beard. "I have known you since you were a very young boy, and now here you sit before me, a man about to embark on the most important day of your life. The day you are to get married. You are very fortunate, your kallah, your bride, is a very frum, religious girl from a good family. Now, I know you wouldn't want to do anything to bring shame upon Rachel or her parents, would you?"

"No, of course not."

"Then, you must stop what you are doing."

Eli was shocked. He hadn't expected the rabbi to say that. *Perhaps he means something else. How could he possibly know what happened between Naomi and me. Perhaps he doesn't really know.* "I don't know what you mean." Eli looked away, knowing that if the rabbi looked into his eyes, he would know he was lying.

"I think you do. But, since you don't want to admit your sin, I will tell you what I know so that we are both clear about what I am trying to say." The rabbi cleared his throat. "I am aware of what happened in the past between you and Naomi Aizenberg. In fact, I am surprised her husband doesn't know. Or maybe he does, and he just doesn't want to acknowledge it. I am also aware that you met with her this morning. This is not a good thing for anyone involved." He sighed again, and once more, he pulled at his beard. "I have treated you like a son. Perhaps I have been too indulgent with you because I knew you needed a strong father figure in your life. I let you talk out of turn, and during our discussions, I let you say things that I might not have allowed the other boys to say. But in this situation, I must put my foot down. I cannot indulge you anymore. You must end it with Naomi Aizenberg for good. In plain words, what I am telling you is that if you are ever going to have a good, solid marriage and a good, solid family with Rachel, this thing with Naomi Aizenberg must end here and now. Do you understand me?"

Eli nodded. "Yes, I understand you very well, Rabbi. And I've ended it today. I am so ashamed that you found out about this."

The rabbi nodded. "It would be worse if your kallah or her family found out. It would not only end your chances for a good marriage, but you would carry the shanda, this shameful situation, with you throughout your life."

"Yes, that's true." Eli hung his head. "But, Rabbi, Naomi and I haven't spoken in years. How did you know there was ever anything between us?"

"I see the way you look at each other when you see her at shul. I knew five years ago, when you and she were meeting every week. I was worried about you then, and I was relieved when it stopped. But I am worried again now."

"You needn't worry. I am going away. As soon as Rachel and I are married, we are moving to England. She has a cousin there who says they have a small congregation that is in need of a rabbi. It's on the outskirts of London."

"And do you think you are qualified for this job?"

"You always said I had a brilliant mind."

"Yes, and you do. But I don't know that you have what it takes to lead people. You see, I am not certain how firm you are in your religious beliefs, and I have found myself questioning your moral character."

"Do you want to know the truth?" Eli said.

"Yes, I want to know whatever you want to tell me," the rabbi answered.

"I am in love with her. Naomi, I mean. She is my bashert. I know it. I have always known it. And the bond between us is so strong that when I am near her, I forget what is right and wrong."

"Then it's a good thing that you are going away from our village. Both you and Naomi will be better off once you are gone."

"I know you are right. And thank you for taking the time to talk to me, Rabbi."

"Come and talk to me anytime. Especially if you are feeling that you must see Naomi. I will help you to stay on the right track."

"Thank you."

"Go to the classroom. I'm sure your student is waiting for you."

Eli left the rabbi's office and walked toward the classroom. He was filled with a million conflicting emotions. But no matter how much he loved Naomi, he knew that the best thing he could do for her and himself was to leave the neighborhood.

CHAPTER FORTY-ONE

Dovi Greenspan was struggling with the Hebrew words from his Torah portion when Eli walked into the classroom. Eli sat down quietly across from Dovi and tried to pay attention, but the boy's clumsy attempt at reading in Hebrew was getting on his nerves.

Eli, having always been a quick learner, had mastered Hebrew rapidly, and he found it difficult to watch boys with less ability, especially now when he had so much on his mind.

"Why don't we reschedule your lesson. I won't charge you for the next one or this one since I was late."

Dovi nodded and smiled brightly.

He's a lazy boy, and he's glad not to have to work, Eli thought. "All right, I'll see you next week."

Dovi gathered his books and was gone in an instant.

Eli sighed as he watched Dovi go. *He will have an easier time than me in life. His parents have found him a trade, and he won't be a scholar. He'll marry and raise a bunch of children. From the time I was a child, I was considered to be intelligent. Everyone thought that was a gift, but in fact, too much has always been expected of me.*

Eli felt old and tired from thinking and agonizing too much. He picked up his coat and then went back to his room, where his roommate, Ari, was getting ready for lunch. "How was your tutoring session?" Ari asked.

"It was with Dovi Greenspan. Poor boy is an amoretz. He's as dim as an unlit room." Eli shook his head. "Most of these boys are not very bright. It makes it difficult to teach them. I often ask myself why I am still tutoring. I don't spend any of the money I earn anymore."

"Of course you are getting the ones who are not so smart. They are the ones who need help with their bar mitzvah lessons. The smart ones don't need a tutor."

"Yes, you're right," Eli said. "I should try to have more patience and understanding."

"You've been tutoring for almost ten years. I thought you did it as a mitzvah. I thought it made you feel good to help these boys."

"At first I did it because I wanted extra money, because of Naomi. I wanted to give her things. I know that doesn't make sense to you because you've never been in love."

"And after witnessing what love has done to you, I hope I never experience it," Ari said.

"It can be beautiful. In fact, it can be the most beautiful thing in the world. But it can also be painful when it is not meant to be."

"I'm sorry. I didn't mean to put it that way," Ari said, gently patting Eli on the shoulder. "So, if you don't need the money anymore, and you don't like it, why not just quit?"

"I thought about it after Naomi and I broke up. But I kept on tutoring because it filled my time and my empty heart. However, now that I am getting married, it feels like an overwhelming responsibility that I just don't need. So, I guess I am going to stop."

"You're in a bad mood," Ari said. "Is there anything I can say to make you feel better?"

"No, there's nothing. And you're right, I am in a terrible mood. I saw Naomi today. I told her that I am leaving for England. It was like living the whole heartbreaking end of our relationship all over again. And then to make matters even worse, Rabbi Geldman was waiting for me outside of our room when I returned."

"Oh no. What did he want?"

"He knows about me and Naomi. He's always known."

"Oy vey. What happened? What did you say when he told you he knew?"

"What could I say? I told him the truth, that I am leaving for England, so the relationship between Naomi and me is over. But he didn't seem to believe me."

"Well, you can't make him believe you. All you can do is what is right. And you're doing that by leaving here and starting over with Rachel in a new place. Did you tell him that you are planning on becoming a rabbi?"

"Actually, yes. And . . . do you know what he said? He told me that he didn't think I would make a good rabbi."

"Why? Because haven't you been in training to be a rabbi?"

"That's not the reason. Of course, I have been training to be a rabbi. But Rabbi Geldman said he questions my moral character."

"Oh." Ari frowned. "Did you tell him how long you and Naomi have been broken up? Did you tell him you haven't spoken to her for years?"

"I did. But he can tell how I feel about her. He knows. You know how he is. He seems to know everything."

"Yes, that's very true," Ari said, then he sighed. "Well, I will miss you when you go, but it's good that you're getting away from here. And you're very lucky, my friend. You are marrying a lovely girl from a good family. Your father-in-law is wealthy, and he's promised that you can spend all of your time studying and never work if you choose. So, in reality, you don't need to take that job as a rabbi. You won't be needing the money."

"Yes, that's all true."

"I wish something like that would happen to me. So far, I haven't been as lucky. I think it's because I walk with a limp. No girl's father wants a son-in-law with a defect. The family is too afraid that my children will be born with a deformity."

"I hate to hear that, but you're probably right. You know how petty people are."

"Yes, I know. I've been subjected to it all my life," Ari said, "but not you. You are handsome. You are smart. You can get away with having an affair and nothing bad happens to you. Instead, you marry a rich beauty. Ahhh, such a life you have, kenahora. Nu, it should only happen to me."

"You know I wish only the best for you, Ari."

"I know. You're my best friend."

CHAPTER FORTY-TWO

HERSCHEL AIZENBERG HAD JUST RETURNED TO HIS OFFICE. HE WAS IN A terrible mood. It was late afternoon, and although Frieda, his secretary, was more than curious about where he'd been, she dared not question him. Instead, she smiled and greeted him warmly. Then she asked him if she could get him anything.

"No, you can go home for today," he said coldly. "I will see you in the morning."

"Are you sure? You're looking pale."

"Go, I said. Go home. I have work to do."

"Perhaps it's something I can help you with?" Frieda offered. When Herschel was struggling with something, it hurt her heart. She wanted to take all of his pain away. If she could, she would give him the world. But he thought of her as nothing but an employee, and perhaps as an old friend because he'd known her since they were children. However, he never loved her, but to her, he was the sun, the moon, and a reason for living.

"No. You can't help me. Go home. I have to do it alone."

She nodded and looked down at the floor. Then she went into the front office to get her coat and hat. She took them down off the coatrack. But she wasn't satisfied. Frieda couldn't leave him like this.

She had to try to make him feel better. She walked back into Herschel's office. "Did you eat the lunch I brought for you?"

"I'm not hungry. Please, just leave. Just go home. I need to be alone right now."

She nodded. He could be very mean when she pressed him to speak. So, she picked up her handbag and walked out the door. It had been a long time since he'd eaten the food she brought for him. A few months ago, he'd started going out each day for long lunches. His work was suffering, and Frieda wondered who he was meeting when he was gone.

Naomi was no longer her rival. Now, it was someone else. She was certain that when he was out with his clients, some girl he'd met in Warsaw had caught his eye. Frieda had no idea who she was, but she knew of her existence because one afternoon when Herschel was gone from the office, she rummaged through his desk in search of evidence. Receipts for hotel rooms and expensive lunches, along with two receipts from a local jeweler lined the bottom of his desk drawer. Frieda sank down into Herschel's chair. She was defeated again. This time it was another woman, not Naomi, who had stolen him from her. And she knew that Herschel Aizenberg was living a double life. But how long could that go on?

CHAPTER FORTY-THREE

♊

After Frieda left the office, Herschel got up and locked the door. Then he sat down at his desk and pulled out a bottle of whiskey. He took a swig directly from the bottle. *How did everything in his life go so wrong?* he thought as he put his head in his hands. And he began to remember.

On a day in September, when the sun was that golden yellow that only happened at the end of a long, hot summer, he walked to a restaurant near his office. He'd grown tired of Jewish food, and he'd given up keeping kosher. It had begun when some of his non-Jewish clients had taken him for lunch meetings. At first he'd been reluctant to eat the food he knew was treif, not kosher. However, as time passed, he gave in and started to try a bit of this, then a bit of that. Before he realized it, Herschel found that he'd come to enjoy eating out.

He walked into one of his favorite restaurants and asked to be seated at a table near the window. One of his favorite pastimes was having a drink and watching the people walk by. He especially loved watching the women with skirts short enough to show their calves, and blouses with sleeves above the elbow. Once in a while he would catch a glimpse of the white delicate skin that covered a collarbone or just a hint of cleavage. This sent his heart racing.

Forbidden thoughts clouded his mind. These were the kind of girls a man could truly allow himself to enjoy. He wondered what their breasts looked like, and he thought of holding them in his hands. Then he thought of his wife and felt a pang of guilt. *Naomi is a beautiful woman, but she must be respected and never thought of in such a vulgar way. A man should never think of doing dirty things like this with the mother of his children. But with shiksas, it's all right. And as long as Naomi never finds out, no one gets hurt.*

He ordered his food, a sausage on a roll with sauerkraut, and a beer. Then he sat back gazing out the window. Men in suits hurried by. Women pushing babies in prams walked slowly as they looked into the shop windows. Couples strolled down the street hand in hand. He watched them and wondered what it would be like to have a lover, and that was the first time he saw her. She was walking and talking with another girl. Her blonde, wavy hair fell loose over her shoulders. The white blouse she wore was unbuttoned just low enough to show a tiny bit of her collarbone. But what really caught his eye and sent his blood coursing through his veins was the dark gray skirt she wore. It had a slit that revealed her shapely calves with each step she took. He had to meet her. The blonde and her friend stopped in front of the bus stop, which was located just outside of the restaurant. Herschel couldn't believe his luck. He decided then and there that he was going to invite her to lunch. Quickly, he raised his hand to summon the waiter, who rushed over to the table because he had served Herschel before, and Herschel had given him a good tip.

"You see that girl outside by the bus stop, the one with the blonde hair?"

"Yes, sir," the waiter said.

"Go outside and invite her and her girlfriend into the restaurant. Tell her that a gentleman would like to buy them both lunch."

"But I have customers, sir."

"Go and do as I say," Herschel said as he slipped a bill into the waiter's hand.

The waiter nodded and walked outside.

Herschel saw the shock on the girl's pretty face when the waiter was speaking to her. She and her girlfriend giggled. Herschel wished he could hear what they were saying. But then he felt butterflies in his stomach when they stood up and followed the waiter into the restaurant. The waiter nodded and winked at Herschel as he showed the two girls to the table where he sat.

"I'm Herschel," he said.

"I'm Julia, and this is my friend Berta," the pretty blonde said, smiling brightly.

The girls studied the menu. When the waiter returned, he took their orders. Herschel wasn't surprised when they both ordered the most expensive thing on the menu, steak. But he didn't care. He enjoyed glimpsing bits of cleavage as Julia was eating. She ate quickly. Then once she'd finished, she began chatting about how she had lost her job at a factory. "I've been out of work, and it's been very hard, because not only did my family have to make due without my salary, but my sister got sick last summer. So she had to take time off from her job too. Money has been very tight for us. But my sister has been doing much better, and she is trying to find work now, just like I am."

"Hmm, that's terrible," he said as he pretended to listen. But the truth was he didn't care what she had to say. He was undressing her in his mind and thoroughly enjoying the fantasy.

"Perhaps you two girls would like to have lunch with me again. Tomorrow?" Herschel asked.

"I'm sorry, I can't. I have to work," Berta said.

Good. I didn't want you here anyway. I was hoping to have lunch alone with Julia. "How about you? You said you lost your job, so perhaps you might enjoy having a quick lunch with me?"

She nodded. "Sure. Why not."

"How about noon? I'll meet you here?"

"All right."

That night Herschel went home and cut off his payot and shaved his beard. *She'll like me better if I look more like the other men in her world,* he thought. Then he looked in the mirror and compared himself to the men he worked with, who lived outside of the town. *I can't say that I am handsome. It would be a lie. My features are too coarse and pronounced. My eyes are too deep set and dark. My eyebrows are thick, and my hair is very gray. But I am tall and well built. So, as soon as I can, I will go to the tailor and purchase a good suit that fits me perfectly. Then I might not be handsome, but at least I will look distinguished.*

That night he walked slowly into the kitchen for dinner. Naomi looked up from the pot she was stirring and saw that he'd shaved his beard and cut off his payot. Her mouth fell open with surprise. "What happened, Herschel? Why did you cut off your payot and shave off your beard?"

He was annoyed that he had to answer to her. But he thought it better to answer than to leave her wondering. So he took a deep breath and said, "You know that I work in a job where impressions are important. Most of my clients are goyim. They live in the city. And they don't really trust Jews. If I want them to trust me with their business, I need to look like one of them. I can't look like an old Jew from this backward shtetl where we live. In fact, I have been thinking about moving us out of here."

"Please don't, Herschel. Is it necessary? It's bad enough that my sister has left here. If you move us to Warsaw, then I won't even be able to see Sarah anymore. And what about Shoshana? She is almost of marriageable age. There are nice boys here in our neighborhood. If you move us, who knows what can happen. She might marry a secular Jew, or worse, a goy. I am begging you not to do this," she said desperately. She no longer seemed to care about the radical change in his appearance.

"For now, I am staying where we are. But if I change my mind, I'll let you know."

Naomi nodded. She stared at him. The look on her face told him that she wasn't convinced. Still, she didn't say anything else about it, and he was glad to be left alone. He didn't want to have to justify the changes he'd made in his appearance any further.

The following day when Herschel walked into his office, Frieda was not as easy on him as Naomi had been. Frieda stared at him. Her mouth fell open, and he knew she was shocked and horrified that he'd made such a radical change in his appearance. "You look like one of them," she said. "You look like a goy."

"That's the point. I want to look more like one of my clients so that they feel more comfortable trusting me with their legal issues."

"I don't like it. It's not right. You are changing, and I am worried about you."

Frieda always had a way of getting on his nerves. Because of this he had a tendency to be meaner and coarser toward her than he was toward anyone else. "Mind your own business. I don't have to defend my actions to you. Now, go back to your desk and do some work. That's what I pay you for."

She turned quickly and almost ran back to her desk. Since she didn't look at him, he figured that she was probably crying. When she pried into his life, and he put her in her place, she usually ended up crying. *Well, let her cry it out. I don't care if she quits. I can find another secretary easily. One that won't ask me so many personal questions. Maybe I could hire Julia. I would love to have her in the office with me all day. We would be alone and have plenty of time together. But it's probably a bad idea. Things could get messy. She would be too close to my family. And my tata, my father, always said not to shit where you eat.*

At eleven forty-five, Frieda knocked on the door to Herschel's office. "What do you want?" he asked.

"I brought you lunch from home again."

"If I haven't told you yet, I will tell you now. Stop bringing me food. I don't keep kosher anymore. I meet with clients during lunch. Do you understand me?"

"Yes," she said in a small voice.

"Good," he said in a condescending tone. "Now, I'm leaving. I'm going out to meet a client," he said as he stood up and opened the door. He was wearing his suit coat, and he was ready to leave. "If I am not back by five, lock up and go home."

She nodded.

He saw that she was crying, but he ignored it and walked out the door. As he made his way to the restaurant, he thought, *After lunch today, I am going to see a tailor here in town, and I do need to have some stylish suits made. No more old-fashioned clothes for me.*

Herschel arrived at the restaurant at exactly twelve o'clock. He looked around for Julia, but she wasn't there. She was either late or not coming. Either way, he was furious. No woman had ever treated him like this. But this one was different; she was a not one of the obedient girls he knew who had been raised to be frum. This one was like a wild bird. She was a different breed. She was a shiksa, forbidden and unknown, and that was what he liked about her.

He ordered a glass of wine and waited.

By twelve thirty, Herschel was livid. Julia was still nowhere in sight. He ordered another glass of wine. *I'm drinking on an empty stomach. This always gives me heartburn*, he thought, shaking his head but downing the glass of wine anyway. At twelve forty-five, he decided to face the fact that she wasn't coming. He motioned for the waiter to bring his check. He waited for the waiter to arrive. And then she walked in. Her golden hair looked like a halo around her face when she turned to scan the restaurant searching for him. Their eyes met and she smiled. Then she walked toward him, and as she did she slipped off her coat. He stood up the way he'd seen other men do when a lady walked over to the table. He pulled out her chair, once again imitating what he'd learned from the non-Jewish men he worked with. Julia laid her coat and handbag on the unused chair beside her. She smoothed her black skirt and sat down. He pushed her chair in and then returned to his seat.

"Sorry, I'm late. I had a job interview," she said.

Before she got there, he rehearsed all the angry lines he planned to say to her. But now that she was sitting across from him, he forgot his anger and smiled. "It's all right. I know you need a job."

"I do. I can't go on much longer this way. I have gone through my entire savings."

Herschel considered hiring her. But if he did, he would be forced to fire Frieda because Frieda would know immediately what his intentions were with Julia, and vengeful Frieda wouldn't hesitate to tell his wife. Besides that, and more importantly, Herschel knew that

Frieda was the backbone of his law firm. She handled everything for him. And he knew that although he didn't have any feelings for her, he could trust her because she was in love with him. Without Frieda at his side, he would be overwhelmed with work. She researched his cases, scheduled his meetings, and even kept the office spotless. No, he wouldn't hire Julia. But, depending on how things went this afternoon, he might just offer her an arrangement. He'd heard other married men talk about the women they kept on the side. And the idea intrigued him. But first he had to see just how far she was willing to go.

"You must be hungry?" he said, then without waiting for her answer, he added, "Let's order."

He watched her as she ate and wondered what it would be like to bed her. Things had never been exciting for him in the bedroom. How could they be? *Naomi is beautiful; there's no doubt about that, but she is also a frum girl who is my wife and the mother of my children. That is the kind of girl a man marries. Sex with a woman like Naomi isn't meant for pleasure; it's an obligation that a husband performs in order to produce children. Julia is a different story. She is the kind of girl a man can do things with that, until now, existed only in my imagination,* he thought.

I might like to rent an apartment for her where I could go to see her whenever it pleases me to do so. I don't earn as much disposable cash as I would like, but I make enough that I could afford to give her a modest amount of money for living expenses. And since she is out of work, she might be interested. So, how does a man approach discussing such an arrangement with a girl? She might get offended and slap me or walk out of the restaurant and refuse to see me again. He took a long, deep breath. Julia didn't seem to notice that he was deep in thought because she was busy wolfing down her food. From the way she was gobbling up her steak, Herschel figured she probably hadn't eaten since the previous day when he bought her lunch. *So what if she walks out? What did I lose? Nothing. I'll wait until she's done eating like a horse, and then I'll talk to her.*

Julia was so immersed in eating that she didn't even look up. But once she finished, she gently blotted her lips with her napkin. Then she looked up at him and smiled. "That was delicious," she said.

"Would you like dessert?"

"Oh yes, please."

"What would you like?"

"A slice of karpatka," she said, smiling. "Would that be all right?"

He let out a short laugh because it was a delicious custard-filled type of pie, and it was the most expensive dessert on the menu. And he couldn't help but think, *She's such a shiksa, custard pie with steak, milk with meat. Oy vey.* "Sure, why not?" he said.

"Would you like one too?"

He'd just eaten chicken, and although he no longer kept kosher, he was not used to eating milk and meat together. He'd done it once or twice, but it always gave him a stomachache. So he shook his head. "No, not for me."

While she closed her eyes and savored the sweet pie, he watched her. *I wonder if that's how she would look during sex,* he thought. When she was finished with the last morsel of pie, she licked the fork.

He waited for minute, then he said, "I would like to speak with you about something."

"Of course. What is it?"

"I like you. I find you attractive."

She smiled.

"What do you think of me?"

"I think you look a lot better without that long beard and those odd-looking long sideburns." She giggled.

He managed to smile. This wasn't going as well as he had hoped. He wanted her to say that she found him appealing. He tried again. "I am glad you approve of the changes. But that's not my question. My question is . . . do you like me?"

"Well, of course I like you, Herschel." Then she added, "Herschel is your name, isn't it? I hope I remembered it correctly."

"Yes, Herschel is my name." He was losing patience. She had just insulted him. How dare she be so flippant about forgetting his name. *I just bought this girl two expensive lunches, and she acts like I am a nobody. I am just going to ask her outright. What do I care if she's offended? It will either be yes or no, but no more of this tiptoeing around when I talk to her.* "Listen, I have a proposition for you."

"Oh?" she said, and her eyes opened wide.

"I want to set you up in an apartment. I'll give you money for food and clothes. But I want to be your lover."

"You get right to the point, don't you?" she said, shaking her head. Then she laughed. "I should have expected it. You people are clumsy around women."

"What people?" he asked. He was insulted now.

"You Orthodox Jewish fellas. I have a feeling you don't have a lot of experience with women."

"Never mind about the offer. Thanks for joining me for lunch." Herschel raised his hand for the waiter. "Check, please," he said, offended.

Julia reached over and touched his hand. "Wait. I didn't say no."

He put his hand down and looked directly into her eyes. "So, that means yes?"

"Yes," she said casually.

His breath caught in his throat. Herschel smiled. He forgot that he was offended. He was too pleased by her answer. "Can you find a reasonably priced flat somewhere near here?"

"Sure."

"All right, I'll meet you here for lunch tomorrow, and you can give me the details."

"And how about paying for the flat?"

"Here." He handed her a wad of bills. "But don't disappear, because this is only the beginning. There's more where that came from."

"I wouldn't think of it."

Herschel left the restaurant. *My plans of going to the tailor to have some suits made will have to be put on hold for now. I can't afford both this girl and a new wardrobe. And for right now, I'd rather explore this thing with her. But eventually, I'll have some more modern clothes made.*

And that was how it began. All morning on the following day

Herschel was filled with anticipation. When he was just coming into puberty, he and some of his friends had whispered about girls like Julia; a couple of their fathers' said that "Jewish girls were for marriage but shiksas were for practice." They talked about the things they would do if they ever had the opportunity to have sex with a wild shiksa. But they knew better than to ever speak of such things out loud because if the rabbi or the scholars ever heard them say such things, they would be in trouble. *Well, I am not a boy anymore. I am a man now, and a successful man. I will do as I please. No one will tell me what is right or what is wrong. I have always wanted to venture out of this small-minded world where I grew up. And now is my chance. This girl is everything that Naomi is not. So I intend to explore this until I have had my fill.*

The next day, Herschel left the office early for his meeting with Julia at the same restaurant for lunch. He felt light on his feet as he walked down the familiar streets. People were staring at him less since he'd shaved and cut his payot, and that gave him confidence. Entering the restaurant, he nodded to the maître d' who smiled at him. Then he glanced over at his regular table, and there she was, her blonde hair falling in waves like a golden ocean. She looked around and their eyes met. He walked over and sat down.

"You're early today," he said.

"I knew you were not pleased at my being late yesterday," she said, "so I made sure to get here on time."

He nodded and smiled. *That's good. She is already starting to know who's boss. I like it that she wants to please me.* "Did you find a flat?" he asked her.

"I did. It's not far from here. I think you'll approve," she said, smiling. Then the waiter came, and they placed their order.

After they finished eating, he paid the check and then followed her to the furnished apartment she rented which was only a few streets away from this restaurant and his office. When they arrived, she turned to him and smiled, then she unlocked the door. He walked inside and looked around. *This will be the place where I will explore all the things I have fantasized about over the years*, he thought. His feet tingled, his hands too, but he didn't say a word.

"What do you think?" she asked brightly.

"It's nice," he said, thinking it was probably going to be too expensive for him to keep this up for a long time. *I'm sure once I try all of the things I want to try, I'll probably tire of her. I can manage the cost of this for a few months.* He sat down in a chair. "It's comfortable," he said clumsily.

She leaned down and kissed him. He had to try hard to keep his hands from trembling. Then she slipped her dress over her head and stood in front of him in her thin white slip. He'd never seen a woman so undressed in the light of day. She had not even drawn the shades. Sunlight poured in, and he saw the curve of her breasts. *I have never known a woman so brazen as she.* Even though he and Naomi had been married for many years, she'd never acted this way. He had not moved from the chair. He was mesmerized by her. Julia reached down and took his hand. She led him to the bedroom, where she slowly undressed him. Herschel had never felt so nervous or been so excited. When she touched his manhood, he felt himself release almost immediately. His face turned red with embarrassment. But he didn't say a word. Instead, he just got up and got dressed. Then he turned to her and said, "Lunch tomorrow?"

"Sure. Same time, same place?" she asked casually.

"Yes," he answered, and without looking at her, he walked out the door. The cold wind on his face felt good. He was glad to be out of there. After his premature ejaculation, he'd felt embarrassed. *Well, it doesn't matter. I'll do better tomorrow*, he thought as he hurried back to his office. He wanted to collect some papers on a case he was working on and then head for home.

When he entered the office, Frieda was at her desk staring at him.

She makes me so uncomfortable. I feel like my clothes are askew or something, and she can somehow tell where I have been.

"You were gone for a long time. I was starting to worry," Frieda said.

"I'll be meeting with clients after lunch for the next few weeks.

So, don't expect me to return right away. And you might as well stop bringing food for me every day. If I wanted someone to pack me a lunch, I would tell my wife to do it. As it stands, I like to eat out."

"All right," she said in a small voice. He knew he hurt her feelings, but he didn't care. She was always in his business, and he was sick and tired of it. Besides that, this thing he was doing with Julia had set his mind spinning. He felt ashamed of what had transpired today. His body had betrayed him, making him look like a young virgin instead of a successful businessman. However, it didn't matter because even though he was embarrassed, he knew he was going to continue. It was just too exciting to stop now.

The following afternoon, he went to the restaurant to meet Julia. She was sitting at their regular table waiting for him.

"Good afternoon, Mr. Aizenberg," the maître d' said when Herschel walked into the restaurant. "The young lady is already here waiting for you."

Herschel nodded, but he made a mental note that he was going to make plans to go to different restaurants each day from now on. He didn't want his name to become known anywhere. What he was doing was not something to be proud of and he knew that. So it was better that he remained anonymous.

"Hello," he said as he sat down beside Julia at the table. *I'll tell her after lunch that I decided that we are going to start meeting at different places from now on.*

But he completely forgot, because after they finished eating, she said to him, "Has anyone ever kissed your manhood?"

He almost fell off his chair. "What?" he asked her.

"Come on, let's go back to the apartment," she said as she reached across the table and squeezed his hand. "I have a surprise for you. I know you're going to like it."

She shocked him, she intrigued him; but most of all she excited him.

From that day forward, he lost control of his emotions. All he could think of was her, and he could hardly wait until the next time he would be with her. At first she was satisfied with the modest allowance he gave her. But as time passed, she began to demand more money. He found that he was starting to dip into the money that he gave Naomi to buy food each week. But it didn't matter; he didn't care about anything else but Julia.

When he'd first met her and he'd fantasized that she would be willing to do things he had only imagined, he was right. And when he said she was a wild bird, he now knew that she was an eagle. Most days they met for lunch. Other days they didn't have lunch but instead went straight to her apartment. He saw her every day, and he found he wasn't growing tired of her at all. In fact, when he wasn't with her he was obsessing about her, remembering what had happened between them earlier.

His business was suffering. He began to feel trapped in his marriage and in his life. He thought that he should probably try to go and talk to someone to break this spell Julia had over him. But how could he ever tell the rabbi what he'd done? He began to feel like he'd made a mistake, a terrible, irreparable mistake. *I have allowed this woman into my life, and like the treif food I have been putting into my body, this relationship between us is dirty. But I can't leave her. She's cast a spell over me. I want her more and more every time I am with her. What have I done to myself? What have I done to my family?*

These thoughts flooded his mind, but as soon as he saw her, he forgot his fears and let her lead him back to her bed.

One night he lay in his bed listening to Naomi breathing softly in the bed next to his. He couldn't bear living this double life anymore. It was difficult to go home each day when all he wanted was to stay with Julia. Besides that, it was getting too expensive to keep both his family and his mistress. Herschel sighed softly. He felt bad for Naomi, but he was ready to leave the little shtetl, leave his wife and his children, and begin a new life with the woman who held him captive.

He imagined how it would be to be married to Julia, to know that each night she would take him to places he'd never before thought possible. Quietly, ever so quietly, he got out of bed and took his suitcase out of the closet. Then he began to pack his things. He glanced over at his wife. She was still asleep. He pushed thoughts of his children out of his mind. They would manage without him somehow, even if they had to take charity.

When he'd finished packing, he went to look at the twins. They were wrapped up in each other's arms, sleeping soundly. He felt his heart ache. Then he looked in on Shoshana. She was going to need a father to choose a decent husband for her. *But I am not a good father. I am not worthy of my family. They'll be better off without me*, he rationalized. Then he looked at the small roll of money that he had in his pocket and separated it into two halves. He laid half of the money down on his bed to leave for Naomi. Then he stuffed the other half of the bills back into his pocket.

He put on his coat, then picked up his shoes and walked barefoot out the door so the clicking of his heels on the floor would not wake anyone in his family. The thought of facing them was unbearable. Herschel felt a pang of guilt but he fought it. Once he was outside, he put on his shoes and headed straight for the apartment where he knew Julia would be asleep. He thought of her hair strewn across the pillow and her body naked and warm under the covers, and all of his guilt dissolved.

I must tell Julia how I am feeling about her, about us. I can't bear to be away from her for any length of time. If there really is such a thing as love, I am in love. So I'll tell her that I think Naomi and I should get divorced. And I will offer to marry her and take care of her. I hope she will understand that I must continue to support Naomi and the girls, which will mean that we won't have as much money as she would like. But I'll work harder if it means that I can come home to her each night.

He arrived at Julia's apartment at three o'clock in the morning. He had a key. *She'll be asleep. I'll climb into bed with her and get some rest. Then in the morning I will tell her everything I came here to say*, he thought as he quietly turned his key in the lock. The apartment was dark and quiet, but it was neat and clean too. He realized that he was hungry from the walk, so he took a couple of crackers from a bag on the shelf in the pantry and ate them quickly. Then he removed his coat and hat and walked to the bedroom where his sweetest memories lay. There was no light in the room, except a small beam that filtered in from the full moon through the uncovered window. Herschel Aizenberg looked down at his sleeping girlfriend. She looked just as he'd imagined she would. Her golden hair spread softly across the pillow. Herschel felt his breath catch in his throat, but then he saw something, and a pain shot through his heart. He reached up and clutched his chest.

CHAPTER FORTY-FOUR

NAOMI STIRRED IN HER SLEEP. SOMETHING WASN'T RIGHT. SHE FELT IT, and it woke her up. Sitting up in bed, she glanced over at Herschel's bed. For some odd reason she wasn't surprised to find that he wasn't there. But she didn't think he was gone forever. She thought she would find him in the kitchen unable to sleep. Lately he'd been even more distant than usual. Something was weighing heavily on his mind, something that was bothering him enough for him to lose sleep over it. This had never happened before in all the years they'd been married.

Unlike Naomi, who could not rest if the least little thing was on her mind, Herschel was a sound sleeper. It seemed nothing bothered him. A few minutes after he lay his head on his pillow, he was fast asleep and stayed asleep, snoring softly, until he had to get up for work in the morning. Naomi remembered the horrible night after Herschel's mother passed away. It was early in their marriage. His mother had been a widow for many years when she died. Naomi had expected Herschel to be devastated, broken, and weeping. She'd expected to sit with him and hold his hand, comforting him through the night. So she was surprised to find Herschel fast asleep when she came out of the bathroom to go to bed that evening. That was many years ago. However, it was the beginning of Naomi's learning to live with her husband's cold and distant nature.

As she pulled her robe down from the hook on the wall and put it on, she thought to herself, *Nothing keeps him awake. What could this possibly be? I am worried because this is so unlike him. I hope he is not ill. That would be the worst thing. I hope that my sins have not hurt him. Hashem, please don't punish Herschel for what I have done. Perhaps there is something, anything, I can do for him. I doubt he'll want to talk to me about it. But I can offer to make him a cup of tea. And, of course, if for some reason, he does decide to talk to me, I would be happy to offer to listen.*

Naomi walked into the kitchen and looked around. She gasped. No one was there. Herschel's hat and coat were gone. She ran to the bathroom and flung open the door just to make sure he was not there. But she knew the room would be empty. Then she looked in the bedroom she shared with Herschel, just to be sure she had not been mistaken. His bed was empty. On top of the quilt, she saw the roll of money. *What is going on here?* Quietly, she peeked into the twins' room and then into Shoshana's. Her children were fast asleep. She went into the kitchen and put on a pot of water to boil for tea. Then she sat down at her kitchen table and waited. She wasn't sure what she was waiting for. *Where is Herschel? Will he come home, or has he left us?*

CHAPTER FORTY-FIVE

JULIA TURNED OVER AND OPENED HER EYES. "HERSCHEL WHAT ARE YOU doing here? How dare you enter my apartment in the middle of the night without any warning."

"Who is this?" Herschel said, pointing to the naked man who lay beside Julia on the bed. "And what is he doing here?"

"That's none of your business."

"None of my business? He's sleeping in the apartment I pay for. Laying in the bed I pay for. I would say that is my business."

"You pay me for my time. I pay for the bed. When you're not here, I decide who sleeps in it," she said, sitting up without bothering to cover her naked breasts with the sheet.

Julia was beautiful, but at this moment Herschel found her to be ugly, coarse, and vulgar.

The man woke up. His blond hair was standing straight up from his forehead, but even so, he was handsome. He sat up quickly. "Who is this? What are you doing here in the middle of the night?" he said to Herschel.

"I don't answer to you," Herschel said angrily. "Get up, get dressed, and get out of here."

"You get out of here," the man said.

"This is my apartment. I pay for it. Julia is my mistress."

"Julia is a whore. She belongs to no one and to everyone," the blond man said. "I paid for my time. She is mine tonight."

"You filthy swine," Herschel said, and he rushed over and punched the man in the face. The man was angry. He stood up. He was tall and muscular and strong. He punched Herschel in the jaw, knocking him to the floor.

Julia got out of bed and turned on the light. "For goodness' sake, Flip, what the hell have you done? Look at him, he's bleeding. If I lose him, I'll be back on the street," she said to the man she called Flip.

"This is the end of us. So you can prepare to be back on the street. This place is paid through till the end of the month. Then you are on your own. I can see I made a terrible mistake," Herschel said, standing up and wiping the blood from his nose with a handkerchief he kept in the breast pocket of his suit coat. "Julia, I am a fool. I hate to admit it, but I am. I thought you and I had something special. But . . . I-I-I was wrong. I'm leaving and I won't be back. You can find some other way to pay for the rent on this place. I'm done with you."

Herschel walked into the kitchen where he put on his hat and coat which he failed to button. Then he walked out into the night. Blotting the blood from his face, he walked for hours. Finally the blood dried, and he was exhausted. Dejected, Herschel plopped down on a bench in the park. *I don't know what to do. I have never been religious, but think I need to talk to the rabbi. I need advice from a wise, old father figure. But how am I ever going to tell him what I have done? He will look at me with disgust and he would be right. Still, I need to talk, and there is no one else I can trust.*

The weather was chilly but not frigid. Herschel's heart was broken, and it had left him feeling chilled inside. He sat on that bench alone in the darkness, assessing his life and all of the mistakes he'd made as he waited for the first light of dawn when he could go to the synagogue and ask to speak with the rabbi.

It was a little after eight o'clock in the morning when Herschel stood up and stretched his legs. He had been sitting on the bench in the park for hours. Even when the sun rose and the day began, he could not make himself move. It was a difficult thing for Herschel to admit he was wrong and to ask for help. *But I cannot face this alone, so I must speak to the rabbi, and see if he can give me some advice. Once I tell him what I've done, he will look at me in a different light, and terrible shame will fall upon me.*

This is a great loss to me because I have spent my life making sure that everyone in the village saw me as a shining example. I enjoyed knowing that I was everything that most men in our shtetl wanted to be. When people spoke to me, I saw the respect and admiration in their eyes. Soon the rabbi will know that I am not the man everyone thinks I am. I don't think he will tell the others in the village, but he might. That may well be the price I'll have to pay if I want help, and I need it. No matter the consequences, I must go the rabbi, and I must tell him everything.

Herschel knew where the rabbi's office was. When he was thirteen, his bar mitzvah had taken place in that shul. And when he was man, the rabbi had married him and Naomi. He knew every inch of that building. In fact, he'd made donations for its renovation. As he walked toward the rabbi's study, he thought about Naomi, and a wave of guilt came over him. *What have I been thinking? I have been so selfish. I never gave a thought to her or to the children. All I knew was that this little shiksa made me feel young and excited about life. I am not a good man.*

The door was open to the room in which the rabbi's secretary sat. Herschel thought about running away. But he didn't; he knew he must face the consequences, so he knocked on the door. "Herschel Aizenberg? How can I help you?" Mrs. Musenburg, the secretary, asked.

"Good morning, Mrs. Musenburg. I need to speak with Rabbi Geldman. Is he in?"

"He is. Please, won't you sit down and wait for just a moment? I'll go in and see if the rabbi has time to see you now."

"Thank you," Herschel said as he sat down in a chair across from Mrs. Musenburg's desk.

A few minutes later, she returned. "Rabbi Geldman said to tell you that you should go right into his office. He's waiting for you."

"Thank you again," Herschel said. He walked into the rabbi's study.

"Herschel, it's been a long time. You shaved your beard. You cut off your payot, I see."

Herschel nodded and looked down at the floor.

"Why don't you sit down and tell me why you came here to see me," the rabbi said.

Herschel sat down and put his head in his hands. For a few seconds neither of them said a word, and then Herschel told the rabbi everything.

CHAPTER FORTY-SIX

ELI WALKED PAST THE RABBI'S STUDY. HE WAS ON HIS WAY TO MEET A student when he happened to see Herschel Aizenberg sitting across from the rabbi's desk. He knew it was wrong to eavesdrop. But he had to be sure that Naomi was all right. So he hid on the side of the door where he would not be seen and listened.

Herschel poured his heart out. And Eli felt his face fill with tears. Herschel had been discontented. How could he be unhappy with Naomi when Eli would have given his life to be her husband. If only he could go in there and tell Herschel to divorce his wife. *Just let her go.* If only he could tell him how much he loved Naomi. But he had promised Naomi that he would never tell Herschel about the two of them. And he would never break a promise to her. He owed her that much.

The rabbi had gently suggested ways to fix the marriage. And Eli fell to his haunches as he listened. He put his head in his hands. *Things should have been so different. If only she had been mine . . .*

CHAPTER FORTY-SEVEN

HERSCHEL LEFT THE RABBI'S STUDY WITH A NEW PERSPECTIVE ON LIFE. He hummed softly to himself as he walked home.

When Herschel walked into his house, Naomi was sitting at the kitchen table with a cup of tea in her hand. She looked at him, and he saw deep worry lines between her eyes. "Herschel, where have you been? I've been worried sick. Are you all right?"

"Yes," he said. "I am."

"What happened? Where did you go?"

He took off his coat and laid it down on a chair. Then he sat down across from her and smiled. "That tea sure smells good," he said.

"You want a cup?"

"I'd love a cup." His hands were shaking. Naomi glanced at him. He was much nicer to her than usual, and she wondered what was going on.

She stood up and took a clean cup down from the shelf and poured him some tea. Then she sat down, folded her hands in her lap, and waited.

Herschel sipped the tea for several moments before he said, "It's good. It's hot." Then he added, "I have a lot to talk to you about."

She nodded. "Please tell me what's going on," she said.

CHAPTER FORTY-EIGHT

NAOMI LISTENED WITHOUT SAYING A WORD AS HERSCHEL TOLD HER about his affair with Julia.

"I don't know if you can find it in your heart to forgive me. You are a good girl, a frum girl. I should be ashamed of myself. There is no doubt in my mind that you have always been a good wife and a wonderful mother too. You don't deserve to be treated this way." He hesitated a moment, then he sighed. "Naomi, I am sorry. Can you please find it in your pure heart to forgive me?"

She sighed as she ran her index finger around the side of the teacup. For a moment she was silent. Then she looked into his eyes and shook her head. "I'm not such a good girl. I'm not as frum as you think I am, and I could be a better wife."

"What do you mean?"

"I had an affair too." The words spilled from her lips. "I knew it was wrong, but I did it anyway. It ended years ago. I am sorry. I never meant to hurt you."

"You had an affair?" He was shocked. His voice cracked. Herschel stood up and put his head in his hands. "How could you do that? You are the mother of my children. How could you lay with another man?"

"The same way you laid with another woman."

"It's different for a man. You are a mother. A mother should be pure," he said. He was pulling at his hair. "Oy vey. I can't believe this. No matter what I try to do, this day keeps getting worse." Herschel walked to the front door and let himself out. Naomi got up and walked to the door. She stared out after him for a few minutes. Then she sat back down at the table. Tears began to form in her eyes.

"Mama, are you all right?" Perle walked into the kitchen.

Naomi looked up. *How long has she been standing outside the room? Did she hear Herschel and I talking? I pray she didn't or at the very least she doesn't understand what we were saying. The worst thing in the world that we could do is hurt our little ones.*

"I'm all right," Naomi answered, wiping the tears from her eyes. "How long have you been standing outside this room?"

"I just got up, Mama," Perle said, "Have you been crying?"

"No. I am fine. I promise. Now, where are your sisters? You three girls should eat some breakfast."

"I'll go and get Shoshana and Bluma. I'll be right back."

Naomi managed a smile.

Shoshana helped Naomi prepare some hot cereal, and they all sat together at the table and ate. Naomi moved the cereal around in her bowl, but she couldn't eat a bite. She felt like she was falling off a cliff, and there was nothing she could do to stop whatever might come next.

After Naomi's daughters were done eating, they got dressed and went to the barn to collect the eggs from the chickens while Naomi cleaned the kitchen and washed the dishes. After she finished, she went into her room to put on some clothes to go to the market. And then she heard the front door open. Her heart raced. It was too soon for her daughters to be done with their chores. *It has to be Herschel,* she thought. Her hands were trembling. *He's probably come back here to tell me he's leaving me and the children.*

"Naomi," Herschel said. His voice was soft as he walked into their bedroom. "Neither of us are perfect. You made a mistake. I made one too. I gave it some thought, and I feel that the best thing for us to do is to forgive each other and find a way to make this marriage work for us. We have beautiful children together. And a nice home."

She looked at him. This was the most honest and heartfelt thing he'd ever said to her. "Can I ask you something? I know it's none of my business, and you can tell me if you don't want to answer. But was the woman who you were seeing, Frieda?"

"No, it wasn't Frieda who turned my head. It was a shiksa."

"A shiksa? Someone you work with?"

"No, just a young woman I met. I shouldn't have done it." Then he added, "You know Frieda was never a threat to our marriage. I never had any interest in her. But I think Frieda suspects something."

"You do? Why?"

"She's so nosy. You know that about her."

"I do. And I also know that she hates me. She always has."

"She's jealous of you," Herschel said. Then he hesitated. "Do you think it would be good for our marriage if I were to let Frieda go? I suppose I could hire a new secretary."

"Yes, maybe it would be better if she wasn't always such a big part of our lives."

"Then I'll do it. And, for both of our sakes, I'll hire an old woman to work with me. Someone with experience."

"An old woman, so you won't be interested." Naomi started laughing. She couldn't help herself. Herschel saw her laugh, and it was contagious. He started laughing too.

"Do you think we could try to show more appreciation for each other? I know I would like nothing more than to feel appreciated," she said, and for the first time since they were married, she felt at ease talking to him.

"I've always appreciated everything you have done for me."

"But it's nice to hear please and thank you sometimes. Would you mind doing that for me?"

"Of course not. It's the least I can do after what I have done."

"And what can I do for you?" she asked. "How can I make our marriage better?"

He looked away and sighed. "How do I say this to you?"

"Whatever you have to say, just say it."

"I am ashamed."

"Please, Herschel, just say it."

"All right. Nu, so you want this marriage to be better? So do I. I want it very badly," he said, then he cleared his throat.

"All right. And . . . so . . . what can I do?"

"Don't just be my wife, Naomi. Be my lover."

She blushed. "I was hardly expecting that." Then she smiled. "But all right. I'm willing to give it a try."

CHAPTER FORTY-NINE

WHEN HERSCHEL TOLD FRIEDA HE HAD TO LET HER GO, FRIEDA WAS shattered. She couldn't believe that he cared so little for her after all she had done to integrate herself into his life. *I am the backbone of this business*, she thought as she cleaned out her desk. *Once I am gone, and he sees how much I did for him, he will change his mind and ask me to come back.*

But he didn't. And once she was packed, he didn't even walk into her office to say goodbye. Instead, he stayed in his own office with the door locked. When she was ready to go, she knocked on his door. "I'm leaving," she said.

"Go."

That's all he has to say to me. Just go. Nothing more. I mean nothing to him. I never have. She didn't answer. There was nothing more to say. Tears ran down her cheeks as she picked up her things and walked out the door.

For the next week, she lay on the sofa in her parents' living room prostrate with grief. She'd made Herschel Aizenberg the main focus of her life, and now he was done with her. *What am I going to do? I am in my late thirties, far past marriageable age, and I have no man, no children, no job, and no Herschel. I was certain that if I stood by him and made myself an important part of his life, he would see my value and divorce Naomi for me. But he didn't. And it wasn't as if he has been a good and pious man. I know he was unfaithful. I followed him. I saw them together. My Herschel with that floozy—that blonde shiksa.*

Finally, Frieda's mother sat down on the sofa beside her and said, "Stop lying on the couch and feeling sorry for yourself. That will do you no good at all. You have secretarial experience. Why don't you go into the city and find another job? You might be too old to find a husband here in our religious neighborhood, but among the secular Jews, you could find someone."

"I don't want anyone but Herschel."

"I know how you feel about him. But that's all over. If you are going to survive this, you need to forget about him. You did the best you could. You gave him everything. And he turned away from you. Now you must try to build a life of your own that doesn't include him."

Frieda nodded. She knew her mother was right. And she missed working. She missed having a place to go each morning, and she loved solving problems at work. It gave her a sense of purpose. So the following day she forced herself out of bed. It had been a week she since took a bath. It felt good to bathe. The warm water was like the caress of a lover on her skin. She lathered up her body and hair, and for a few minutes she inhaled the clean scent of the soap. Then she rinsed her hair and body. After she dried herself with a thick towel, Frieda put on a clean and modest dress, smeared a light stain of red lipstick on her small mouth and a dash of rouge on her cheeks. Now, she was ready to go.

"I'm on my way into the city to look for work," Frieda said to her mother who was in the kitchen.

"Eat something first?"

"I can't. I'm too nervous. I'll eat when I get home."

Her mother nodded. "Good luck."

Frieda smiled.

She wasn't a pretty woman. But when she glanced into the mirror, she decided that she looked professional. And more importantly, she could type, take dictation, and compose a convincing letter. Within an hour of arriving in the city, she had a job working as secretary for another lawyer.

It was a good job. She had to admit, she enjoyed her work. But a day didn't go by that she didn't miss Herschel. In fact, during her lunch hour she would walk by his office hoping to run into him. She would wait outside his office until it was time to return to her own job, thinking he might go out for lunch. She had no idea what she would say to him. But she longed to see him anyway. She needn't have concerned herself with what she would say, because It never happened. She never saw him. Herschel had stopped going out for lunch. Naomi packed him food each day.

CHAPTER FIFTY

FOUR YEARS PASSED. ELI MARRIED RACHEL, AND THE TWO OF THEM LEFT for England. Things improved between Naomi and Herschel. Both of them tried to give what they could to make the marriage work. Their relationship was not perfect by any means, but they were doing better. Sometimes on a soft summer night, when the nightbirds sang, and the wind whistled through the trees, Naomi's thoughts would still turn to Eli. She remembered everything about him, the warmth of his smile, the depth of his eyes, but most of all, the love they shared. *I hope he is all right*, she thought, and she wished that she could be so selfless as to wish him and his wife happiness in their marriage bed. But she couldn't. Even now, after all this time, it was still painful to think of Eli kissing another woman. Naomi wondered if Herschel ever thought about the Polish girl he'd been in love with. But she never asked him. In fact, after that night, five years ago, when they decided to work on making their marriage better, neither of them ever brought up their indiscretions again.

Herschel kept his promise and hired a new secretary. She was an older woman who was efficient but not nearly as capable as Frieda had been. Still, Herschel never complained.

The years had been kind to Shoshana. She was a beautiful girl just about to turn seventeen. And one night after the children went to bed, Herschel told Naomi that they had waited long enough. "It's time to make a match for Shoshana," he said.

"Do you have anyone in mind?"

"I was thinking about Albert Hendler. He's handsome and smart. He also has a good job working for his parents' business."

"Yes, all of that is true. And any girl would be happy to have him," Naomi said, but she thought, *I wonder if Shoshana will be happy about this?* "Do you think that perhaps we should discuss it with Shoshana?"

"No," Herschel said adamantly. "I am her father. I will make the decision," Herschel said firmly.

"All right," Naomi said. She was tired and wanted to avoid any possible disagreement. But as she looked at her husband, she thought, *He has changed a little, but not enough. He still has to have the last say in everything.* She sighed.

"I'm going out tomorrow night after dinner to speak with Mr. Hendler about the match."

Naomi nodded.

CHAPTER FIFTY-ONE

WHEN HERSCHEL RETURNED HOME LATE THE FOLLOWING EVENING, Naomi was waiting up for him in their bedroom.

"So, what happened?" she asked.

"Hendler was very happy. He agreed to the match and said his son would be ecstatic to have such a lovely kallah."

"I'm glad," she said. Then she hesitated. "I think you should talk to Shoshana. I really think you should have spoken with her before you went to see Mr. Hendler. What if she doesn't like Albert?"

"She'll like him. What's not to like? He's handsome; he will be a good provider." Herschel patted Naomi's shoulder. "So, I've decided that we'll have the Hendler family over for dinner on Sunday night. That way, the young couple can meet each other in the proper setting."

"All right. I'll take care of everything," she said.

Then he added sheepishly, "Thank you."

She smiled. "You're welcome."

Naomi decided to make a brisket and kishka. As she walked to the market, she thought about Miriam. I'll have to send her a letter telling her that Herschel has decided upon a chassan, a husband for Shoshana. Soon my precious daughter will be a kallah, a bride. *I wish*

I could talk to Eli right now. After all, she is his child too. Sometimes I wish Eli and Shoshana could speak to each other. But I know it's best this way. She doesn't know that Herschel isn't her father, and he doesn't know either. They have a good relationship. So, even though I feel guilty, for their sake I should take this secret to my grave.

CHAPTER FIFTY-TWO

ALBERT AND HIS FAMILY CAME FOR DINNER ON THAT SUNDAY NIGHT. HIS mother brought a cake and a box of chocolate candy. She handed it Naomi who thought, *Well, at least he comes from a good family. They have manners. And he is very handsome.*

All through dinner Naomi watched Shoshana and Albert eyeing each other and then looking away. *They are both so young and shy. But I think Shoshana likes him.*

After the Hendlers left that evening, Naomi went to Shoshana's room.

Naomi knocked softly. "Can I come in?" she asked.

"Yes, of course, Mama," Shoshana said as she was getting ready for bed.

Naomi looked at her daughter. *She is like an angel in her white nightdress.* "So, what did you think of Albert?" Naomi asked.

"He's handsome. But the truth is I don't know anything about him. He seems nice."

"Of course, you know your father has arranged a match for you two."

"I know. And I suppose I am happy about it. I mean, he is nice looking and he has a good job. I don't know what else there is to look for."

"You seem unsure."

"I sometimes feel like I don't want to get married. I know that here in our Jewish shtetl, marriage is the most important thing. But I often wonder what life is like outside of here. I wonder how secular women live."

"Oh, Shoshana, don't wonder about things like that. They will only hurt you."

"Did you ever wonder, Mama?"

"No . . . not about that. But I did wonder about so many other things. And you know what? I found out that it's better not to think about things you know you shouldn't do. You will only hurt yourself. Learn to be happy with what you have."

Shoshana nodded. "Maybe you're right. And as far as Albert is concerned, he would make a good husband. I can't complain. He is definitely the best of all the young men that I have seen in our town."

"So you will have a chance to get to know him better over these next few months while we plan the wedding."

"Yes," Shoshana said.

The following day Shoshana went to see Neta to tell her the news. She knocked on the door. Sarah, Neta's mother, answered.

"Come in," Sarah said. "How is your mother?"

"She's fine." Shoshana smiled. "You should go and see her sometime."

"I should. I am always so busy," Sarah said, tsking. "There is always so much to be done." Then she smiled. "Neta is making challah in the kitchen."

"Is it all right if I go in and speak to her?"

"Of course."

Neta was braiding the dough when Shoshana walked in. "Look at this braid. It's perfect," Neta said, smiling. "Of course, I had to do it over three times to get it right. But now, I must say, I am quite proud of it."

"It looks wonderful. You are such a good baker. I wish I were better at it."

"You hate it. So you don't practice. If you practiced, you'd be good at it," Neta said. "You want some tea? I'll put a pot of water on to boil."

"Sure. That would be lovely," Shoshana said. "My father made a match for me. I'm betrothed."

A bright smile came over Neta's face. She hugged her friend tightly. "Mazel tov! Who is he?"

"Albert Hendler."

"The most handsome boy in town. I would have expected no less. I am so happy for you. Are you excited?"

"I don't know. Maybe I am just scared."

"Most girls are scared. It will be wonderful. I wish my father would find me a match already. He hasn't even started looking, and I am already seventeen. Practically an old maid."

"You are not an old maid. Girls are getting married a little bit later these days. Besides, you're just the right age." Shoshana smiled reassuringly

"I have always wanted to have a husband and a family. I am not scared; I'm ready."

"I know you are, Neta. And I am sure your father will find you a good match very soon."

CHAPTER FIFTY-THREE

NAOMI AND SHOSHANA WERE INCREDIBLY BUSY WITH PLANS FOR THE wedding. Early one morning, Naomi took her wedding dress out of storage. Shoshana was awake, so Naomi began fitting the dress to her daughter. *It has to be perfect*, she thought, and just then Perle and Bluma walked into the room.

"Last night I had a dream that the sky was on fire," Perle said, her eyes wide and glassy.

"Another bad dream?" Naomi got up and left her sewing machine. She ran over and hugged Perle.

"She woke up crying during the night. But I comforted her," Bluma said.

"Oh, Perle. Everything is all right," Naomi said softly. "You have been having these dreams for years, and none of them have come true. Praise Hashem. So, perhaps your papa is right. Maybe they are only just bad dreams. Maybe they mean nothing at all." Naomi wanted to believe this to be true. After all, she was grateful that not one of the premonitions in Perle's dreams had come to pass.

But Perle did not answer. She just shook her head.

Then Naomi remembered the flags, the red-and-black flags with the black spider in the center. She couldn't overlook that the same flag had shown up in both of their dreams. Naomi closed her eyes and saw the flag clearly. And she shivered.

But something happened in Warsaw. Something sinister that would shake up the entire city. It would change things for the worse for the Polish people, but not nearly as badly as it would affect the Jews.

CHAPTER FIFTY-FOUR

♊

At five twenty in the morning on the first of September in the year 1939, Herschel and Naomi Aizenberg were sleeping soundly in their beds when the earth seemed to explode. They were awakened by a loud deafening sound. Then the ground beneath them shook.

"Herschel!" Naomi sat up in her bed.

Shoshana, Bluma, and Perle came running into their parents' room. "Mama, Papa? What's going on?"

Another loud explosion followed. Naomi jumped out of bed and ran to the window with Herschel at her side. In the distance, giant fingers of red fire were reaching for the sky. Again, the earth trembled.

Naomi hugged her children, holding them tightly to her. "What is this?" she asked Herschel.

"I think we're being bombed."

The people who lived in the shtetl had begun gathering outside. Screams and cries filled the air along with heavy charcoal-gray smoke.

A few streets away, Frieda was awake. "I must go to Herschel," she said to her parents. But her mother grabbed her arm.

"Stay here with your family. This could be the end of all of us."

"I know, and if I must die, the last thing I want is to see Herschel."

Her father shook her. "Herschel is with his wife and children. Stay away from them. Especially now."

She put her head in her hands and began to weep. But she didn't move to get dressed. Two more bombs exploded. Frieda ran out of her house still in her nightdress. She ran all the way to Herschel's home and began banging her fists on the door.

"Herschel, Herschel. It's me. Let me in."

Naomi opened the door. "What are you doing here?" she asked.

"Is Herschel all right?"

"He's fine. He's with his family. Go home and be with yours." She slammed the door in Frieda's face.

Bombs were exploding all around her, but Frieda didn't care. All she wanted was to be with Herschel during this terrifying thing that was happening. But he had not even come to the door. As she walked up the street toward her parents' home, a bomb fell directly upon Frieda's house. She let out a piercing scream. Then she began running toward the house. "My parents are inside there," she yelled. But no one was paying attention.

Frieda's parents never knew what hit them. They were gone in an instant.

CHAPTER FIFTY-FIVE

FOR TWO WEEKS, THE BOMBS RAINED DOWN UPON WARSAW. THE
Aizenbergs stayed at home together huddled in terror. Naomi was
forced to go to the market because they were completely out of food.
It was there that she overheard the news that Frieda's family had
been killed by the direct hit of a bomb. She shivered as she ran
home carrying the few things she was able to purchase. She thought
about telling Herschel what she'd heard about Frieda but decided
against it. *What is the point? He has enough to worry about. Best to leave
it alone. He'll find out when things go back to normal, and he returns to
work.*

Herschel did not return to work. In fact, he had not yet returned
to his office on the day that Nazis marched into Warsaw. He was still
at home with his family trying to make sense of what the future
might look like for them.

And then it happened. It was horrible, unreal, just like Naomi's
dream. The soldiers marched into the little Jewish village. Germans!
Nazis! It was a pogrom. The soldiers were hollering, "Jewish swine.
Miserable, filthy Jewish swine. Come out of your houses, or we will
drag you out. They were rough and cruel as they rounded up every
living person in that little Jewish neighborhood. It was not only the

children as it had been in Naomi's dream. It was everyone: men, women, children, the young and the old.

Herschel turned to Naomi. "Stay here. I am going outside to see what is happening," he said.

"Be careful."

"I will," Herschel said, then he walked out the door.

There was chaos in the streets. People were crying, begging, screaming. Terrified. There was a gunshot. Naomi tried to see who had been killed but she couldn't. All she saw was the form of a woman lying facedown in the dirt.

An old man, who Herschel remembered as having given Herschel and his friends a bag of nuts when Herschel was just a boy, was lying dead in the middle of the street.

"What happened to him?" Herschel asked the man's fourteen-year-old grandson, who was standing by the body and weeping.

"One of those soldiers shot and killed him for not moving fast enough. I should have done something. I should have torn the bastard to pieces. But I am a coward. I hate myself I didn't do anything. I just stood there shaking like a helpless fool while they killed my grandpa."

A Nazi grabbed the boy. And then another grabbed Herschel. They were thrown onto the back of a truck.

Herschel was appalled, but he saw that he was powerless, so he did not try to fight. Then a Nazi with a gun broke the door open and rushed into the Aizenberg home. He grabbed Naomi. The Nazi picked Naomi up and tossed her on the back of an open-air truck, like she was a doll. She scraped her face on the wooden truck bed. Shoshana, Bluma, and Perle began to scream. A young Nazi hit Bluma with his fist and she fell forward. Blood spurted out of the open wound. Naomi leapt off the truck. She fell facedown into the dirt, but got up as fast as she could and ran toward her daughter. The Nazi saw her. His face grew red with anger as he smashed her hip with the butt of his rifle. Pain shot through her and she fell to her knees. "Get in the truck, all three of you," he said to Naomi and the girls. They did as he commanded. The twins ran to their mother and clung to her. Naomi's chin quivered. Shoshana sat quietly, tears running down her cheeks, her arms wrapped around her shoulders. With the hem of her skirt, Naomi gently wiped the blood that was still oozing from Bluma's lip, and when Bluma squeezed in closer to her mother, Naomi felt the white hot shooting pain in her hip again. Then she remembered this was just as it had happened in the dream she'd had so long ago.

Herschel was not in the same truck as his family. He looked around him, his eyes wide with shock and disbelief. For the first time in his life, he had no control over what was to come. He dared not speak. But when he looked out at the ground, he saw a woman lying dead. She had been shot. He looked closer and saw the side of her face. It was Frieda. She lay dead, facedown in the dirt.

The engine of the truck roared as the vehicle sprang to life. The Aizenbergs glanced at each other. The trucks formed a line and began to move. Herschel kept his eyes locked on his family, who were in the truck right behind him. Perle began gagging. She was about to vomit, but the armed guard hit her in the stomach with the butt of his rifle, knocking the air out of her. Now Perle was panting unable to catch her breath. Bluma held her sister and began to cry. The family was on their way to somewhere. They didn't know if they would be reunited with their father or not. All they knew was that they were terrified and were traveling into an unknown future. If they had known the truth, that they would be guests of a mob who hated the Jews and were hell-bent on ridding the world of them, they might have tried to fight. But right now all they had left was hope.

As the truck pulled away, Perle turned to her mother and whispered, "Look over there, Mama. These soldiers left their flag there. Do you see it? That's the same flag I saw in my dream."

"Yes," Naomi said. That was all she could manage to say, because she already knew.

AUTHORS NOTE

I always enjoy hearing from my readers, and your thoughts about my work are very important to me. If you enjoyed my novel, please consider telling your friends and posting a short review on Amazon. Word of mouth is an author's best friend.

Also, it would be my honor to have you join my mailing list. As my gift to you for joining, you will receive 3 **free** short stories and my USA Today award-winning novella complimentary in your email! To sign up, just go to my website at www.RobertaKagan.com

I send blessings to each and every one of you,

Roberta

Email: roberta@robertakagan.com

MORE BOOKS BY ROBERTA KAGAN

AVAILABLE ON AMAZON

The Auschwitz Twins Series

The Children's Dream

Jews, The Third Reich, and a Web of Secrets

My Son's Secret

The Stolen Child

A Web of Secrets

A Jewish Family Saga

Not In America

They Never Saw It Coming

When The Dust Settled

The Syndrome That Saved Us

A Holocaust Story Series

The Smallest Crack

The Darkest Canyon

Millions Of Pebbles

Sarah and Solomon

All My Love, Detrick Series

All My Love, Detrick

You Are My Sunshine

The Promised Land

To Be An Israeli

Forever My Homeland

Michal's Destiny Series

Michal's Destiny

A Family Shattered

Watch Over My Child

Another Breath, Another Sunrise

Eidel's Story Series

And . . . Who Is The Real Mother?

Secrets Revealed

New Life, New Land

Another Generation

The Wrath of Eden Series

The Wrath Of Eden

The Angels Song

Stand Alone Novels

One Last Hope

A Flicker Of Light

The Heart Of A Gypsy

ACKNOWLEDGMENTS

I would like to thank my editor, proofreader, and developmental editor for all their help with this project. I couldn't have done it without them.

Paula Grundy of Paula Proofreader
Terrance Grundy of Editerry
Carli Kagan, Developmental Editor

Made in the USA
Coppell, TX
14 April 2022